MAKELESS MADE

BOOK FIVE OF THE GATES OF INLAND

JOHN ROSEGRANT

For Donna and Joey

ALSO BY JOHN ROSEGRANT

The Gates of Inland

Book I: Gatemoodle

Book II: Kintravel

Book III: Rattleman

Book IV: Marrowland

Learn more about John Rosegrant and The Gates of Inland at

johnrosegrantauthor.com

CONTENTS

1

SIGNS OF WAR

A goblin smirking across the heavy plank table. A witch muttering over a pot on the stove. A hobgoblin grinning as he whisked bowls of thick steaming stew from stove to table. And sitting at Dan's right, a gorgeous fairy.

Typical day in Inland.

Abruptly the scene flickered like video with a bad Internet connection. Heavy pressure hit Dan's ears. The fairy turned to him with wide eyes and he saw her mouth moving but heard nothing.

That wasn't so typical.

Finally sound cut through the thick air: the witch calling out strange words as she stirred the pot. The flickering stopped and her voice subsided again to muttering.

The hobgoblin had paused, bowl in hand. Now he placed it in front of the fairy—Dan's girlfriend Maggie—looked across the table at the goblin, and sighed. "And so it begins. There is her sign, Crackerbones."

"'Sign,' Billy?" sneered Crackerbones. He nodded at the

witch, who now stirred silently. "If not for Mother Ferny's brew, that sign would have shaken our walls. We can't absorb too many signs like that one."

Dan looked at the massive beams that formed Gatemoodle's walls. The trees must have grown for hundreds of years before they were hewn and shaped into the great rustic hall, and the hall wound with spells had probably stood for thousands more. Did Sister really have enough magic to threaten them?

Mother Ferny joined the other two Gatekeepers and Dan and Maggie at the table. "Your journey here was truly uneventful?" she asked.

Dan nodded and took a bite of stew. Billy Portman's cooking was delicious as always. "How did you know to make enough for us? We didn't tell you we were coming."

Billy just winked.

Dan shoveled in a few more bites. He and Maggie had a lot to tell the Gatekeepers, and a lot to ask them, but he was hungry after three days of hard travel. He decided to start with a question so he could eat while he listened to the answer. He reached for a hot muffin and asked, "What sign do you mean?"

Crackerbones shook his head. "Uh-uh, Quest Boy. Wrong topic. The sign didn't come until you arrived, because it's you Sister wants. She might not even trouble us if we weren't helping you. So tell me, what good are you doing? We brought you to Inland to find First Changing Beast. Where is First Changing Beast?"

Dan and Maggie exchanged looks. Crackerbones had always been the surly Gatekeeper, "joking" that he and his goblin warriors might eat Dan. Luckily, Dan and Maggie finally did have a solid lead where to find First Changing Beast.

But Dan had a bite to swallow, so Billy spoke next. "Crackerbones, you know as well as I that Sister wishes to control all the

Gates of Inland." The Gates of Inland!—that was what Dan's quest was all about. The gates between this magical world and the normal world (Outland) had been slowly closing for many centuries. This was miserable for the normal world, as magic and beauty drained away, and maybe even worse for the inhabitants of Inland, who needed contact with the normal world, even its food, to thrive. First Changing Beast was a mysterious figure who had long been lost, but the Gatekeepers believed that if Dan could free the Beast it would ensure that the Gates of Inland remained open.

"She will attempt to wrest away our power and seize control of our hall even if Dan returns forever to Outland and Maggie hides with her fairy folk," continued Billy. "She means to destroy us."

"All the more reason that we need First Changing Beast." Crackerbones tapped his forefinger with its dirty claw on the table in front of Dan. "Where. Is. First. Changing Beast?"

Dan swallowed the last of his stew. "In the Shadowlands!"

The Shadowlands was an eerie in-between world, neither Inland nor Outland. Things that happened there could be unreal, real, or mere hints at the real, but whether real, unreal, or hinting, it was usually scary. Dan had encountered First Changing Beast (dubbed FCB by his friend Josh to save time) a few times when he had fallen into the Shadowlands. He explained that he had finally figured out that these weren't just hints about where in Inland to find FCB; he only encountered FCB in the Shadowlands because FCB was stuck there.

"And however he got there in the first place, Sister is keeping him there. Last time I was in the Shadowlands, FCB made sure I saw what was going on. Sister controlled him and forced him to give her his blood to drink by saying weird words: 'Minik Mingarria.' Then First Changing Beast told me that whoever understands the dual nature of the truename will be able to use it—whatever that means."

"My father was frightened at the idea that Sister might know First Changing Beast's truename," put in Maggie. "But if Minik Mingarria is the truename of Sister and not the Beast, my father had no explanation for how speaking her own true-name could control him."

Billy jumped up. "You have been busy since last we saw you! So many threads to follow. You have found your father, and we wish to learn who he is, and if he will give you away at your wedding." Dan and Maggie blushed. It still wasn't easy getting used to the idea that they were going to fulfill a prophecy by getting married.

Billy continued, "But most urgent is that we understand about First Changing Beast and Sister."

As if to underline this comment, the room began again to flicker silently. Mother Ferny hurried to the stove and stirred and chanted until things settled back to normal.

Billy sat down and then stood up again immediately. "You have done well, Dan and Maggie! Finally we know where First Changing Beast is trapped: in the Shadowlands. No wonder the Beast has been so hard to locate, for that is the land between, the land of which it cannot be asked if it is real or not, because both answers are both true and false. We must all ponder how you can free the Beast once you find it there.

"And finally we know how Sister has become so powerful. She steals and wields the power of First Changing Beast!"

As Mother Ferny stepped back to the table, the corners of her mouth quirked up. "I felt certain she was not using our old witchcraft—yet certain as I was, I am reassured to hear your proof. 'Earth, water, fire, and air met together in a garden fair.' Witches may turn wicked, but still they remember the garden, still their magic has elemental depth. Sister's magic is strong but it is also cold and brittle, a perversion of the garden." The room flickered once, and Mother Ferny gestured and called out a strange word. Then she spread her arms. "As you just felt."

"But who is more elemental than First Changing Beast?" asked Crackerbones, still tapping his claw on the table. "If she is using the Beast's power, why do we not feel its depth? And how can Minik Mingarria be his truename? We all know First Changing Beast has no truename. This mortal fool's information is wrong and useless."

Dan stood and leaned over the table and shouted, "Crackerbones, why don't you take your dirty claws and sharp teeth and go back to your mines? Maggie and I have just been through more crap than you can imagine, and our friends Josh and Alice too, to find this stuff out. And we'd be on our way to FCB right now except that you guys sent a magpie to tell us that Gatemoodle was almost under attack, and that Graciela has information for us." That had been at the end of their last adventure. Their good friend Graciela was the daughter of a Maya shaman, so she'd had the power to send notice from Outland that she had a message for them. Josh and Alice had gone back to Outland to find Graciela so she could bring them the message.

Crackerbones stood up too, hand on his sword. Maggie pulled Dan back to his chair, and he only struggled a little because he realized he was no match for Crackerbones in a swordfight. He glanced at the corner by Gatemoodle's massive wooden doors, where he had left his bow and arrows. But bow against sword would be cheating ...

Billy hopped up on the table. "Cracker, hands off your sword. Dan, calm yourself. You must remember that it is hard for a goblin to be, how do you say it in Outland? A 'good guy.' Mother, the walls."

Billy and Mother Ferny began walking around the great hall, stroking the walls and murmuring. After a few heartbeats, Crackerbones joined them, and Billy nodded to him and gave a small smile. They completed the circuit and returned to the table.

Crackerbones bowed. He frowned, but said, "My apologies, quester."

Dan bowed clumsily, "And mine. I'm sorry, I don't know why I got so mad."

"I do," said Billy. "As you will recall, this hall is wound with many ancient spells of harmony. Goblins, witches, hobgoblins ... we are not always friends either, but the enchanted halls enable us to work in amity on our great task of preserving what gates we can. Sister shook the spells when she shook the walls. I'm glad this was merely a spell she set to alert her army when you arrived, and not a full attack."

Billy smiled. "And we have set things aright. Now, our esteemed goblin gatekeeper speaks the truth when he says that First Changing Beast has no truename. That is why we believed him eternally free. Dan, are you certain that Minik Mingarria is a truename?"

Dan nodded. "FCB looked at me to make sure I got the message, but he was speaking to Sister, and he said, 'The holder of the twofold meaning will wield the truename you have spoken.'"

"So Minik Mingarria is Sister's truename?" asked Mother Ferny with a frown. Without waiting for an answer, she continued, "This is something new: one person's truename controlling another person."

"Perhaps if we knew who Sister is ..." said Billy.

"We know! We found out!" said Dan.

"Sister is the mortal child for whom I was switched," said Maggie. "And as I am the daughter of the King and Queen of the Fairies, Sister was raised as a fairy princess."

The Gatekeepers turned to face her. Crackerbones even stopped tapping the table. Maggie explained how she and Dan had found their way to the Marrowland of the Fairies and learned not only that she was the royal daughter and Sister her mortal changeling, but that Dan's therapist back in Outland, Dr. Green, was actually her older brother, Prince of the Fairies. The switch of Maggie for Sister had created a terrible rift in the royal family, for Maggie was left with a human mother who abused her, and so the King of the Fairies abused the mortal changeling in return, in order to keep symmetry between the worlds according to the Old Ways. The Prince had rebelled against the Old Ways and tried to protect the girl, whom they named Sally Wandil, and the enraged King had banished the Prince to Outland and cursed him to forget his origins. Sally grew up strange and cruel as her father abused her, and began visiting First Changing Beast and taking his power, although no one understood this was happening at the time. When she was sixteen she fled the Marrowland on the wings of red ravens.

"So Dr. Green *is* of our world," muttered Billy. "I thought so."

"I saw you there!" cried Dan.

Everyone turned to him with puzzled looks.

"After my very first therapy session with Dr. Green, I saw, uh, a little old man with silver hair in the waiting room." Dan glanced to see if Billy would be OK with that description, but the hobgoblin merely smiled. "I thought it was you, but when I asked Dr. Green he couldn't tell me."

"He no longer knows himself," said Billy, shaking his head.

"I visited him because I perceived a faded aura of Inland, but he could say neither yea nor nay. Faint pictures of his old life he may have from time to time, or glimmering feelings, but mostly it is a hole in his mind. He helps his patients with their mysteries and suffering but still waits to heal his own."

"Yeah, yeah," interjected Crackerbones. "The Prince of the Fairies has his suffering and mystery, but it is no mystery that we will be suffering a vicious attack from Sister soon enough. Back to business. How do we stop Sister? And how does Dan find and free First Changing Beast? Where in the Shadowlands is he? In what sort of trap?"

"He's in a cave with prehistoric paintings," said Dan. "That's where I've usually seen him in the Shadowlands, and just before coming here we found the Inland entrance. It's guarded by a dragon who blocked us until we could solve a riddle, and we did solve it after we left—it was telling us that entering the last cavern was entering the Shadowlands—so the dragon will let us in now! And I don't think he's in any special trap besides the Shadowlands itself. He always looked like he belongs in that cave, and other times I've seen him he wasn't in any trap either. Billy, why are you shaking your head?"

"It is good that you came to Gatemoodle rather than going straightaway after First Changing Beast in the caves," answered Billy. "As you just said, you have also seen First Changing Beast other places."

"Yeah, like Shadowlands Stonehenge."

"And I am sure you have seen many other things in the Shadowlands, random things that have in common only that they trouble you or attract you. Even a terrestrial entrance to the Shadowlands will open to a place that is mind as much as world."

"Then that's even better!" replied Dan. "First Changing

Beast is totally on my mind, so any trip I take to the Shadow-lands will lead me to him. OK, now you're all shaking your heads."

"Sister is smarter than you," said Crackerbones.

"If you saw her there, she saw you," said Mother Ferny.

"She will have twisted the shadow paths so that you cannot sense him," said Billy.

"How can she do that if the Shadowlands are in my mind?" protested Dan. But even as he said it, he remembered Sister there changing in front of his eyes so that she looked like the female avatar of First Changing Beast and then the old Mexican Rattleman. Dan's Shadowland mind was not trustworthy.

"Not *in* your mind," answered Billy. "*Of* your mind and of the world as well."

Dan shook his head and slumped his shoulders. "Then maybe I'm wrong too about the trap, maybe he's in some special trap that I never saw because of some weird Shadowlands reason."

"Perhaps," said Billy. "But perhaps the absence of a trap is a true perception, since you never saw one in any of your contacts with First Changing Beast, and Sister did not know of you at the beginning and so would not have known to disguise a trap from you. Perhaps the Shadowlands itself is the trap."

"But I can get in and out of the Shadowlands, and Maggie too, and probably lots of people," said Dan. "So why can't First Changing Beast? Why does he need me to free him?"

Billy furrowed his brow. "As I said before, we must all ponder this."

Everyone fell silent. Maggie cleared her throat and said, "Even if we do not yet know the nature of the trap from which Dan must free the Beast, I think I know how to find our way there. Rather than searching for the Beast, we will track Sister.

When we feel her in the Shadowlands, we will follow her to the Beast."

Everyone looked at her. "We have not the power to track Sister," said Mother Ferny. "Nor have you the power to defeat Sister in a Shadowlands battle."

"But I will have the power to track Sister, for you will aid my learning, Mother Ferny," said Maggie. "Already I am close. Sister has been able to feel my whereabouts for some time."

"Indeed, that is how she knew to begin her attack just now," said Billy.

Maggie nodded. "Since the Marrowland, where I learned who Sister is—not only that she is my mortal changeling, but *who* she is, struggling to survive my father's abuse and my mother's weakness, I have been able to sense her. Mother Ferny, can you not teach me to aim this power to know where she is precisely?"

"That I can do, child," said the witch. "But I do not wish to send you to a fight you must lose."

"We won't lose it if we learn the twofold meaning of Minik Mingarria," said Dan.

"And how will you do that?" asked Crackerbones, with a sneer that he barely stifled.

"You are the wisest people that I know in Inland," answered Dan. "Can you not tell me?"

The Gatekeepers looked at each other. "We cannot," said Billy.

"Then I'll ask the wisest person I know in Outland. Dr. Green."

"My big brother!" said Maggie in a tone of wonderment. "But how can he help us? He no longer knows about Inland."

"I'm not sure I can explain it," said Dan. "I feel like I must already know the twofold meaning of Minik Mingarria, that the understanding is somewhere inside me. Otherwise, why would First Changing Beast have looked at me like that? And why would you Gatekeepers have chosen me for the quest? You've never been able to explain that. Even Maggie's fairy mother thinks I'm the right one, she told us so when she gave us the backstory about Sister and Dr. Green. But I was chosen for some reason. I must be able to free First Changing Beast, and that means going through Sister. Anyway, Dr. Green has always been good at helping me figure out what's inside me."

"I think your idea is a good one," said Billy with a nod. "Even if his mind does not know it, Jack Green still is akin with Inland deep in his bones. That will help him guide your thoughts."

"Well, what are you waiting for?" asked Crackerbones. "My scouts girdle Gatemoodle aboveground and below and they have reported no enemies, but Sister and her armies will be upon us sooner than we like."

"Uhh. I can't go straight to Outland. I don't have Breaklock."

"Fool!" snapped Crackerbones. In the same moment Mother Ferny gasped, "Oh!" Billy just stared.

It was about the reaction Dan expected. Breaklock, created by witch magic and nature magic from a branch of the Mayan world tree and Pacal's bracelet, was a precious amulet that could make a gate between the worlds upon demand. Although many lusted after it, it had been bequeathed to Dan to help him on his quest.

"But don't worry," he said. "Josh and Alice are taking it to Graciela so she can come here and deliver her message. And maybe you don't have any idea what her message is about, but we do. She was trying to discover the truth about what happened between her aunt and Maggie's Outland father—the birth father of Sister. Graciela's aunt and Maggie's Outland father were lovers, and then Maggie's fairy father did something to him."

"And this is not important only to me, so that I know my heritage," put in Maggie. "Before my fairy father cursed him, my fairy mother put a charm on him, so that whoever loved both his daughters—me and Sister—would heal Sister. I still worry that my fairy father killed him, but if not, Sister's birth father may be the one who can stop Sister's evil by loving her as well as me." She looked down briefly. "I believe he loved me as a toddler, and who better to love Sister than her birth father?"

Dan didn't feel like mentioning that Maggie's fairy mother thought that Dan was probably the person who could save Sister by loving her as well as Maggie. Yuck, talk about zero chance.

"You bear up well under grim discoveries about your two sets of parents," said Mother Ferny.

Maggie shrugged and took Dan's hand. "I am accustomed to it by now. Dan helps."

"Indeed you did well to send for Graciela," said Billy. "This is a large vine in the tangle around Sister, and may help us solve her."

"In fact, I thought Graciela might be here before us," said Dan. "Only ... I didn't know a war would be starting. Could she be in trouble with enemy soldiers?"

"Is she good enough to open a gate right inside this hall?" retorted Crackerbones. "If not, she had better arrive soon, or you have given both her and Breaklock to our enemies."

"Perhaps not," said Maggie. Everyone turned to her, but she said, "Wait!" and ran to the door. She sang out two clear notes, and after a moment a magpie landed on her shoulder and nibbled her earlobe. Maggie whispered and it took off swiftly. Maggie ran back to the table, saying, "My magpies have not seen Graciela but will continue to search. As for Sister, I do not think she will approach Gatemoodle anytime soon. I sense her at the outskirts of the Marrowland."

"That's right!" said Dan. "Your father the King told us he was girding for her attack. Maybe she hates him so much that she means to defeat him and his fairy army before challenging Gatemoodle. Whew. Graciela should be safe." He looked toward the door, wishing for her knock.

"What kind of attack do you fear, Billy?" asked Maggie. "Once before goblins besieged Gatemoodle, and even brought the Unlight, but could not break down your doors."

Dan shivered at the thought of the Unlight. Iron was deadly to Inland creatures, and Sister had somehow used iron to create Unlight, a seeping grayness that sapped will and life from all it struck. Sister had also been able to immunize against iron some creatures that worked for her, so they were able to wield it with deadly effect. Luckily, there didn't seem to be much iron available in Inland.

Billy was answering Maggie. "Even then we were trapped inside, and would have starved if you had not come and rescued us with your Outland magic." Dan thought that had been about the weirdest thing in all his adventures—he had accidentally discovered that cell phones neutralized iron and Unlight both. Not all cell phones, though, only ones that had been given as a present. He fingered the iPhone in his pocket. Josh and his other friends had given it to him.

"It is clear from the news you bring us that Sister has tapped more and more power from First Changing Beast," continued Billy. "If she comes herself with the Unlight, I fear it will be more than we and the old hall can bear. As for what her armies will be ..."

"To understand war, go not to hobgoblins or witches. Go to

a goblin," interrupted Crackerbones. "She will send Gragguts's warriors." Crackerbones spat. He had been chief of the local goblins until recently, but Gragguts had deposed him and only small bands remained loyal to Crackerbones. "I have learned that she has animated sticks and grass bound in human form that she calls malkins, that respond to her will alone. And most of the giants will fight for her. Noggles too, but we need not fear them this far from salt water. Beyond that, all races are corruptible: human, dwarf, kobold, gnome, redcap, thrumkin, bulbeggar, and all the rest. We will know sooner than we like.

"Your news is good that Sister is not near, but do not be overly heartened. I fear her armies are big enough that she can attack in two places at once. Even as she leads an attack on the Marrowland, she can send an army to weaken Gatemoodle and come for the kill after finishing the fairies."

"Like we told you, the King of the Fairies is a horrible person," said Dan. "But I got the impression that he and his fighters are tough. Maybe Sister won't win there."

"All the same, we must do more to prepare," said Crackerbones. "At least the dwarves from the local mines are wily enough to realize that Gragguts's boys are a worse threat to them than my band, so they have joined us. Goblin and dwarf, we block all the underground passages and can emerge as needed."

"I worry about the creek side though," said Billy. A shallow lazy creek wound to the east of Gatemoodle. Beyond it was a wide field of lush grass and wildflowers, and beyond that a great woodland. It was from that direction that Dan and Maggie had traveled. "Maggie, was there any sign of the Moss Maidens? Have they returned? Their woodland glamour would be protection indeed."

Maggie's eyes grew damp. "Alas, no. As you know they are

my cousins who first welcomed me here, although they blessed my departure to search for my true family. Now that I have seen and spoken to my father and mother, I like the Moss Maidens even better, and hoped against hope that I would find them in their old groves. But when Sister's Unlight came against them, they fled beyond my ken. Only Iralia's heart remains. What did you call her spell, Mother Ferny?"

"Makeless Making, an ancient and powerful spell. Even the strongest magicians avoid it, for it comes at great cost. With it the caster can grant to someone whatever freedom she likes, but at the moment of casting she loses a freedom of her own, and will not know what she has lost until after. Iralia gave her deep groves freedom from the Unlight. But she lost her body and the freedom it gives. Her heart dwells in the trees, but never again will she dance or sing, even if her sisters should return."

Dan was sad for Maggie, and sad for the Moss Maidens, but Crackerbones was as unsentimental as usual. "I never thought they would help. We must dam the creek, as I have said. That flooded field will be impassable."

"But we know not what water spirits Sister may have corrupted," protested Mother Ferny. "And we cannot be certain that we are safe from her noggles. Maggitch was working on a spell to free the noggles from their need for salt. She made much progress although she never had the chance to finish."

Mother Ferny dipped her head to Dan and Maggie. Maggitch was a witch who had worked for Sister, and on Dan and Maggie's first trip to Inland she had enslaved Maggie by speaking her truename. Dan had only been able to free Maggie by finding an ally strong enough to slay Maggitch. And that gave him an idea about protecting the creek. But before he could say anything, a knock came on the door.

"Graciela!" said Dan. He jumped up and strode to the door. Even as thick and tall as it was, it opened smoothly and silently on its great brass hinges.

But it wasn't Graciela standing there.

It was a broad, scar-faced, armor-clad goblin who gnashed his sharp teeth at Dan as he held out a drawn sword in his right hand.

Only after Dan staggered back from the wicked-looking notched blade did he notice the dirty white cloth tied to its tip.

"Gragguts," said Crackerbones.

"Hello, brother," said the other goblin, pointing at the white cloth that fluttered in a breeze from the open door. "Today is not the day that we discover whose blade has the deepest bite."

"What business have you to justify a parley?" asked Crackerbones.

"Business of the Golden Lady, of course."

"Pah! Do not bring talk of a golden lady into our great hall. She has gone by Sister up till now, and Sister she remains." Billy and Mother Ferny nodded at Crackerbones's words.

"But it will not be your hall for long," said Gragguts. He swung his sword at the thick doorpost, and snarled when it rebounded without leaving a scratch. "Where is your vaunted ancient courtesy? Will you not invite me in? Will you not serve me some of your famous Outland food?"

"Please enter and be seated," said Billy in a flat voice. "We have exactly one bowl left of stew."

Gragguts strode to the table with an athlete's confident posture. Billy scooped stew from the bottom of the pot into a bowl, but as he turned from the stove his feet somehow got tangled, he stumbled against a shelf, and a small vial spilled into the bowl.

"One of your poisons, hobgoblin?" asked Gragguts.

"My apologies," said Billy. "You will not want this now. And that was the last of it."

Dan caught Mother Ferny's wink and smiled. Billy had never been clumsy before.

Gragguts glowered. "Never mind. Soon enough we will control the Gates and have access to all the Outland food we want." He slammed his hand on the table. "But we wish to avoid bloodshed. Goblin against goblin, brother against brother, this is not good. We give you your due, Crackerbones, you are doughty and you lead your band well. Drula and her dwarves are a powerful army. But we have the numbers, and we have the giants, and we have the Unlight. We will wade through your blood to this very hall. And yes, I well understand that we will not take the hall with force of arms." He nodded to Cracker-bones, Mother Ferny, and last to Billy. "You do not look like much, especially when you pretend to stumble with my food, but I know that even wielding the Unlight my troops cannot conquer you.

"But when we have cleared the way she will come, the Golden Lady, floating above the corpses of your soldiers. And before the Golden Lady wielding the Unlight you will fall. These timbers will shudder, crack, and dry to dust. She will shrivel you all like frogs in the desert sun." Gragguts looked at Maggie and Dan and licked his lips. "And she will take this one, and this one, and have her way with them.

"All this can be avoided. All you need do is give me the fairy and the mortal now."

"You waste our time and yours as well with this absurd request, Gragguts," answered Billy. Dan looked at him closely. Billy had always reminded him of a warm grandfather, but something different rang in his voice now. "Perhaps you truly came only for my cooking, since you cannot have thought we would agree to these terms. But before we send you out, consider this: you resent and resist the authority of Crackerbones your brother. Do you truly wish to serve a tyrant, whether she goes by Sister or by Golden Lady? She serves only her own desires, and will toss you aside as soon as you do not please her. Come back! Come back to Crackerbones and the old Inland."

"The old Inland is no more, and you know it," said Gragguts. "Its gates are mostly gone and all your efforts barely keep the last ones ajar. Sister will open them wide and make Inland new, flourishing, and strong. She only requires allegiance."

"Water and wind ..." said Mother Ferny.

"... mountain and rock ..." said Crackerbones.

"... Passion and thought," said Billy. "None give allegiance, nor do we. Begone."

"Fairy girl?" said Gragguts. "Mortal boy? Have you more sense than these old gibberers? Do you even know who they really are? Come with me."

Dan and Maggie just stared at him.

Gragguts shrugged. "Easy now, hard later, but you will come." Then he pounded his chest with his right hand. "Crackerbones, our swords will meet in the coming battle and you will fall."

"I said begone," repeated Billy. The door swung open and Gragguts stumbled out as though someone were pushing him between the shoulder blades. The door slammed behind him.

Billy picked up the last bowl of stew and took a bite. "Would anybody care for some? A bit too much salt, but still tasty."

2

POWER TALES

*D*an gazed at Maggie's leg as she raised it from her tub. She flipped water with her toes and with perfect aim landed the drops on Dan's head.

Mother Ferny had understood that they were sore and grubby after three days hiking from Iralia's grove, so water had been heated and sent up in the dumbwaiter to Dan and Maggie's loft room. They each had a small tub to soak in; not as fun as sharing a regular size tub, but somehow appropriate to the rustic feel of Gatemoodle.

Dan karate-chopped water at Maggie but completely missed. She laughed and sank back. He raised his arm for another splash, but instead lowered it into the tub quietly.

"It's hard to believe there's really going to be a war," said Dan. "What if Graciela is out there caught by the enemy? I hoped Josh and Alice would come back with her, but now I hope they don't. None of them are fighters. I guess if they do come I'll have to take them right back to Outland when I go to see Dr. Green."

"I too worry about Graciela," said Maggie, "for her safety, and, selfish though this may be, so that I may hear what she learned about my Outland father. He was the only one of my four parents who treated me well. We do not even know if my fairy father's spell left him alive." She sighed. "I hope my magpies sight Graciela soon."

Dan saw tears in Maggie's eyes. "I wonder if that Makeless Making could be used to free your Outland father from your fairy father's spell," he said. "And I wonder if it can be used to stop the war. I'm going to ask them at the war council tomorrow, but I guess they would have told us if it could. Maybe the risk is too great. Iralia was very brave."

"Yes. I miss her."

They soaked away aches in silence, and then Maggie said, "I never knew that Gragguts and Crackerbones were brothers."

"Me neither," said Dan. "It's pretty hard to like Crackerbones, but meeting his wife Loosejaw last time we were here, and now seeing he's got family troubles, kind of humanizes him. If 'humanizes' is a word that can even be used for a goblin. 'Goblinizes?'"

"I guess we'll see Loosejaw again tomorrow, and Drula too."

"Yep," said Dan. "Drula was always nice to us, but I didn't know she was important enough to lead the dwarves. I'm happy for her."

"My old Outland self worries about how slow they are here to organize for the battle," said Maggie. "Not until this morning did Crackerbones send out summons for a war council, but it sounds as though Gragguts's army is already on the move. Yet my fairy self is happy with their meandering pace. And I like it that they said the meeting will run from dawn to dusk, although I do not understand why it will need so much time. It is mysterious."

"I think meandering mystery is part of what Sister intends to change," said Dan. "Get things efficiently organized here more like Outland. And it does give an advantage for stuff like war. What a depressing idea." After a pause he added, "I wonder how long it will take them to assemble for the council. And I wonder where Graciela is."

"If she is anywhere near, my magpies should know by nightfall."

But no word had come when darkness fell.

DAN'S first question at least was answered by the clang of a bell while it was still dark. Dan and Maggie dressed by candlelight and made their way downstairs. Several figures murmured around the big table. Dan and Maggie took seats between Billy and Mother Ferny. As the light grew, they made out Crackerbones next to his wife, Loosejaw, who smiled at them and then slapped her jaw back into place. Drula sat next to the red dwarf Fir Darrig; they smiled and nodded. A large chair sat empty.

Billy nodded at it. "The wodewoses send word that their sunstones do not favor either side. They will not come. I do not know what delays Boe. We will have to proceed without him."

Crackerbones shrugged. "Perhaps we are better off without him. He cares for his precious road, but does not care who walks upon it."

"Nay, he fears Sister as much as we do. Boe wants roads that are free, but Sister wants all roads to lead to her. Now, breakfast first."

Dan and Maggie looked at each other and raised their eyebrows as food was brought. Boe Bulbeggar was a man who could turn into a big black dog and looked a little like a dog in any case. Kind of scary, but he had helped protect them from Sister and her goblins before. He would be a fierce ally.

"Oatmeal with fruits that concentrate the sun that shone as they grew," said Billy, setting bowls on the table. "Sun to help us grow today." Dan wondered what Billy meant, but after taking a bite full of piercing flavors had attention only for the food. As he licked the last of it from his spoon, he heard Fir Darrig speaking.

"I wield the Outland jewelry that is Unlight's bane." Fir Darrig lifted his necklace of cell phones that Dan and Maggie had given him on past trips, little knowing that they would turn out to be the Outland spell that defeated Outland iron.

"And I have another one, given me by my friends," said Dan, pulling his iPhone from his pocket.

Smiles rippled around the table. "That is good," said Billy.

"Drula's people and ours guard the mines and mountains," said Crackerbones. "If the bulbeggars protect the road, we have only the creek side to worry about. Again I say we should flood it."

"Blocking a woodland invasion but opening ourselves to invasion by water," said Mother Ferny, "does not seem wise."

"I have an idea!" said Dan.

Crackerbones snorted, but Loosejaw elbowed him and said, "Listen to Ironbreaker."

"Well, I'm friends with Nellie Longarms," said Dan. He paused a moment, gazing at the strange people sitting around the table. Of all of them, and all the other weird creatures he had met in Inland, he might be fondest of the water spirit Nellie Longarms—not counting Maggie, of course, who was giving him a look he couldn't quite identify. Maggie was always suspicious that Dan mainly liked Nellie for her looks. In fact, he didn't understand himself exactly why Nellie meant so much to him, but there was no time to try to figure it out now. "She's helped me, and Maggie too, a bunch of times." As long as he always promised to give her Outland food—he hoped Graciela would bring some canned tuna when she came. If she came. He glanced at the door.

Crackerbones was shaking his head. "Nellie has never taken sides. Whoever walks by her river, goblin, dwarf, or human, fears her."

"But Nellie says we even have a mental connection that happened because she thrice helped me," said Dan. "So I'm pretty sure she'll come help us if I ask her. She has a friend, Jenny Greenteeth. I bet no noggles could get by them."

"I don't know what Nellie sees in him, but believe me, she likes Dan," said Maggie. Her arms were crossed but at least she was smiling.

"Then this is a good plan!" exclaimed Billy. Even Cracker-bones nodded.

"Nellie might bring other friends too," said Fir Darrig.

"Only one problem," said Dan. "Nellie needs deep water, and this hall sits on low ground, not much above the river. If we flood it deep enough for her, Gatemoodle will be flooded too.'

"That is no problem," said Crackerbones.

Dan saw Billy's eyes twinkling, but he wasn't reassured. He remembered something else from *World of Warcraft* and a bunch of movies. "Wait ... Gatemoodle is set in this valley. River on one side, hills and mountains on the other. Attackers will have the high ground, doesn't that give them a huge advantage?"

"That is no problem," said Crackerbones again. Billy's eyes were still twinkling. Inland meandering and mystery and lack of planning were cool in a way, but—were these guys nuts? The enemy would just rain down arrows.

Mother Ferny didn't seem worried either as she said, "The last piece of our planning is to know whether Sister will lead the attack. Maggie, do you sense her whereabouts?"

"She remains near the Marrowland. Perhaps she concentrates on attacking our father."

"That is good!" said Crackerbones. "I am confident we can withstand Gragguts's attack if she does not come. That is, we can withstand it if the bulbeggar arrives to help." He looked at the door.

"As for that, we can only wait and hope," said Billy. "But now is time for preparation. Our planning is done."

"Planning is done?" said Dan. "What about military strategy, and where to station troops, and trenches and bulwarks and—"

"Now is time to prepare," repeated Billy.

"But wait, I have another idea!" said Dan. "Maggie and I were talking last night: how about using Makeless Making to stop the war?"

"The cost would be worse than the war itself," said Mother Ferny. "Iralia gave up her body, and that was to contest only one pot of Unlight, and even that was a mighty act. We know not how much Unlight we face, and how many soldiers. Even if we reach to other friends not here, there are not enough of us to join in a Makeless Making with power enough to stop the war. And although it is never known ahead of time what freedom is being surrendered to create the Makeless Making, we can be certain it would render us defenseless. Sister would stroll unmolested into Gatemoodle."

"How about after the Makeless Making, have some other people do a Makeless Making to undo the losses from the first one?" Even as he said it, Dan knew it couldn't be that simple.

"Makeless Making cannot be unmade by Makeless Making," replied Mother Ferny.

Dan looked at Maggie. "Different question then. Once Graciela gets here and tells us whatever Maggie's fairy father did to her Outland father, could Makeless Making undo it?"

"I am sorry, children," said Mother Ferny. "Makeless Making must be performed quickly after the event it is intended to change. The more time that passes, the less power it will have."

"We know that what you have learned about your parents grieves you, Maggie," said Billy. "Let us hope that Graciela brings news that is less painful, but now time passes. It is time to prepare."

"OK, but one more thing: at least tell me how we're going to dam the creek and when I should call Nellie Longarms," said Dan.

"You will call Nellie Longarms after you dam the creek," said Mother Ferny.

"But—" said Dan.

"You will dam it with the help of those you call," added Mother Ferny.

"But—"

Dan closed his mouth when Billy frowned at him and repeated, "Now is the time to prepare."

"It is ours to begin," said Crackerbones and Loosejaw in one voice.

"And mine to begin with you," said Drula.

They began telling stories. Dan looked around the table to see if anyone shared his bafflement, but all were listening intently. Even Maggie put her finger to her lips and turned to the speakers.

Dan sighed and started to pay attention.

Drula was talking about the darkness underground, and how it is deeper than the middle of a starless moonless night aboveground. She talked about the creatures that navigate the lightless passages, bats and blind crayfish and dragons and their whelps. She spoke about unexpected breezes in the deep places that hint at unknown passages to openings in the earth. She spoke about the textures of rocks.

At some point Dan realized it was no longer Drula's voice but Loosejaw's, praising the hardness of granite, the sparkle of mica, black hornblende and pink feldspar and quartzite of many colors; flint and chert that could be flaked into tools, marble that could be shaped into pleasing columns. Then she was back in the caves, telling of the joy that ores took winding through the dross, the joys that goblins took following the ore, green copper, pallid gold, glinting silver, and the flash of gems in lamplight: sapphire blue, ruby red, the white fire of diamonds.

Now it was Crackerbones's voice describing cold mud between the toes, cold water that swept away the mud, underground drips and drops that lightless day after lightless night, year after year, century after century, crystallized into stalactites, stalagmites, columns, straws, and dripstones, ancient pools fed by nameless streams, streams that found their way in and out of caves, not sure if they preferred the fresh air or the calm embrace of the earth.

The two goblins chanted with voices like rock scraping skin, and the dwarf joined in with her voice smooth as a polished jewel. Dan was no longer sure of their exact words, but he followed the chant into the hearts of mountains and the lungs of the earth. He had lost track of time but knew it could not be much past midday, yet Gatemoodle had grown dim like the corner of a cavern. The voices faded to the swish of bat wings, and then were gone, but Dan's dream continued and he felt a tremor in the hall, and gentle movement like a boat accepting the swells of a peaceful sea.

Mother Ferny began telling stories about roots and stalks, tendrils and trunks, leaves swaying in the breeze, rattling in the wind, spattered with rain or drinking in sunlight. She talked about reticent lichens, quiet mosses, and mighty trunks heaving their branches toward the sky. She talked of thorns and brambles, of poison ivy and poison sumac and toadstools whose poison waited hours after being eaten before gripping the heart in cold death. She spoke of savory golden brown mushrooms, and green smelly walnut husks hiding nutty treasure, and berries waiting within the thorns to be found.

As she talked, sunlight returned to Gatemoodle, and squirrels leaped among the branches, and deer cropped the leaves, and a bear stepped into a clearing, and Fir Darrig's voice stepped into Mother Ferny's. Fir Darrig told the animals' tales: the bear heedless of thorns raking berries into his mouth with juice-stained paws; the rabbits leaving tracks in fresh white snow beneath a fresh white moon as owls mourned; a fox leaping headfirst into the snow to catch a vole that shrieked as it died; the bats that Drula had sung out of the caves, now swooping and snaring insects in their basket mouths; the white pennants of deer tails as they fled the leaping cougar. And Mother Ferny and Fir Darrig told stories of marshes becoming fields, of fields becoming thickets, of thickets becoming woods, and woods burning back to fields, and always the wildlife changing as the plants changed.

In late afternoon sunlight, Fir Darrig told stories about the secrets that pond turtles keep, and tortoises swaying beneath their shells beneath the desert sun, and Dan relaxed in the warm breeze and felt Gatemoodle swaying as though it rode the shell of a giant tortoise.

Wait. What? Was Gatemoodle really swaying? Dan looked around but no one else appeared worried.

Fir spoke about his own pony named Turtle, and Maggie laughed, for Turtle had been their helper and companion on their first trip to Gatemoodle. Dan worried that he was being lulled but couldn't resist joining her laughter as Fir told stories about Turtle facing down noggles and Oakmen.

Then Maggie began to tell the story of when she and Dan had truenamed each other. It had been the only plan Dan could come up with to protect Maggie when Sister tried to truename her, so when Sister caught them they had spoken each other's truenames in the nick of time. Clumsily, like at his first high school dance, Dan began to tell the story with Maggie, and then his words and Maggie's harmonized. They told of how they had first felt wonderful, like they had found true love purer than any knight and lady, clearer than a mountain brook, fresher than lilac on a late spring breeze, a love that included and needed no one else. But then they told how a rift grew between themselves and the rest of the world, and the rift widened, and Dan told how Maggie was everything and he was nothing and he was Maggie, and Maggie told how Dan was everything and she was nothing and she was Dan, and they told of their conjoined nightmare of solitude, broken only with the help of dear friends Josh and Alice. As they told this story Dan remembered the moment when the spell was broken and he recovered his real love for Maggie, and his heart beat deep and strong.

But that lurch wasn't my heart! Something really was shaking Gatemoodle, and no one noticed but Dan. He imagined giants pushing against the timbers, rocking Gatemoodle off its foundation. He imagined goblins burrowing underneath, about to break through the floor. Or even dragons buffeting the old hall with their wings. If no one else would do anything, it was up to Dan. He began to stand.

Billy Portman said, "Now I tell my stories last. Listen all! Listen, Dan!" Dan still longed for his bow, but his legs refused to take his ears away from Billy's words. Billy said that Dan and Maggie's tale had reminded him of households sick and households healthy. He spoke of thresholds that none could pass without permission, and warm well-tended hearths, and rooms and minds that took on each other's shape from long living together, and beds for resting and lovemaking and giving birth, and especially of the kitchen. He spoke of great stoves and little stoves and cooking over the hearth; he spoke of pots and pans blackened from long use, and plates whole, chipped, repaired, and discarded, and cupboards full and empty, and the magic of spices and the blending of flavors. And he spoke of flour and oil and yeast becoming dough that grew to be beaten down and then grow again until in the oven's embrace it became a crusty loaf. And as Billy spoke, Gatemoodle seemed to swell and sigh, and settle back to rest.

Gradually Dan became aware that no more stories were being told. He and Maggie were holding hands. He waited for the light to return as he returned from his dreamlike state, but the darkness remained; they had talked all the day long without a bite since breakfast. As far as Dan knew Billy had been at the table the whole time, but now the hobgoblin was passing out thick slabs of warm freshly baked brown bread with butter and jam.

Someone knocked at the door. Everyone at the table glanced up, but kept their seats and kept chewing. The knocking came again. Mother Ferny sighed, swallowed, stood, and waved her hands and muttered. Candles and hanging lamps flickered into life, and Dan saw Billy walk heedlessly to the door.

Had no one else felt Gatemoodle shaking? Did no one else recognize the danger?

Dan sprinted for his bow and arrow. Billy ignored him as the knocking came again, louder. Billy reached the door and threw it wide.

A big black dog walked in with the nighttime, and beside him walked a young woman.

"Graciela!" shouted Dan and Maggie.

"Hello, everyone," said Graciela. Then she ran into the room and hugged Maggie. Dan threw down his bow and ran to them, and Graciela hugged him too, although an awkward inch remained between their bodies. Dan and Graciela had clinched and kissed once, after their epic battle with Sister in the Natural History Museum, before they realized what they were doing and pushed apart. When they pulled back this time Dan wasn't sure if it was too quick or too slow.

"Since when has Gatemoodle been on top of a high ridge?" asked Graciela.

Dan strode past a smiling Billy to the still-open door and stepped outside. Under moon and star he saw a landscape transformed. No longer in a valley, the great hall and its outbuildings now rested on a wide ridge at least one hundred feet high. In front of Dan the pathway wound down the narrow axis of the ridge to join the roadway. To his left the drop-off was steep, and he heard the creek swishing by below. To his right the ridge sloped more gently into a valley that then rose again into the ridges and hills.

"Awesome!" said Dan, turning back inside. "How did you do that?"

"You were here," said Billy.

"You heard all, and you took part," added Mother Ferny.

"I heard a bunch of stories that kind of put me in a trance is all," said Dan.

"You heard stories of the great web." Billy paused and smiled. "Long before your Outland computer World Wide Web, there has been a world wide web of life, the web that weaves and is woven by First Changing Beast."

"OK, the earth and plants and animals all interacting in a web, that's ecology stuff, that makes sense," said Dan. "But Maggie's and my stories about love, and your stories about the home, I don't see how those fit in."

Billy furrowed his brow. "All Outland seems to share your ignorance. Perhaps that is one reason that the gates between our worlds have been closing. And that gives me an idea about how First Changing Beast is trapped ..."

"What's your idea?" asked Dan.

Billy shook his head. "I must consider it more. But however that may be, the web heard us, including our stories of love and the hearth, and knew our need, and responded."

Dan wasn't at all sure he understood, but right now he was more concerned about Graciela. She sat beside Maggie, stuffing bread in her mouth with buttery fingers. No wonder: she was even skinnier than usual, her clothes were dirty, her glasses were filmy, and her long black hair was snarled; she must have had a hard journey. Somehow her disheveled state made her half-Maya features even more striking than usual. Dan pulled his eyes away and smiled at Maggie as she worked her fingers through Graciela's tangles.

Graciela swallowed, wiped her fingers on a napkin, and said, "I'm sorry to be so rude. Thank you for the delicious bread, Billy. Boe and I haven't had much to eat. Let me have one more piece and I'll tell you about it."

Dan was eager to hear from Graciela, but sudden exhaustion struck him such a blow that he crumpled onto the bench. Maggie sagged and her fingers dropped from Graciela's hair. Even Billy, Mother Ferny, the goblins, and the dwarves looked drained.

"You are welcome to all Gatemoodle has to offer, Graciela," said Billy. "But you are worn from traveling, and we are deeply weary from our storytelling. We must sleep now and listen to your tale in the morning light."

"But I can tell you what happened to Maggie's human father!" said Graciela. In a lower voice she added, "If you really want to know."

"Oh, I do," sighed Maggie. But she laid her head on the table and closed her eyes.

"Tomorrow will be early enough," said Graciela. She almost sounded relieved. To Dan and Maggie she added, "You guys go to bed. I remember the way to my room. I need a little more bread now."

Maggie trudged upstairs, but Dan stayed a moment longer, even though he had to lean on the table. "How are Josh and Alice?" he asked.

"They're OK," said Graciela through a mouthful. "I think they feel a little guilty about not coming back with me, but some of what you guys went through before they left really freaked them out. But they said they have to come back in time for your wedding. Best Man and Maid of Honor, true?"

"True," answered Dan. "I guess I'm glad they aren't here. I miss them, but there's going to be a war, and they aren't fighters, so I would have had to just take them back right away. I should take you back tomorrow too."

"Uh-uh," said Graciela. "Are you forgetting my quest to take Sister down?" On her first trip to Inland, Sister's men had captured Graciela and done something to her—she'd never said exactly what—before Dan and Josh rescued her. "For what she did to me, and for what she's trying to do to you guys. And now for what I just learned she did to my aunt and Maggie's father. Want me to tell you now, not wait till tomorrow?"

"It wouldn't be fair to hear before Maggie," mumbled Dan. Curious as he was, he had slumped against the table and laid his head in his arms.

Graciela shook him. "That must have been some story-telling," she said. "Go to bed."

The last thing Dan remembered as he struggled up the stairs was Graciela buttering a piece of bread while the black dog crunched on a big bone.

WHEN DAN AWOKE the next morning, Maggie was sitting on the edge of the bed, taking deep breaths. "You go on down," she said. "Now that it has come to it, I am nervous about Graciela's news."

"I can stay with you till you're ready."

Maggie shook her head. "I just need a moment alone to compose myself."

Graciela came down soon after Dan, rubbing her eyes and yawning, and took a seat beside him. She had met the three Gatekeepers before but not the others, so Billy introduced them.

"Welcome, Shaman Daughter," said Loosejaw.

Graciela looked at Billy, who winked. "I'm pleased to meet you all," said Graciela. "And I already said this once to Billy, but I guess I need to say it to the rest of you: I'm proud to be my father's daughter, but I'm my own person. Call me Graciela."

"We were really worried, Graciela," said Dan. "Why did it take so long to get here?"

"I tried to make a gate open right here," answered Graciela. "Oh, and here's Breaklock." Dan noticed Crackerbones narrow his eyes and lick his lips as she passed him the precious amulet. "But I guess the one location I had made a gate before was in the back of my mind, so this one ended up opening by that little pool, remember?"

Dan nodded and sighed. That was the gate he and Maggie had used, with Boe Bulbeggar's help, to lure Sister into Outland a while back, resulting in all sorts of adventures that mostly backfired and culminated in Sister learning Maggie's truename ...

"At least I knew the way to Gatemoodle from there," continued Graciela. "When I got down to the path, Boe Bulbeggar was sitting on a boulder, almost like he was waiting for me. Hey, where is Boe now?"

"He breakfasted before dawn, and now he roams the road searching for any threat," said Billy.

Graciela nodded. "He was in his creepy almost-human form when he met me, but I remembered you telling me how he helped you, Dan, so I wasn't too scared. He said that war was brewing but scouts of the enemy would fear him. That was seven days ago."

"But it's only a four-day walk to Gatemoodle from there!" said Dan. "What happened?" Then he counted on his fingers. "Wait a minute. It's only been five days since we said goodbye to Josh and Alice and sent them to find you with Breaklock."

"Story time travels in loops, slower and faster as the mind lingers and then hungers for more," said Billy. "We do not count like you, but enough time has passed for Graciela's journey."

Dan had encountered enough weirdness about Inland time

in his past visits that he took this in stride and turned back to Graciela.

"Boe and I hadn't been walking for more than a couple hours when we spotted some goblins. Boe switched into dog form and was after them like lightning and they ran for their lives. I felt pretty safe after that. But then we came to a long straight stretch and in the distance, maybe half a mile away, was some guy walking slowly toward us. I didn't get a very good look, because Boe immediately hustled me into the under-brush, but it looked like a tall guy in formal clothes, even wearing a top hat. Boe seemed scared, even though this dude looked totally nonthreatening to me. Boe said we didn't want to hear anything from him, called him Skriker."

"Oh no!" said Maggie. Dan hadn't heard her come down the stairs.

"What's the big deal?" asked Graciela. "Boe wouldn't explain it. Said it would scare me."

"Maggie and I ran into him once before," said Dan. "He's not dangerous himself, but he has an awful wail. You didn't hear him?" Graciela shook her head, and Dan said, "Thank God."

"But that's why it took us so long to get here. He seemed to be dogging our journey ... well, speaking of dogging, Boe switched back into dog form and stayed there, said he would be able to smell if Skriker was near. He would only let us travel by night."

"That explains why my magpies did not espy you," inter-rupted Maggie.

"And even at night he kept guiding us away from the road, finding places to hide in the shrubbery. Once or twice I saw the —Skriker—through the branches, and he was just an old skinny gent. Since Boe was in dog form he couldn't explain even if he wanted. What's the big deal?"

"Skriker is a Doom-caller," said Mother Ferny. "He wails, and someone who hears the wail, or someone close to them, will die."

"Oh," said Graciela in a small voice. "OK, but we never heard him."

"If he followed you in this direction, one of us will hear his wail sooner than we like," said Crackerbones. All of them— Billy, Mother Ferny, Crackerbones, Loosejaw, Drula, and Fir Darrig—looked at each other, and at Dan, Maggie, and Graciela.

Crackerbones shrugged. "We already knew we faced war," he said. "We should not be surprised by death, not even by our own."

3

A CRY AT NOON

*D*an looked around the silent table. "Well, we haven't heard him yet. Can't we do something? Block Skriker from coming closer? Wear earplugs? Yeah, pretend I didn't say that last thing."

"No good will come from attempting to avoid Skriker," said Billy. "We would have to flee Gatemoodle, when our presence here is needed to defend it. And many a traveler has fled Skriker only to be startled by his shriek just before they plummeted over a cliff or into a sucking swamp because of their heedless flight. Perhaps he is merely passing through on his way to some doomed soul far from here. Or perhaps he will wail for one of the enemy when they arrive. What will be, will be."

"And speaking of the enemy arriving, it's time for you to get busy damming the creek, Quest Boy," said Crackerbones.

"But Maggie's here now. We need to learn what Graciela found out."

Crackerbones glowered. "One important thing delays

another. I do not believe that news about the other father will aid us against Sister as much as our defenses will."

"We must choose between these two actions with the heart," said Mother Ferny.

"Tell us your tale, Graciela," said Billy.

"DAN AND MAGGIE know the first part of this already, but for the rest of you: my Tia Josefina was like a mother to me after my own mother died. I lived most of the year in New York with my mother's relatives, but whenever I returned to Mexico it was Tia Josi's embrace that I looked forward to. She told me that she had once been in love but had lost her lover, but at least to my child's eyes she seemed to have accepted this fate. She happily told me that I too would fall in love one day. But when I returned to Mexico for the summer of my thirteenth year, everything had changed. Tia Josi was cruel and aloof, and even my Papi the Shaman could not explain it.

"Recently Dan and Maggie and I learned from Mrs. Westerley—Maggie and Sister's mortal mother—that her ex-husband—Maggie and Sister's mortal father—had fallen in love with a Mexican woman named Josi. Mrs. Westerley thought that someone, either the Rattleman or Josi, had killed him."

"Not the Rattleman," said Dan. "The Rattleman is Dr. Green, and he's Maggie's brother, and he's been a good guy all along." Graciela looked startled. "I'll explain later."

"OK," Graciela resumed, "so just before coming here I went back to my little Mexican village to find out once and for all what had happened. Like usual, Josi would not speak to me and only told me go away. She spent all her time alone in her room;

it had gotten so bad that Papi and Mama Anita brought her food to eat there.

"But when I told Papi what was going on with Sister, and what we had learned from Mrs. Westerley, he said the time had come to solve this riddle. Turns out he had met Dr. Green long before at a conference of shamans and therapists, and he knew right away that Dr. Green was from Inland, even though Green hardly remembered it himself. Papi tried to use his powers to intuit more, but he didn't get much farther than a glimpse of Sister and the certainty that she was a dangerous relative.

"A couple weeks after the conference, Mr. Westerley showed up on his motorcycle. Lots of Americanos into psychedelic drugs used to come because my father is a master of magic mushrooms and other plants for his shamanism, but Mr. Westerley just wanted to talk, and he mentioned he was in therapy with Dr. Green."

"That is so weird," interrupted Dan. "That is too much coincidence, that he and I would both go into therapy with the same person."

"I do not think it sounds like coincidence," said Maggie. "Dr. Green—my brother—tried to help Sister as a baby when our fairy father was abusing her. When our fairy father banished Dr. Green to Outland, he tried to help my mortal father there, which was a form of helping me."

"OK, yeah," said Dan. "But I don't fit in that."

"Of course you do," said Billy. "Remember, you chose Dr. Green as a therapist right after we chose you to find First Changing Beast. You and Mr. Westerley are entangled in the healing of Inland. Perhaps the rest of Graciela's story will tell us how."

"OK, so," said Graciela. "It was definitely Tom Westerley who became Tia Josi's lover. They were very happy, but one day she came back from a trip and Papi knew something was wrong. Always before she had ridden back with Mr. Westerley on his motorcycle, but this time she came by bus, alone. But when Papi asked her what had happened, she said she couldn't remember. Papi wasn't even sure she remembered Tom."

"That's because their fairy mother cast a forgetting spell after whatever happened," said Dan. "But then why did your aunt turn mean when you were a teenager?"

"Just let me finish," said Graciela. "When I confronted Tia Josi with the name Tom Westerley, it finally broke her out of her mean shell and she started crying. I was mad and I demanded to know the same thing you just asked. She said that when I started to develop a woman's body it provoked her and she remembered that she and Tom had gotten to Inland by stealing and eating a bunch of Papi's magic mushrooms, and while they were there someone told them that he needed to have a different lover. In her crazy state she imagined that lover would be me.

"Papi said we had to go to Inland to consult with the aluxob." Aluxob were little people, kind of like Mayan dwarves, who were friendly to Dan when he was in Inland Mexico. "Papi is only able to visit Inland briefly, and only by eating magic mushrooms, and I sure didn't want to eat them, and neither did Josi after what had happened the other time, but Papi said he could carry both of us there if we meditated and held his hands.

"Dan, remember how the aluxob left to escape the People from the Sea?" Dan nodded emphatically. The People from the Sea were like Vikings who had colonized Inland Mexico, and Sister had turned them prejudiced against "Big Noses"—people with Mayan features, like the aluxob and Graciela. They were the ones who had captured Graciela and done something to her that she never talked about.

"We found a couple aluxob scouts who had stayed behind," continued Graciela. "And the first thing they told us that you all need to know is that the People from the Sea have sailed to join Sister's war."

Graciela paused to drink some water. Crackerbones whispered something to Loosejaw, who left quietly.

"Apparently the Fairy Queen's forgetting spell didn't work on the aluxob, so they finally told us what had happened: Josi and Tom were visiting with them when suddenly the Fairy Queen appeared with a little girl. I assume that was Sister?" Dan and Maggie nodded. "The Fairy Queen cast a spell that whoever could love both of Tom's daughters would heal them. That's what mixed into Josi's bad trip so that she thought Tom would love me. But as soon as she cast her spell the Fairy King appeared and cast his own."

Face pale, Maggie asked, "Did he kill Tom?"

"No. But ... you won't like this ... he turned him into a giant blue deer."

"Oh my god!" exclaimed Maggie.

"We met a huge blue deer once who was kind to us," said Dan. "Maggie, do you think that was your father?"

"I don't know, I don't know! And my fairy father hunts and slays blue deer. Oh, he is a terrible person!" She buried her face in Dan's chest.

"I'm sorry to bring such news," said Graciela. "I'm nearly done. That's when the Fairy Queen cast her forgetting spell, and immediately she and the girl and the King disappeared.

"But maybe this will help you feel better. The next winter, when the great deer shed his antlers, he gave them to the aluxob. Apparently the little people can understand animals, because he told them to make a horn from one of the tines. He said that in a time of need he will come when the right person blows on it."

Graciela held out a small bone-white horn with a turquoise mouthpiece.

Maggie pushed it away. "You keep it. You are as likely as I to be the right person."

THEY ALL FELL silent until Billy startled them by placing a big pot of delicious smelling soup on the table. Dan was doubly startled to realize it was lunchtime already.

"I am not hungry," said Maggie. "I wish to go to our room and think."

Dan heard his stomach grumble and he gazed at the soup, but he said, "I'll go with you."

"No need," said Maggie. "I wish to be alone."

"And you are needed here, Dan," said Mother Ferny as Maggie ran up the stairs. "You must eat quickly and then call your totem animal."

"Uhh. But I don't have a totem animal?"

"Of course you do. Eat quickly."

After Dan gulped down his soup, Mother Ferny said, "Come with me."

Dan was worried about Maggie, but he was also glad for a diversion. He had been afraid the Gatekeepers would want to discuss that thing about someone loving both Maggie and Sister. Mother Ferny was already at the door selecting a cloak from the rack, so Dan jumped up and followed her. "Take one," she said. "A rain is about to fall that will help us flood the field." Dan shrugged into a thick hooded cloak and they opened the door as the first thunder groaned overhead.

Dan paused and peered around for Skriker. No matter what Billy said, he planned to jump back inside and slam the door if he caught sight of the tall, skinny gentleman. But only Mother Ferny was in view, hurrying down the path before a curtain of rain swept in from the north. Dan caught up with her just as she turned left off the path and headed for the creek.

Before they had changed the landscape with their stories, Gatemoodle had rested in a gentle valley, bordered by a quiet creek and then a wide grassy field that eventually gave way to wild woodland. The creek still flowed alongside the wide field, its swishes and burbles mingling with the patter of raindrops. But on the side where Dan and Mother Ferny stood, the ground surged into the steep ridge on which Gatemoodle now rested.

"You see how a dam built against that cliff will give us a deep lake," said Mother Ferny. She raised her voice to be heard over thunder. "There will be a mighty storm in the mountains and rising waters."

"Then it would have to be a super strong dam, and super-long too," replied Dan. "It would have to go all across that field until it reaches higher ground in the woods."

"Of course," said Mother Ferny.

Of course? "But that will take forever to build, and I don't know anything about building dams. And I'm not trying to be difficult, but I really don't have a totem animal."

"Of course you do. What is that around your neck?"

Dan fingered the amulet he wore on a chain. "It's the transition symbol I need for the gate-creating ceremony."

"And why is it a transition symbol for you?"

"Well, it's the foot of my old stuffed beaver, Fuzzy Fat-Tail." Dan looked over his shoulder to make sure none of his friends were listening nearby. "When Billy first contacted me I was having mixed-up feelings about wanting to grow up but still liking some kid stuff, and Fat-Tail symbolized that. But I don't know why his foot still works as a transition symbol, because I'm over that now." He thought about how strong he had grown in Inland, and he thought about sleeping with Maggie. "Playing with stuffed animals is totally kid stuff."

"Do not draw too thick a veil over childhood," said Mother Ferny. "Of course you no longer desire to play with stuffed animals. But giving up stuffed animals does not mean giving up play, it merely means no longer playing as a child. Do you not know that play is a serious matter? That play is lifelong, unless you choose to live a life of death?"

Dan was silent.

"Now is a moment when you must play with roots deep in your past," Mother Ferny went on. "Take Fuzzy Fat-Tail's foot, and return in your mind to the feeling at the center of your play."

Dan held the foot in his hand and looked at it. At first he just felt stupid. The rain started falling harder, and Dan cupped his other hand over the damp and bedraggled foot, feeling a little sorry for Fuzzy Fat-Tail. What did Mother Ferny mean? Dan didn't have many memories of his stuffed beaver anymore. OK, there was that time when he had punted it all around the house, somehow knowing it wouldn't get hurt. And he knew that when he was really young he used to sleep with it in his bed, but that was hardly even a memory, it was mostly something his parents told him about when he got older.

"Not those memories," said Mother Ferny. "Go deeper."

Dan closed his eyes. He was pretty sure he was failing at Mother Ferny's task. Lightning flashed even through his closed lids, and instead of thinking about Fuzzy Fat-Tail he listened to the thunder. He loved thunder and lightning. So did his brother Theo. Dan remembered how surprised he had been when he got to be a teenager and his mother told him she was terrified of thunder. She had always hidden that from him so he wouldn't get scared like her—awesome, Mom! Then Dan remembered, or maybe imagined, watching through the kitchen window while lightning crackled like dragon fire and thunder roared like giants.

Then, as though struck by a sudden dart, Dan felt that he was no place, that he was every place, that he was small and the world was before him and all around him huger than imagining, mighty and magnificent, fierce and colossal, everything and nothing, and Dan stood there all by himself and yet was safe because he was not alone.

Dan heard a crack and opened his eyes. Something swam downstream toward him, only a fuzzy whiskery face showing above the water. The crack came again as the animal raised a flat tail and slapped it against the stream. A beaver, of course! It waddled across the lawn, stopped in front of Dan, and reared up on its hind legs, using its tail as a prop. It looked into Dan's eyes and for a moment he thought it might speak to him the way he had imagined Fuzzy Fat-Tail doing all those years ago. After all, there were talking beavers in Narnia. But this beaver merely patted Dan's knee with one paw, dropped back to all fours, and waddled back into the water.

Another crack, and another. Beaver after beaver swam down from the mountains and trundled through the field until they reached the thickets and woods, and began to gnaw. And as the rain soaked Dan and Fuzzy Fat-Tail's foot, the trees began to fall, and a dam rose to meet the rising mountain waters. Dan was dimly aware that Mother Ferny patted his shoulder and trudged up the path to the hall. He pushed wet hair from his eyes, watched the beavers work, and smiled.

DAN RETURNED to Gatemoodle just as Mother Ferny stepped out again with Graciela and Maggie. Graciela waved and said, "When Mother Ferny told us what you just did with the beavers, I mentioned that I used to have an araña doll—a spider."

"And I told her that means she can help me with the webs," said Mother Ferny.

"I am only along to watch," said Maggie. "I felt cooped up in the room by myself. Want to come?"

This time Mother Ferny turned off the path to the right. They dipped into a valley on the side of the ridge away from the stream, and then climbed into the hills that Dan knew lay above a warren of goblin and dwarf tunnels. Dan hurried to catch up. Crackerbones and Drula seemed to think they controlled the tunnels, but the protection of a friendly witch would be handy too.

Before long they entered a beech grove. Thick ferns covered the ground, and the greens would have been pretty against the silvery bark if the rain hadn't made everything dim and sodden. Mother Ferny took Graciela's hand and began to chant quietly. Dan had no idea why Graciela wasn't told to access her "totem" the same way he had. The two women closed their eyes.

Nothing happened. Dan shifted from foot to squelching foot and began to regret coming. Then Mother Ferny and Graciela each held out a hand. Dan squinted through the rain to see what they were doing, and stepped closer.

Good thing he wasn't an arachnophobe; Josh would have hated this. Spiders were dropping on threads from tree to hand. Just regular spiders, not huge Hobbit-story ones, but there were a lot of them. The leaves were crawling with spiders.

Then Dan thought he saw something move behind him. He squinted. Something was there that he couldn't quite make out, something a lot bigger than spiders. Dan looked back at Mother Ferny and Graciela, but they were deep in concentration. He caught Maggie's eye, felt at his side for his sword, and then walked slowly toward the thing, trying to brush rain from his face so he could get a clear look.

Dan froze. What if it was Skriker? He grabbed Maggie's hand and started to back up, but then almost laughed. The creature had made a sound, and it wasn't Skriker's awful wail but a gentle whinny. Turtle! Just at the edge of the grove stood Fir Darrig's pony with the silly name Turtle. Turtle had been a huge help on Dan and Maggie's first Inland journey, not only as a pack beast but as a reassuring friend. She had even faced down the angry noggles that had chased them one time. Dan smiled at Maggie; she was even fonder of Turtle than he was.

But what was Fir Darrig doing leaving his pony out in the pouring rain? Dan stepped forward to greet her and lead her down to the stable. Turtle nickered and looked at Maggie and him in that way she had that almost seemed like smiling. Wet, her mane looked even softer than usual. Dan and Maggie reached out to stroke it.

"Dan! Maggie! No!" cried Mother Ferny.

Turtle's brown eyes became hot red coals. Dan was flooded with terror and he tried to pull back but those red eyes locked onto his and his arm kept moving forward. Maggie was reaching forward too and he wanted to push her away but those red eyes commanded his will. Then, just before their fingertips touched the pony's mane, she stamped and snorted. Her skin started twitching like flies were biting her. Spiders! More spiders than Dan could count dropped from overhead and bit the pony. She rolled over and twisted against the ground, then leaped up and galloped away. Dan couldn't be sure because of the rain, but it looked like she dove into a hole.

"I am sorry, children," said Mother Ferny. "Let us return to the hall. The spiders know their work now."

"What's wrong with Turtle?"

Mother Ferny shook her head. "Turtle is warm and dry in the stable, safely eating oats. I do not know how a tatterfoal could come so close to Gatemoodle. Some evil of Sister's, or did we stir up more than we wished when we raised the ridge? If you had touched her she would have had you on her back and borne you away."

"To where?"

Mother Ferny didn't answer.

DAN AND MAGGIE huddled by the big stove and held their hands close to the fire, unsure if their shivers were from cold or fear. When Mother Ferny told the others what had happened, Fir Darrig went to the stable to let Turtle run free. "For," said he, "neither tatterfoal nor shag pony will stay where Turtle tells them to leave."

Dan meant to ask Graciela how the spiders were supposed to help in the war—biting that horse had come in handy, but surely there weren't enough spiders to do in many enemies. But Maggie brought up a completely different subject first. "I already asked Alice to be my maid of honor, Graciela. But it would please me if you would be a maid of honor too."

"Really? Me? Sure! And thank you. But ..."

"But what?"

"Don't get mad at me. But why are you two getting married

at all? I mean, is that even a thing anymore? It's not like your parents are bossing you around or anything."

Dan had to admit to himself that he still had the same thought somewhere in the back of his mind, but he stayed quiet and watched. Maggie stiffened but then smiled and said, "We find ourselves in a prophecy that a mortal and fairy must wed for the good of Inland. And since we love each other, why not?"

She looked at Dan, who nodded and said, "It's like with changelings. Inland needs to partake of Outland to stay strong, and once every five hundred years, marriage with a mortal serves the same purpose. I'm the lucky one." He smiled and took Maggie's hand.

"Oh," said Graciela. "I guess that makes as much sense as anything else here. I'll be honored to be in your wedding party."

Dan realized now was their first quiet chance to talk about Graciela's news. "Hey, Maggie. So your mortal father got changed into a blue deer. Maybe even the one who helped us before."

Maggie frowned and nodded.

"And Graciela brought a horn to call him. Shall we try?"

"Was not it to be used in time of need, Graciela?" asked Maggie.

"That's right."

"Well, I do not *need* to meet him. All my parents have turned out such disappointments."

"I understand, I guess," said Dan. "Maybe the time of need will be when we catch up to Sister. If he can really love her as well as you, she's supposed to heal, which I'm pretty sure means she'll stop trying to destroy everything and, uh, kill us."

"How could anybody love Sister, unless they were as awful as her?" asked Graciela.

Dan nodded. "I've been thinking about that a lot because Maggie's fairy mother thinks I might be the one who loves Sister and Maggie both. I can't imagine it. If the blue deer can't do it, we'll have to figure out the dual meaning of Minik Mingarria." He caught Graciela up on that part of their adventures, finishing with, "But figuring that out seems almost as impossible as loving Sister."

THE NEXT DAY dawned sunny and clear. Crackerbones and Loosejaw were out scouting, and Billy said there was nothing more to be done unless they returned with news that the enemy approached, so Dan decided to check on how the beavers were doing. He paused briefly on the threshold to look in all directions for Skriker, even though he wasn't much worried anymore because Skriker had had plenty of time to wail at them if that was his intention. The sun sparkled off rain-sodden grass, birds sang, and it just wasn't a day to be scared on.

When Dan reached the bottom of the ridge, he grinned. "Busy as a beaver" was no joke. A dam of mud and tightly woven sticks about twelve feet high stretched from cliff to forest, and the entire grassy field was now a placid lake. The beavers had routed the outflow to the forest side of the dam so that any noggles who came up the creek would have the lake between them and Gatemoodle.

Dan would have liked another glimpse of his "totem" animals. He climbed onto the dam and walked out to the middle, scanning the surface. There! A furry face skimmed toward him through the water, and a large beaver climbed out and sat in front of him. Dan wondered if it was the same one that he had seen the day before. It looked him in the eye, touched his knee, dove back into the lake, and slapped its tail on the water. Immediately, ten, fifty, a hundred or more beavers rose to the surface, slapped their tails, and departed upstream for the mountains.

Dan sat and laughed, then gathered his thoughts to call Nellie Longarms. He didn't really know how his mental connection with her worked, so he hoped he merely needed to think about her. He owed her a lot. When Dan and Maggie first met her, she had threatened to eat them, but the thing about Nellie was that she couldn't breathe if she left the water, so they were able to elude her. There had been something in their conversation that made Dan think Nellie liked him, although he didn't know why she would, so when Maggie was captured by the witch Maggitch, Dan went back for Nellie's help. And then she had kissed him—the first woman Dan had ever kissed—because that enabled him to breathe underwater like her. They swam to where Maggie was held captive, and Nellie kissed him another time so he could live on land again, and then she had battled Maggitch and drowned her.

Then there was the time in Mexico that Nellie had saved Josh and him from being drowned by her weird cousin, La Llorona. And the time she had helped Maggie and him travel under the oceans. And the time she had saved Josh and Alice and him from Sister's malkins, and told them how to reach Fairyland where Maggie was a captive ... no wonder Dan was fond of her.

Except another thing about Nellie was that she ate people whom she caught by her waters. Dan was pretty sure she ate whomever she could catch, including careless human children. So she was definitely at least as bad as she was good, and he shouldn't like her at all, but somehow it just made this enigmatic and beautiful creature even more intriguing. Dan really wanted to see her again.

So why wasn't she showing up? Dan stood and started to pace. Crackerbones and everyone would be really pissed at him if he failed to bring Nellie to protect them, but even more than that, he missed her.

Duh! Part of his deal with Nellie was that he had to bring her Outland food. Trouble is, he didn't have any with him. But Billy would! Dan ran back to Gatemoodle.

Sure enough, Billy pulled a couple loaves of Wonder Bread, a favorite of goblins, out of the cupboard. He said he wanted fresh air so he walked out to the middle of the dam with Dan and laid the loaves down.

Nothing.

Dan groaned when he saw Crackerbones approach. The goblin studied the water as he walked across the dam, and said, "Well, Quest Boy? Where is your amphibian friend?"

Dan crossed his arms and said nothing.

"Giants have been sighted in the mountains. War will be upon us tomorrow. Nellie Longarms better come soon or we must break the dam and release the water. Mother Ferny has learned with certainty that noggles can travel in fresh water now. This lake is just an invitation for them to attack if Nellie Longarms can't defend it for us. Good job, Quest Boy." Crackerbones wadded up a piece of Wonder Bread and shoved it in his mouth.

Billy sighed and looked at the sky. "Nearly lunchtime. I will go prepare something, and perhaps Nellie will join us later. Oh, but here come Maggie and Graciela."

The women reached them and Maggie said, "We just wanted to see how you're doing."

"Not great," said Dan. "Nellie hasn't shown up, not even for this Outland food." He pointed at the Wonder Bread.

Graciela slapped her forehead. "I'm an idiot! I totally forgot! Josh made me bring some cans of tuna. He said that's what you always have for Nellie. I'll run and get it."

In a few minutes Graciela returned and handed Dan three cans that he placed on the sticks at his feet.

Immediately a long arm shot out of the water. All of them, even Crackerbones and Billy, jumped back as it seized a can and pulled it under the surface. Then Nellie took hold of the edge of the dam with her other arm and pulled herself into the air. Water sluiced from her blond hair and down her lithe figure seductively draped in garments of weeds. She bit into the can, metal and all, chewed and swallowed.

Then she smiled and licked her lips and pointy teeth. "Hello, Dan Outlander. Hello, Maggie Fairy. And hello to you, Crackerbones and old Billy. It is long since Nellie saw you. And who is the mortal girl who stares at Nellie?"

"Hello, Nellie," said Dan. "It's great to see you. This is our friend Graciela. Graciela, this is Nellie Longarms."

Graciela flinched as Nellie reached out and poked her shoulder even though she was standing well back from the water. "Nellie is pleased to meet Graciela Mortal, friend of Dan Outlander."

Then came the terrible shriek. A tall, skinny man clad in an old-fashioned long black coat stood at the other end of the dam. He took off his top hat, tilted back his throat, and wailed again in an awful tremolo. And again. Without looking at them he replaced his hat, turned, and strode into the forest.

Dan looked around and shivered. Him and Maggie and Graciela. Billy and Crackerbones. And Nellie Longarms. For whom did Skriker call?

4

CHANGE IN THE WATERS

*N*ellie dipped underwater and back up. She wiped water from her face and for a moment Dan wondered if it had been tears. She unfolded a long arm and pointed to where Skriker had disappeared in the trees. "Nellie has never before heard old Skriker. Nellie is glad Jenny Greenteeth has not yet arrived, or Peg Powler or Nan O' the Well. Nellie's cousins were not marked."

"Wait a minute," said Dan. "I thought hearing Skriker could mean a loved one might die, not necessarily that one of the people who hears him will die." He felt guilty as soon as he said it—wishing the doom on someone else, maybe one of Nellie's weird cousins.

"Three wails, each immediately following the last, places the doom on one who hears," said Billy.

"I've heard Skriker, more than once," growled Cracker-bones. "A warrior does." He shrugged.

"Let's go back in," said Graciela, hugging herself.

"Come back and visit Nellie, Dan Outlander." The water spirit sank under the surface.

THEY ATE A SOMBER LUNCH. The smile had left even Billy's face as he served them. Loosejaw returned from scouting and when she heard about Skriker she peered at Crackerbones from lowered eyes and then pulled him into a jarring hug. She reported that three Giants had been spotted on the next ridge over, waiting like statues as goblins and kobolds flocked to them. As if to underline her words, a slow drum began beating *Boom ... Boom ... Boom*. It sounded mournful and lonely to Dan.

"War is almost upon us," said Billy. "It is time we make some decisions. Dan, as the master of Breaklock, you can open a door to the safety of Outland at will. You—"

"I was thinking the same thing," said Dan. "Graciela, it doesn't make any sense for you to stay here."

"What good do you think it would do me to run away?" she responded. "If Skriker was calling for me, I'd probably get hit by a truck or something as soon as I stepped through the gate."

"Indeed, the one marked by Skriker cannot escape his or her doom whether here or in Outland," said Billy. "But when the attack comes many may fall, Skriker or no, and from that attack Outland provides sanctuary. Yet it is not Graciela who must leave us."

"Graciela will help me with the spiderwork," put in Mother Ferny.

"It is you, Dan, who must leave," said Billy. "It is you upon whom all our hopes of freeing First Changing Beast and defeating Sister depend. If we repel this attack but you are slain, all our efforts will be as dry leaves in the wind."

Dan gulped and felt his face turning red, but his answer was firm. "No. Absolutely no. I am not leaving Maggie, or Graciela, or any of you to fight without me. Do you take me for a coward?"

Billy frowned. "We ask this not only for your protection, Dan. Have you forgotten that you also have a task in Outland: to speak to Dr. Green about the meaning of Minik Mingarria?"

"Still no. That can wait until after the battle. Minik Mingarria doesn't matter until I meet Sister face to face."

"Couldn't you talk to Green and return in time for the battle, Dan?" asked Maggie. She explained to the others that when she and Dan truenamed each other the flow of time had been altered for them, and from that Dan had learned the trick of aiming Breaklock in time as well as space.

Dan shook his head. "Not sure," he said. "Since we released each other, my grasp of that magic time is fading. I might get it wrong." This was a lie, but in Dan's anger about being told to leave Inland he didn't even feel guilty.

"And it still would not serve to keep Dan safe," said Billy. "We must insist about this. You stay in Outland until we send word that the battle is over."

"Or what?"

Billy sighed. "We will confine you to your room."

"Like mean parents," exclaimed Dan. "But you can't! Breaklock, remember? I've even learned how to use it to travel inside Inland. So I can escape any room you put me in and return to wherever I want." He saw the three gatekeepers look at each other. "You're probably thinking about overpowering me and taking Breaklock. Sure, that would be easy, with magic or muscle, either one. But you know what? If you do that, I quit. I've been through a lot for you guys. Well, that's not quite fair, I did it all for Maggie and me too. And I've loved it, even when

I've hated it. But I won't keep it up if it means abandoning my friends to fight without me. Not Maggie, not Graciela—and not the rest of you either. If you try to make me, you can find First Changing Beast by yourselves."

Boom ... Boom ... Boom.

Maggie edged closer to Dan on his right, and then Graciela did the same on his left.

To Dan's astonishment, it was Crackerbones who spoke up for him. "Let the boy stay. I have seen his bowmanship, and I reckon that he can help in the fighting. How about a compromise? You stay and fight with us, but that means you acknowledge me as War Chief. You cannot roam about wherever you wish. I will station you here at the hall, where if the fighting draws close you can fire down from our ridge."

Dan nodded. "Thank you, Crackerbones. I accept that."

Billy looked at Mother Ferny and sighed. "Very well."

AFTER LUNCH, Maggie and Graciela went off with Mother Ferny. She was going to have Graciela help her with the spiderwork, whatever that meant, and teach Maggie how more precisely to locate Sister. Crackerbones and Loosejaw went off to do something military. Billy bustled around the stove looking grumpy. Dan decided to go outside.

He wandered to the stable in search of Turtle, feeling like it would be restorative to pat that friendly horse face. But Turtle was gone, probably out chasing off tatterfoals and shag ponies. Dan meandered to the road, wondering what Boe Bulbeggar was up to, but Boe was not in sight, just the road with some strange black blotches. Dan's feet turned toward the new lake. He crossed to the far side of the dam and stared where Skriker had melted into the trees. Then he went and sat down in the middle.

Nellie Longarms had mentioned her cousins Jenny Green-teeth, Peg Powler, and Nan o' the Well, and Dan wasn't sure it was safe to meet any of them. Nellie's cousin La Llorona had nearly drowned him long ago. But somehow Dan wasn't worried.

"Hello, Dan Outlander." Nellie Longarms pulled out of the water and sat beside him, feet submerged. She was as beautiful as always. But except for those arms—her hands dangled in the water near her feet even though she sat with a straight back—she was smaller than Dan remembered.

"Hello, Nellie. I'm afraid I don't have any more Outland food for you."

She flipped hair from her face and lightly touched Dan's knee. "Nellie knows. Nellie does not mind." She turned and looked at him. "Nellie releases Dan from the agreement. Dan can visit Nellie even if he does not bring Outland food."

"Thanks, Nellie. Wow, that's nice of you. I'll still bring it whenever I can, just as a gift. You've helped me in so many ways."

"And Dan has helped Nellie."

Dan didn't know what she meant, but when he started to ask he choked up for some reason. He was glad for the diversion created by a big splash in the middle of the lake.

"Jenny has arrived," said Nellie.

"I'm glad Jenny and your other cousins didn't hear Skriker. I'm sorry you did. And it's my fault. Once again you come to help me and put yourself at risk. I hate Skriker."

Nellie shrugged. "Skriker does not kill. Skriker only warns those already chosen."

"That very first time you helped us, Nellie." Dan wasn't sure what he was starting to say, but he continued. "The first time Maggie and I came to Inland, and we didn't know anything, and Maggitch caught Maggie, and I asked for your help. You killed Maggitch for us, and saved Maggie, but Maggitch was a witch, you could have been killed yourself, and all I had for you in return was an Outland apple."

"It was a fine apple." Nellie flashed her catlike teeth at Dan in a smile. "But that was not all. Does Dan not know? Nellie sensed change in the waters even then. She senses more now. The waters taste different."

Dan poked a finger into the lake and brought it to his mouth.

Nellie laughed. "You have a stiff mind, Dan Outlander. Not waters of the tongue. Waters of the spirit."

"Is it a change for the better or for the worse?"

But Nellie stood and dove into the lake, a perfect arc, a rainbow, and disappeared without a splash.

Boom. Boom. Boom.

Fir Darrig came out of Gatemoodle just as Dan was about to pass in. Even though batteries and electricity didn't function in Inland, he had magically gotten one of the iPhones working. The screen shifted through the rainbow like a child repeating Roy G. Biv and showed a .gif of a dragon that started out with its tail in its mouth and then undulated and blew fire at the viewer. Except as Dan watched, he realized it ran a little too long for a .gif and didn't repeat precisely; even when the dragon took its tail back into its mouth, it continued to shift minutely.

"I take it to our troops. Whoever gazes into its glow will no longer be cursed if touched by iron. A sharp iron blade will still cut, but no more fatally than a blade of bronze."

"Where are our troops?" asked Dan. Only a dozen or so dwarves stood on the ridge side facing the mountains.

"They are amassing in the tunnels. I go there now."

Boom. Boom. Boom.

The women were still off doing whatever they were doing. Dan took his bow and went to the stables for a bale of straw to use as a target. His bow and arrows were a gift from the fairies, and they shot straighter and truer than any weapon he had used before, but their precision would be no use if he was rusty. As Dan drew back his bowstring, he heard wingbeats overhead and beheld magpies, flocks of magpies descending on the trees and the roof of the hall. Maggie must have called them.

Boom. Boom. Boom.

Dan practiced until dusk. When he returned to the hall he saw that dozens of dwarves had taken up position on the north end of the ridge facing the mountains, and an equal number of goblins "manned" the south end. A smaller number of goblins waited on the lake side, keeping watch on the still water in case more noggles showed up than Nellie and her cousins could handle.

Boom. Boom. Boom.

DAN WAS DYING to talk to Maggie and Graciela. He wanted to know what they had been up to with Mother Ferny, but mostly he just wanted some ordinary conversation. He'd been in fights in Inland, and he had slain a noggle, some goblins, and even a human, one of the People from the Sea corrupted by Sister. But those had all been one-on-one affairs, or at most small skirmishes. The biggest battle Dan had seen was the Siege of Gate-moodle, when a giant and some goblins had tried to capture the hall and the Gatekeepers, and even then the only deaths (one at Dan's hands) had been the giant and a couple enemy goblin sentries. This was going to be another affair entirely. Even without Skriker's call, a lot of people were going to die. And who had Skriker marked? For a moment Dan realized he was hoping it was Crackerbones, but the thought felt unworthy and he tried to push it out of his head.

But Maggie and Graciela weren't at the supper table, and Crackerbones and Drula were out with the troops. Dan couldn't figure out if Billy was mad at him for refusing to run to Outland, or if it just seemed that way because Dan felt guilty, but in either case Billy was silent and sat at the far end of the table.

Luckily Loosejaw was there. She slapped Dan on the back so hard he dropped his food, and said, "Greetings, Ironbreaker!"

"It's good to see you, Loosejaw." They had first met when Loosejaw's band had captured him and Maggie and threatened to kill them, but Dan had saved Loosejaw's life and they had become friends.

"This will be different than the siege," said Loosejaw. She took a big bite of beef and slapped her jaw into place as she chewed.

"Have you ever been in this big a battle?" asked Dan.

Loosejaw shook her head. "Nor have any of us. Sister's doing. Movements, alliances, great wars: she is teaching us to fight the way it is done in your world."

"What about the rift between Crackerbones's band—your band—and Gragguts's?"

"Oh, sure, lives were going to be lost there. You have seen it so already. But in the end my husband and Gragguts will have it out hand to hand. And we have often battled dwarves—some of the very same dwarves who now take up stations beside us!" Loosejaw shook her head and slapped her jaw into place. "But we never thought to wipe them out and take all their tunnels, and they never tried to do that to us. And what about the bulbeggars? Bulbeggars have always devoured the stray traveler who irks them, but they have never fought in an alliance. Times change."

"I'm sorry my world is intruding on yours like this. I came here to get away from things like that."

"Not your fault. And you will free First Changing Beast and set things right!" Loosejaw slammed him in the back again.

"I hope so." Dan breathed in and out deeply. "I'm ... I'm scared." He stared at his plate.

"As am I. Cracker has been in more fights than any of us, and he will tell you that only fools feel no fear before battle."

Dan looked at Loosejaw. "I'm glad you were not there to hear Skriker wail."

"And I am sorry that you were."

At that moment Maggie finally came in. She hurried to Dan's side and kissed him on the cheek. She had bags under her eyes and her hair hung limply in a way Dan had never seen since Maggie had learned she was a fairy, but she was smiling.

"I have news," she said. "Billy, Loosejaw, for you too. Mother Ferny taught me to sharpen my perception of Sister. I already knew she lurked at the edge of the Marrowland, but now I can tell that she is staying in one small spot. She has not moved for hours. I will check again tomorrow to make sure, but the only thing that makes sense is that she is caught in one of Father's traps."

"Really?" asked Dan. "We knew he put traps around—that

one even caught you for a while—but Sister eluded them and taunted your father about how feeble they were. She was all about contempt."

"I know. But she must have fallen into a stronger one."

"I judge this news both good and bad," said Billy. "Good because as long as Sister is confined she cannot join the assault against us. Bad because we had thought her presence near the Marrowland meant that she led an attack there, but now we must assume her army will come against us fresh and in full force."

"Why doesn't she just delay the attack until she gets free?" asked Dan.

"It is a good question," replied Billy. "We can hope it is because the trap will hold for a longer time than her army is willing to wait. I am certain they have been promised feasts of Outland food when they conquer the gatekeepers. Sister has deceived them into thinking that we have access to great quantities, rather than the little we actually bring through the flickering gates. Knowing their unruly hunger, Sister may have authorized her army to attack without her, and if that is the case we have the opportunity to repel them without facing Sister and her Unlight.

"But I think it unlikely that even the King of the Fairies can long hold Sister when she wields the power of First Changing Beast. I think that because of her contempt she did not imagine she could be detained at all, and so gave standing orders to gather and attack after the signal set off by your arrival, Dan. We can only hope that the trap holds her long enough for us to repel her army, and that in this way her contempt comes to our aid."

Dan frowned and looked at his feet. "I guess Crackerbones was right when he said I should leave Gatemoodle. I set off the attack signal by arriving here, and if I go somewhere else they'll call off the attack."

"Nay, Dan," answered Billy. "Tempting as it is to use your guilty feelings to persuade you to depart, I do not wish to trick you. If you had listened with clear ears you would understand that the attack now proceeds with or without you. Sister wants you and Maggie above all else, but her army wants Gatemoodle. I believe it was one of your wisest Outland generals who said that an army travels on its stomach. They are coming."

Boom. Boom. Boom.

DAN AND MAGGIE lay in bed together in their cozy loft room, bathed by gentle candlelight. It felt like resting in an oasis that was about to shrivel under a Sahara sun.

Dan stroked Maggie's hair. "You look totally worn out. Locating Sister must have been hard work."

"It was very hard. Mother Ferny had to urge me over and over how to sharpen my concentration, and when I finally understood the method it was like swimming underwater against a strong current. Luckily, I did not have to experience Sister's feelings like Harry Potter with Lord Voldemort. Yet it is not hard to imagine what they are: loneliness, fear, anger, and hatred."

"Anger and hatred for sure," said Dan. "Loneliness and fear not so obvious to me."

"To me they are perfectly obvious, for I too know what it is to be hated by my parents."

Dan's hand paused a moment in Maggie's hair, and then he resumed stroking, more gently.

Maggie laughed quietly.

Dan pushed himself up on his elbow and looked at her. "What? What is there to laugh about?"

"I just remembered that we all imagined Mother—you know, Outland Mother, Mrs. Westerley—would help us by showing Sister how much she loves her."

"Yeah, that was a big part of the reason that we tricked Sister into Outland for a while. Pretty much a total fail. When Sister tried to catch us in the Marrowland we heard her tell her people that she wanted her mother kept safe, so I guess they made some kind of connection, but it sure doesn't seem to be making Sister any nicer."

"I wonder where Mother Westerley—oh no, I cannot call her that, it sounds like Mother Ferny—I wonder where she is right now?"

"Who knows?" said Dan. "Probably still back in Sister's weird flying palace." When they had first tried to find Maggie's father, they had been fooled by a beautiful palace, only to discover that it was Sister's creatures and not the fairies who dwelt there.

A candle flickered out, leaving just one that distorted the shadow of Dan's quiver of arrows so that it looked like a vase of flowers.

"I haven't heard Graciela come up to her room," said Dan. "I wonder where she is."

"She still had spiderwork to do with Mother Ferny. She will be tired too."

"What is spiderwork, anyway?" asked Dan.

"I do not know exactly. Graciela can tell us tomorrow."

The last candle sputtered out.

"I'm confused about the Skriker thing," said Dan. "Six of us heard him wail. Most of all I don't want you to die. And I don't want to die either, obviously. Or Graciela of course. And I've always liked Billy, and I owe him a lot, and, uh, Nellie Longarms too."

Maggie pinched him.

"Ow!"

Maggie giggled. "It is all right. I no longer worry that you will let Nellie seduce you. I like Nellie too."

"So that leaves Crackerbones. He did rescue us in South America." When they had been threatened by mukis, South American creatures that resembled goblins, Crackerbones had saved them by winning a duel against the muki champion. "But that may be only because he owed me for saving Loosejaw's life. Just now he spoke up for me staying here against the opinion of the other Gatekeepers. But basically he's mean, and insulting, and always talking about letting his goblins eat us. I don't like him. So I hope that he's the one that Skriker meant. But that feels all wrong, like I'm disloyal to one of the team."

"We can do nothing about this," said Maggie, "except to let our wishes go where they will, and fight the battle as best we can."

"Well, I hope you fight the battle beside me. Can you stay with me near the hall? I want to protect you. And, er, I haven't forgotten your knife work. I want you to protect me, too."

"I will have my knife just in case, but my job is to direct my magpies. And yes, I will be with you beside the hall. I can best see my birds from that elevation."

Footsteps came up the ladder, and a door opened and closed. Graciela was finally going to bed.

"Hold me, Dan," said Maggie. She rolled against his side and he snuggled her close.

"Danny?" she murmured.

"Hmm?"

"Let's not die tomorrow."

There didn't seem to be anything to say to this. Dan just hugged Maggie closer, and after what seemed like forever drifted off to sleep.

HE DIDN'T KNOW how much later it was when they were awakened by footsteps and a knock on the door. Had the war started? No, it was Graciela's voice, saying, "Are you guys awake? No way I can sleep. Too nervous."

"Just a minute," said Maggie. She and Dan pulled on clothes and invited Graciela in.

"C'mon," said Graciela. "Let's visit a campfire."

"Uhh, I'm nervous too," said Dan. "But why should we go down there, especially since goblins like to eat people?"

"Then we'll find dwarves instead. But I'm sure Crackerbones has told his goblins not to eat us. Some of the folks I've run into back in America scare me more than goblins, anyway."

"But why go down there?"

"Because I don't like feeling all hoity-toity up here in the hall."

"Let's do it, Dan," said Maggie. "It may be fun. I could do with some fun about now."

"OK," grumbled Dan. "At least tell us about spiderwork while we walk."

"Uh-uh," replied Graciela. "I want to talk to strange people and get my mind off this war."

As they walked into the valley, Dan complained that it was already so dark it would be hard to tell if it was dwarves or goblins until they were right among them. They approached the nearest campfire, but when they were still far enough away that all Dan could see around it was a few shapes with glittering eyes, he recognized a goblin voice. "Let's try the next one," he whispered.

Then he remembered those glittering eyes could see in the dark. "Join us!" called the voice. "We're a mixed-up crew already, you won't make it any worse."

Another goblin added, "And we promise not to eat you. Hee Hee Hee Hee Hee!"

That wasn't real reassuring, but Graciela and Maggie headed over so Dan followed. It turned out to be a man and woman goblin—Wormhair and Ratskin, where'd they get those names, anyway?—and a man and woman dwarf named Lammer and Tanly.

After Dan and his friends introduced themselves, Lammer said, "Since we probably die tomorrow, we figured why not have some fun while we can, do something new, hang out with goblins? Now here comes two Outlanders and a fairy, better yet."

"Not just any Outlanders," said Wormhair. "Aren't you the great Hee-ro?"

"Uhh."

"No denying it. And Cracker tells us you actually have an idea where to find the big ol' Beast, that's why we can't eat you."

"Hee Hee Hee Hee Hee." That was Ratskin. "Drink, Hee-ro! Drink, fairy, and Grassy Ella!" She passed a big jug to Dan, who took a tiny sip and then a swallow.

"It's OK," he said, passing the jug. "Hard cider, I think."

After the jug reached Tanly and she took her pull, she peered at Dan and said, "You're the youngest son, right?"

"Uh, what?"

"Two older brothers, right?"

"No, actually I've just got one brother, and he's younger. Why?"

All the goblins and dwarves groaned. "Maybe you're supposed to be the hero," said Tanly to Graciela. "Two older sisters, right?"

Graciela shook her head and said, "Two younger half-brothers."

"How can you have half a brother?" asked Lammer.

"Don't matter 'cause they only add up to one and they's younger anyway," said Wormhair.

Maggie took her second turn with the jug and giggled. "And I'm an only child."

"Uh-uh," said Dan. "You have an older brother, remember?"

"Hee Hee Hee Hee Hee! More cider for the fairy who doesn't know her own family!"

"Well, what's the big deal about our birth order anyway?" asked Dan.

"Because when Outlanders come blunderin' in here it's generly three brothers or three sisters," answered Lammer. "And the eldest is usually dumber'n a fencepost."

"So's the second," said Tanly.

"And both of 'em's mean as snakes," said Wormhair. "Hoardin' their food, whoppin' us with swords if they've got 'em and sticks if they don't. Third one's the one who's nice to us so we help 'em figure stuff out."

"Dan will be nice to you!" said Graciela and Maggie, laughing. "Will you help him find the Beast?"

"This is the only inspiration we have to share," said Ratskin, passing him the jug again. "Hee Hee!"

Tanly stood up and said, "Since you are the hero, you are supposed to treat people right. I do not know how a younger brother got in the story, but he is important and you must treat him right." She sat back down.

"Hear hear," said the others.

"Wait," said Wormhair. "I think I'm figgering it out." Ratskin giggled while Wormhair continued. "Sometimes it's a only child what comes. Since he's only got one brother and that brother ain't here, maybe he counts as a only child."

"Like who?" asked Tanly.

"Like Jake and the Sunflower Stalk."

"Jack and the Beanstalk," said Dan.

That got a roar of laughter. Wormhair said, "His name was Jake and no one c'n climb a skinny ol' beanstalk. Hell, Jake was lucky to get up a Sunflower Stalk, the fat lummox. But anyway, he clumb it to the troll's lair—"

"He what?" asked Lammer.

"He clumb it to the troll's lair."

"He climbed it," said Lammer.

"That's what I said!"

"No it ain't!"

"HE CLUMB—"

"NO ONE CAN'T CLUMB!"

By now Wormhair and Lammer were standing and bellowing at each other, Ratskin had fallen to the ground with her Hee Hees, and the others were laughing almost as hard.

"Bedtime, boys and girls!" shouted a voice from the darkness. Loosejaw strode into the firelight. "Big day tomorrow and you're keeping everyone awake. Gimme that jug." Loosejaw drained it and slapped her jaw into place.

"But I want to hear about Jake and the Sunflower Stalk," protested Dan.

Tanly swallowed the last of her laughter and said, "We shall tell you after the battle."

❄

DAN JERKED AWAKE the next morning. "Smoke! I smell smoke!"

He and Maggie dressed quickly in the light of first dawn and climbed down to the main floor. Billy, Mother Ferny, and Crackerbones were facing each other near the wood stove, arms crossed.

"Do not fear the smoke, Dan and Maggie," said Billy. "Gatemoodle cannot burn, not unless all of us have fallen first."

"But it is time to take our positions," said Crackerbones. Dan and Maggie followed him out the door.

The smoke came from campfires that dotted the next ridge over. Around the fires stood many goblins and other creatures, squatter and hairier and with noses so long that Dan could make them out even at this distance. Kobolds, he supposed. More goblins and kobolds were pouring up from the other side of the ridge. Some carried flags with a red G—must be for Gragguts. Others planted red raven banners. Then they let out a great hurrah.

Battle-axe in one hand, massive club in the other, a giant strode into view.

5

THE BATTLE BEGINS

*I*t wasn't a loutish, misshapen, fairy-tale giant. The goblins didn't even come up to its knees, and Dan figured that made it twenty feet tall at least. But it was perfectly proportioned, from its long legs to its narrow hips and broad chest and shoulders under lumberjackish clothes.

"Do not quail," said Billy. He reached up and placed one hand on Dan's shoulder and another on Maggie's.

"But Billy, there's a lot more of them than of our guys," said Dan. He pointed to the road and said, "That's the easiest route for their attack, and I see Crackerbones over there arranging his troops, but he doesn't have nearly enough. Not to mention they have a giant."

"Our scouts tell us they have more than one giant," said Billy. "But do not quail. Crackerbones is a great warrior, and we have the high ground. And we know some tricks."

"Like what?"

Billy smiled. "Some that would lose potency if named too early. But ... how big would you say his feet are?"

"What?" said Dan.

"At least four times the size of yours," mused Billy, staring at Dan's feet.

Dan didn't know what had gotten into Billy, but it didn't seem worth pursuing. He wiped his brow and shook his head. Enemy goblins and kobolds surrounded the giant, singing a martial song and waving their banners.

"At least it is like the giant we faced at the siege of Gatemoodle," said Maggie. "Dangerous, yet I am relieved it is not hideous as in the stories."

Dan pulled an arrow from his quiver but held it loosely by his side; the giant and the rest of the enemy forces were too far for a shot. He shook his head again. "It's too soon to be relieved. We got our fairy stories from somewhere."

As if in answer, the handsome giant twirled a huge ax over his head and shouted, "Now, brothers!" Two creatures hulked into view and stopped beside him, towering even taller by their heads and shoulders. Dan glanced over to see Billy's reaction, but the hobgoblin was gone.

These giants wore caveman-style skins, but Dan doubted you could find anybody this ugly no matter how far you went down the evolutionary tree. Their muscles bulged and twisted in the wrong places like old trees knotted and contorted to fight disease. They were so big that even from this distance Dan could see eyes out of line, bent noses, and mouths the wrong size beneath heads of stringy hair and bald patches. Their bare feet were the size of bathtubs, and their Godzilla hands gripped tree trunks ripped from the ground so recently that soil still dribbled from the roots. They bent their heads and listened to the handsome one.

"I guess he got the looks *and* the brains." Dan hadn't noticed Graciela join them. "Mother Ferny says giants don't see well at night, even the handsome ones," she continued. "That's why we get a daylight attack, which is good for the spiderwork."

"And for my magpies," added Maggie. She whistled, and a flock rose from the roof and resettled like a windblown blanket.

"It's gonna take a whole lot of spiders to faze those guys," said Dan.

"It isn't that," said Graciela. "Listen, and especially you, Maggie." But as she began to explain, horns blatted from the left. Just as Dan had worried, a great company of goblins bearing the G banner charged along the road toward Gatemoodle. He ran to the edge of the ridge where the path dipped to join the road and nocked arrow to string. A lone archer wouldn't do much good, but the road was even worse protected than a moment ago because some of the defending dwarves and goblins had moved north to face the giants.

Doom. Doom. Doom.

Gragguts's troops pelted toward the ridge up to Gatemoodle. They were too far for a shot on level ground, but Dan gauged the extra distance his arrow would fly from this height and released the string. The arrow soared high above the road, then angled down and flew true into the banner bearer's chest. It was a great shot, but instead of feeling proud Dan felt sick and like the sickness was going to get worse. The goblin pitched forward, but the one running beside him caught the banner before it struck ground and the attackers slowed not at all. Their wordless roar changed into, "Death! Death! Death!" Dan backed toward the hall, calling to Maggie and Graciela to flee. He halted when he saw the black shapes that he had vaguely noticed strewn about the road rise, twist, and form into great black dogs. The bulbeggars! They charged among the goblins and screaming and yammering replaced the chant of "Death."

But before Dan could see how it would turn out, a greater uproar came from behind him.

The two ugly giants charged, scything their trees above their heads. They gathered speed on the downslope like boulders, and kobolds and goblins swarmed behind them in a landslide. Gatemoodle's defenders hurled spears down from the ridge, and many kobolds and goblins fell, but the weapons merely bounced off the giants' skin. Even with the momentum gained running downhill, they soon slowed to a plod up the ridge to Gatemoodle, but Dan didn't see how anything could withstand them. He fired an arrow that struck one in the chest and fell uselessly aside.

Dan saw Maggie calling to her magpies, but in the din of horns, battle cries, barking, and screams she was inaudible. She ran closer to the hall and called again, and the blanket of magpies rose, tornadoed around her, and then hurtled to an outbuilding next to the stable. Mother Ferny was there and she threw open the doors and the magpies flocked in. Dan looked to Maggie and Graciela and saw them watching with their hands clasped together.

Whatever that was about, Dan had to try to stop the giants. They had almost reached the line of defenders. Maybe their eyes were vulnerable. Dan aimed at the closest one, trying to lead its eye as the giant lumbered and swayed up the ridge. He released the bowstring and held his breath. His aim was good but the giant lurched over a rock and Dan's arrow struck an inch off, right between the eyes, and bounced away. Dan wasn't sure the giant even noticed. It swung its tree trunk and crushed two dwarves as though they were made of eggshell.

Wind lifted Dan's hair and he looked up and saw a flock of magpies carrying a thick-corded net. Straight to the giant they flew and released the net. It fell across his head and body down to his knees and seemed to stick like glue.

"Spiderwork!" Graciela was beside him again. "A sticky web!"

Graciela's eyes looked weird, the irises black and so huge that hardly any white was visible. Dan had seen her like that before, earlier this summer, but it seemed like ages ago, when he and Graci tried to strand Sister in New York City. Graciela had channeled some kind of magical power to battle Sister, and her eyes had gone black and silver. It had been torment for her, so Dan started to ask how she was doing, but she shook her head and pointed at her work. The giant was bellowing and trying to lift his arms but the web held tight. The kobolds and goblins behind him paused and looked at each other, easy victory slipping away. Crackerbones gestured to his goblins and they ran forward and stabbed the giant's feet. It fell back, crushing a kobold too slow to leap aside, and Crackerbones's goblins leaped upon the giant, ran to its head, and began stabbing. The giant writhed, roared, and was still.

The other giant was at the north end of Gatemoodle ridge, and another flock of magpies bore a net toward it. But it had seen what happened to its comrade, and when they dropped the net it swung its tree trunk overhead and swept it aside. The net clung and flopped as the giant tried to smash the nearby dwarves. He glowered at the trunk and smashed it against the ground, trying to shake off the glob of netting, and Drula's dwarves harried its ankles. It kicked many aside, but now the magpies swarmed around its face. They didn't do any real damage but the giant dropped its tree trunk and began swatting at them, and then lumbered away like an elephant maddened by flies. It spotted the lake and picked up speed downhill. The slope to the lake was steep there, but not sheer like farther south.

Dan figured the giant wanted to dive to shake of its tormentors, then swim south and join the attack by the road. He ran across the ridge in time to see the giant churn into the water, sending a small tsunami before it. It bellyflopped under, and the magpies rose into the sky. For a moment the lake seemed empty, and then the giant's head popped above water. It was so big it was probably sitting on the bottom. Magpies flew at it but it swatted them and their crushed bodies floated away. The giant made a horrible sound like cars crashing, and Dan realized it was laughing. Then the sound stopped and the giant's face twisted into the expression of a child being told that he had to stop playing and study math. Its head jerked under water, and then the giant erupted head and torso into the air, looking down and slapping the surface. Suddenly it jerked to one side, and then the other, and then submerged. The lake around it swirled, turned red, and stilled.

Dan raised his arms overhead and cheered, "Nellie's lake!" even as he ran back to check the road. He felt more and more useless up by the hall while all the action was lower down. But Maggie and Graciela were here too, and he had promised Crackerbones ...

The bulbeggars appeared to be in control of the road. Eight or ten of them patrolled it about fifty yards from where the Gatemoodle path joined, and the attacking goblins had fallen back. All the bodies strewn about were goblins. But now something else began. The goblins looked behind and then opened a lane in the middle of the road, shielding their eyes. A small herd of ponies with glowing eyes trotted forward, and even from this distance Dan felt them tugging at his spirit. Tatterfoals! What relief they offered, to ride freely with the wind whistling by his ears, to ride away from battle and death! He blinked and looked down. When he raised his eyes again the tatterfoals and bulbeggars were in a jerky dance, ponies kicking at dogs while the dogs bit at their shanks. Neither seemed to gain an advantage, but the goblins began creeping past them toward Gatemoodle. Dan shouted for Crackerbones, but then spotted him mustering goblins to face the remaining giant.

When Dan looked back, he saw one of the dogs lunge for a pony's throat. But the pony shied and faced the dog eye to eye, and even as jaws reached throat, the dog twisted and contorted into a man in a black cloak. The pony whickered and the man jumped on its back and was borne away from the battle. The same thing happened to another bulbeggar, and the goblins surged forward.

Suddenly Dan thought of Maggie's magpies. Air Force! He sprinted to where she stood looking downslope toward the giant, and shouted, "Maggie! Can you send birds to help over here?"

"All that I can spare must harry the giant," replied Maggie. "Because remember, Sister has magpies too!"

A dozen or so magpies darted around the giant's face so that he couldn't swing his ax without them pecking at his eyes. But most of the birds were higher up, tangled with other magpies, bloody feathers drifting earthward.

Dan saw tear streaks in the dust on Maggie's face. He hugged her and said, "I feel useless up here, but looks like the battle's coming to us sooner than we like, anyway." He pulled an arrow from his quiver as he ran back to check the road. Twenty-some dwarves burst from roadside shrubs and fell on the goblins that had sneaked past the bulbeggars and tatterfoals; surprised, the goblins were driven back. But only six bulbeggars remained, and soon they would be spirited away by the ponies and the path to Gatemoodle would be open. Already the dwarf band had been halted and slowly driven back.

Hooves clattered behind Dan. He whirled and aimed but it was Turtle, Turtle with Fir Darrig on her back like a smiling red Buddha. They trotted down the path and Turtle whinnied. The tatterfoals froze, eyes rolling, jaws frothing. The bulbeggars left them and charged the goblins who wailed in dismay. The tatterfoals turned and fled back the way they had come, bowling over some of Gragguts's goblins. Fir Darrig carried no weapon other than his necklace of iPhones, but the goblins raised no weapon against him. Dan figured he must have some kind of irresistible magic and shouted, "Get 'em, Fir! Destroy the rest of 'em!" But Fir Darrig and Turtle turned and trotted back to the stable. The bulbeggars and dwarves held the road.

Dan's relief didn't last long. He heard Crackerbones shouting Billy's name, but Billy was nowhere in sight. Maggie's magpies and the enemy flock had apparently determined that neither could gain any advantage and so had formed into flight lines facing each other above the handsome giant. Any enemy magpie that swooped out of formation to attack Crackerbones's troops was harried back by one of Maggie's, but any of Maggie's that swooped at the giant was hectored back by enemy birds. With the air attack neutralized, the giant was slowly driving Crackerbones and his goblins back. He swung his great ax at Crackerbones, who ducked under it and stabbed the giant's shin, but kobolds swarmed at Crackerbones and he barely eluded the ax as he leaped back. Another goblin was less lucky. Crackerbones shouted again for Billy. The melee was close enough now for Dan's bow so he put arrow to string, but he couldn't be sure he wouldn't hit one of his own side amid the darting, stabbing, and feinting.

Crackerbones spotted Dan and shouted, "Get Billy! Arrows are no good now!"

Dan figured Billy must have gone into the great hall so he sprinted for the door. But what help would Billy be anyway? He had helped defeat the goblins surrounding Gatemoodle that other time by baking rolls that charmed them into docility, but that wasn't going to work now unless he had baked a few hundred of them. Dan shoved the door open and saw Billy crouched in front of blue flames spouting from the open oven. Any rolls in there would be charred to ash.

"Is Crackerbones ready?" asked Billy before Dan could even speak. "I thought so." He thrust long-handled tongs into the fire, muttering, "Four times the size of Dan's feet," and pulled out an object that looked too small even for one of Dan's toes. Dan craned his neck to see what it was, but Billy dropped it into a ewer of water that spouted so much steam Dan still couldn't see it when Billy pulled it out with his bare hand. Billy strode to a cabinet, tossed aside fabrics and thread, and seized a long buckskin thong that he tied to whatever it was.

"To maintain its power I must maintain the blue flame," said Billy. "It is for you to take this to Cracker. Catch!" He tossed the object and turned back to the stove.

The weight of the thing nearly knocked Dan over, like when you expect to catch a basketball and it turns out to be the heaviest medicine ball in the gym. It was only a simple red leather boot, big enough to fit only a rabbit-sized person, dangling from the long leather thong, but Dan could barely manage it in his right hand as he used his left to push open the door.

He'd been inside only a minute, but the giant had closed half the distance to Gatemoodle. Dan shouted for Crackerbones and the goblin turned to meet him, but two goblins wearing the red G closed on him and he turned back to parry their thrusts.

"To me! To me!" shouted Crackerbones.

Easier said than done. Dan shifted the boot to his left hand and drew his sword, but doubted he could strike true as he struggled to maintain balance. He loped down the hill, but two kobolds saw him and ran to cut him off. They were small and ugly and hairy and carried serrated blades already dripping blood. Dan might be able to deal with one, but not two, and he saw by their wicked smiles that they knew the same.

Suddenly, Maggie was beside Dan, knife in hand. She threw and the nearest kobold gurgled and pitched forward, her knife in its throat. But even more kobolds had broken through the line of Crackerbones's goblins and begun to run at Dan and Maggie. Maggie whistled and her magpies dove on the attackers. The enemy magpies were right behind, and it wasn't clear which flock would carry the moment, but as they battered each other they formed a storm cloud that shielded Dan from the attackers. He darted right, then left toward the giant. Crackerbones loomed into view, bloody sword showing what had happened to his foes. But the giant was right behind.

Dan stretched for Crackerbones and handed him the thong as the giant kicked out at them. Dan jumped aside far enough that just the edge of the giant's toe caught his shoulder, but that was enough that he found himself sprawled on his back a couple yards uphill.

The giant stomped at Crackerbones, who leaned, danced, twisted, and somehow landed on the giant's huge booted foot instead of the foot landing on him. The giant kicked to dislodge him, but in a single motion Crackerbones clasped his arms around the giant's calf to cling on, and knotted the thong with the little boot there like an anklet. The giant kicked again and

Crackerbones let go, flew through the air, and landed on his feet beside Dan.

"Run!" shouted Crackerbones. Maggie was beside them and she took Dan's hand and yanked, and he hauled his aching body up and they ran until they reached the threshold of the hall. But Crackerbones turned to watch instead of going inside, so Dan and Maggie halted next to him.

The giant let out a yell that froze both armies in place. Dan saw the tiny red boot flopping against its ankle, and then he saw red color spreading from it to the top of the giant's boot, and then slowly seep down transforming the natural brown. The giant yanked at the thong but couldn't break it. He yelled again and tried to yank his boot off, but it wouldn't budge. Now that boot was entirely red, and the other was beginning to turn.

The giant gave up yanking at his boots. He saw Crackerbones, snarled, and stepped toward them.

Except the step took him right over their heads. Dan saw the giant land on the far side of the ridge, take another step before he could stop himself, and fly over the edge. A great splashing came from the lake below, and at first Dan thought Nellie and her cousins were demolishing another victim, but then he saw the giant appear on the road. Two more steps and the giant landed among kobolds, crushing those too dumbfounded to jump aside. Onward charged the giant, crashing into trees, each step covering thirty or forty yards. He landed on the ridge behind the attackers, disappeared into the valley, crashed back into sight on the next ridge, and was gone.

Billy stood next to them, laughing quietly. "It is good that the other giants met other fates," he said. "It takes much time to create Seven Leap Boots."

Dan remembered the old story and without thinking corrected Billy. "Seven League Boots."

Billy laughed again. "Oh no, you Outlanders exaggerate. Seven League Boots, that would be fantastical. But each step the length of seven leaps ... 'tis enough, 'twill serve."

Dismay was obvious in the cries of the enemy goblins and kobolds, and they fled. Dwarves and goblins took off after them, but Crackerbones bellowed, "Stay," and on the other side of the ridge Drula also cried, "Stay!" Crackerbones ran to his troops, shouting that they were too few and must not be lured into extending themselves away from the defense of the hall.

Maggie whistled, and her magpies peeled away from the enemy line and swooped onto the roof of the hall. The enemy magpies dipped, rose, and headed for trees on the other side of the valley where Gragguts's troops slowed, stopped, and began to reform.

Something behind Dan clacked and he turned to see Loosejaw massaging her mandible. "We have held the tunnels," she reported. "Hot fighting in the East and North Rotundas, and we lost several, but they lost more and have pulled back, at least for now." She peered across the valley. "Same aboveground, I see."

Drula joined them, her left arm in a sling. "Pulled back, but not pulled away," she said, "and they still outnumber us. They will attack again, but at least we have time for a Slain Truce. Let us get white flags and retrieve our dead."

Our dead! In the turmoil of battle Dan had forgotten all about Skriker. In the group around him were Maggie and Graciela, Billy and Crackerbones—everyone who had heard Skriker except Nellie! He sprinted to the other side of the ridge and looked down at the lake. Except for red still spreading from where the giant had gone under, the surface was flat and empty.

"Nellie!" shouted Dan.

No answer. Could some of the spreading blood be hers?

"Nellie!" Dan shouted even louder. The cliff here was too steep to clamber down so he started for the path that would take him to the road and loop back to the lake. He hoped the bulbeggars were keeping the goblins away.

"Why does Dan Outlander call for Nellie?"

Dan halted and laughed in relief. Nellie smiled at him from the near side of the lake, only her head above water.

"I just wanted to make sure you're OK. Uh, and your cousins too. There's a pause in the battle over here."

"Nellie and her cousins are safe. Nellie and her cousins are bored. One giant was the only foe. No noggles for Nellie." She sank beneath the surface, and then one long arm reached out to wave.

Dan trotted back to where the others stood. A group of four goblins and another of four dwarves moved down the ridge, holding white flags tied to branches. They wailed quietly, almost a chant, as they retrieved the nearest dead and brought them to rest at the back of the hall. They started down to where several other bodies lay, but Drula put her hand on the shoulder of one of the dwarves and said, "Wait."

The goblins halted too, and looked at Drula.

"Why do they send no one after their dead?" asked Drula.

"She asks well," said Crackerbones. "They make no effort to take advantage of the Slain Truce. Gather cautiously."

Wailing again, the gatherers brought back the other bodies that were near them. The remaining dead lay low in the valley, and the white flags moved slower as they approached them. And it was well that they did, because a spear flew down from the next ridge to land in front of their feet.

"No farther!" Gragguts bellowed through a bullhorn.

Crackerbones looked around, and Billy handed him a bullhorn. Crackerbones put it to his mouth and called, "Do you not honor the Slain Truce?'"

"The Slain Truce is no more," shouted Gragguts.

"By whose design?"

"By the design of the Golden Lady!"

Crackerbones spat and said, "Sister wants your dead to rot uncared for, and ours too?"

"The Golden Lady scorns the honor duels of old. She has taught us that respect for the enemy will dull our killing edge. The dead are dead, and not tending ours is a small price to pay for victory. If you wish to tend yours, best send your entire army, for we will slay any who come close."

Billy took the bullhorn and pointed overhead. "Even now the buzzards circle lower. And look! Your own magpies fly to the slain. Will you have them desecrated?"

"We follow the new ways of the Golden Lady," shouted Gragguts.

The gatherers carried their white flags slowly back up the ridge, wailing louder now. It sounded like some of the enemy weren't totally on board with Sister's new ways, because wailing rose from the south end of their line, but Gragguts gestured to a lieutenant and the sound of their grief was cut short.

Mother Ferny carried from the hall shrouds that she said had been long prepared to keep their dead until they could be given proper farewell. These were folded around the few slain who had been safe to retrieve.

While Dan watched, Crackerbones jogged his elbow and asked, "How did Nellie and the others fare against the noggles?"

"She reported there have been no noggles yet at all."

"Ha!" said Crackerbones. "Gragguts was a fool long before he came under Sister's glamour. He never had enough patience to lead, and today he was so confident that the giants would carry him to victory that he did not wait for the noggles."

"Or for the People from the Sea," put in Graciela. "Remember I was told that they are coming too."

"Even Gragguts will have enough sense to await them after this setback," said Crackerbones. "They will join the noggles when their ships land at Innisport. Noggles will swim up the creek and the People will march up the road. The only question is when, and scouts cannot get through to find out."

Maggie looked into the valley, frowned, and shook her head. "Their magpies feed on the slain. It is sick, but it makes for clear flying for my swiftest." She whistled, and one bird flew from the roof to her shoulder. She spoke too quietly for Dan to hear, but the bird circled the roof chattering, and several magpies launched themselves over the lake and out of sight between trees bordering the creek that flowed toward Innisport.

Buzzards and gorcrows descended to join the enemy magpies in their feasting.

As DUSK FADED into full dark, Dan listened with Maggie just outside the hall door. The cooling air whispered to them. The magpie scouts had not returned, and magpies would not fly at night, but if they had seen anything they would tell the nighthawks. Then the nasal call of nighthawks began overhead, but these birds had no message except that they hungered after moths and mosquitoes.

The only other sounds were snuffling, crunching, and occasional growls from animals that had taken over the corpse buffet when the daytime birds left. The breeze from the mountains shifted from cool to cold.

"Let us go in," said Maggie. "They will know where to find me if they come tonight."

"Yeah," said Dan. "I didn't really do that much in the battle, but I'm exhausted and my legs ache as though I'd run a marathon. Adrenaline, I guess."

Inside, Mother Ferny was applying poultices to wounded dwarves and goblins. Fir Darrig tended with his iPhones to some who had been iron-injured. Billy Portman had somehow found the time to prepare loaves of flat bread and big pots of stew.

"I see by your eyes that no word has come to you," said Loosejaw, putting down her spoon and rising.

"No," answered Maggie, "and I am uneasy, for the distance to Innisport and back is not great as the bird flies."

"Perhaps no news is good news, and your friends do not hurry because they see no danger," said Loosejaw. "But I will tell Cracker to have our guards be doubly alert." She raised her voice and said, "All of you rest and heal while you may. We know not how soon we will be called back to battle." She slapped her jaw into place and limped outside.

Dan stretched stiff limbs and headed with Maggie for the food, but then halted. "Where is Graciela?"

"Do not worry," said Billy, walking toward the door with a heavy wooden bowl of stew. "She does spiderwork by lantern light in the stable, lest more giants come in the morning. I bring her supper."

After eating, Dan and Maggie bedded down in a corner. They had given up their comfy rooms so that injured warriors could better rest their wounded bodies. With the combination of stiff muscles and hard floor, Dan felt like he would never get to sleep, but he found himself gasping and jerking awake from a dream of marching footsteps. The hall was quiet and dark except for a glow from the stove that silhouetted Billy. Cracker-bones was walking toward him from the doorway. They whispered together and then Crackerbones strode back outside. Dan thought about Skriker's call, looked at Billy's eyes sparkling in the firelight, and sighed. He fell back asleep thinking, "Not him. Not him."

DAN JERKED AWAKE AGAIN, trying to figure out what the uproar was. By pale dawn light he saw Maggie sprinting for the door. The uproar came from the magpies on the roof! Dan yanked on his boots and ran after Maggie. She seized his hand and pointed at a spot in the air where the road curved out of sight toward Innisport. A block dot hurtled toward them, and after a moment it resolved into a magpie. The flock on the roof rose and sped toward it.

"Look! It is pursued!" cried Maggie.

A red dot grew larger behind it.

"Red raven," said Dan.

The raven closed on the fleeing magpie faster than the flock could reach it. Raven and magpie collided, and the magpie dropped in an explosion of black feathers.

Maggie moaned. "Now we know why no scouts returned with news."

The raven croaked three times and flew lazily to the bend in the road. Dan thought Maggie's magpies would easily catch it, but they pulled up, circled, and then turned back toward Gate-moodle. A cloud of dust rose from around the bend in the road.

Horns blew, and Crackerbones and Drula shouted orders.

Now they could see soldiers marching in the dust. Graciela

ran up from the stable to join Dan and Maggie. Through gritted teeth she said, "The People from the Sea."

Shrill in the quickening light came a voice from the lake: "Noggles in the creek! Noggles approach for Nellie and her cousins!"

"And red ravens mean Sister," said Maggie.

"But you could sense if she was near, right?" protested Dan. "So just her raven has come? Where do you feel Sister?"

Maggie looked like she was near tears. "Nowhere. I have lost her."

"Then I'd better go to Dr. Green to decipher her truename, in case she really is near," said Dan. He handed his bow and quiver to Maggie and pulled out Breaklock and Fuzzy Fat-Tail's foot. "I feel like I'm running away but I'm not, I will make a gate back right here, just a few seconds from now."

He kissed Maggie anyway, deep and hard as though he might not see her again. Then he pictured Dr. Green's office, sharpened the image, and made a gate.

6

OUTLAND INSIGHTS

*D*an had aimed well: he stood directly in front of the entrance to Dr. Green's office. He'd forgotten that if people saw him appear out of thin air they'd freak out, but luckily it was a quiet street with no one around.

Good—unless that meant it was a weekend. Dan had timed the gate so the same number of days had passed in Outland as had passed since he left for Inland, but he had no idea what day of the week that made it. Even though he was going to open the gate back to Inland precisely after he had left so he wouldn't miss anything there, he felt like he'd go crazy if he had to wait around a day or two first. He tried peeking through the waiting room window to see if anyone was inside, but ever since Dan had told Dr. Green about seeing a little old man—the one who turned out to be Billy Portman—through that window, Green had been careful to keep the blinds closed. At least a light was on.

Josh! Josh probably still had his job at the bagel place, and Dan hadn't eaten anything yet that day anyway. Josh could tell him what day of the week it was. And it would be nice to see his old pal. Dan stretched his muscles, now aching from gate-creation as well as battle adrenaline, and headed for downtown.

It was weird walking his hometown streets. Everything looked a little too thin and bright. His eyes hurt from the midmorning sun sparking off windows, so different from Inland's lusters that hinted of colors never before seen. Counting New York, he couldn't have been away more than a few weeks, but he felt like he'd landed in a computer simulation. Dan remembered a term he'd learned from Dr. Green, "derealization," and smiled as he "realized" that the "real" world was less "real" to him than Inland. He'd have to stop thinking of Outland as the real world. Inland had been there all along, giving meaning to people's lives in the old days, giving birth to all sorts of folk tales, beliefs, and enchantments, until the Gates started to close. Maybe Inland was the "real world" and Outland only an extension. But Dr. Green had also talked about how Dan had trouble bringing the two worlds together, integrating them. Did that mean they were both part of a bigger reality? Josh would say that sounded like some of their college dorm mates talking after they'd smoked too much weed, but still ... Like the way Inlanders couldn't get along without Outland food?

Dan had reached the business district where more people were walking about, and some of them gave him long looks. Not only had Dan forgotten about appearing out of thin air, he'd forgotten he was wearing Inland clothes. Luckily he'd changed out of fairy clothes and put on a slightly less weird set he had stored at Gatemoodle: supple leather boots, gray trousers, and a green long-sleeved muslin pullover with embroidery on the V-neck. Not too far from Outland-normal; just far enough that people reacted to the sight of him the way he was reacting to Outland.

Dan stopped and looked more closely at people going in and out of shops. He was supposed to be on a long camping trip, and if someone recognized him he'd have to come up with some bullshit about why he was back in town, which wouldn't be too hard, but what if they told his parents? But he didn't recognize anyone, and the bagel place was only a block away. If Josh was there, his Jeepster would be nearby, and if he could get free they could drive someplace secluded. Dan walked faster.

Crap! His mom, dad, and little brother Theo were walking out of the bagel place! Dan darted behind a big maple tree that grew near the sidewalk. He could hear their voices growing louder; he'd have to sidle around and keep the tree trunk between them as they walked by.

Theo was saying, "... hear from him anymore."

"Well, he's having his summer in the mountains, and I'm sure he's out of cell phone range," said his father.

"You know what I mean," said Theo. "Ever since he went to college he's been kind of a jerk. Hardly gets in touch at all, and I bet he never takes me camping like he used to promise."

"I miss him too," said his mother. "But college kids don't necessarily pull away forever. Josh was real nice when he sold us these bagels."

The last of their conversation Dan could hear was his father saying, "You've had your phases too, Theo. What about soccer ..."

Phases? Dan slapped the tree trunk so hard he broke off a chunk of bark. He wasn't in some stupid phase. His hand bled and he scraped a little bark out of the cut. He nursed his pain and anger because those were fighting feelings that he could use when he returned to the battle. Unlike that other feeling that was trying to grow in his belly.

Dan trotted to the bagel place, peered through the door—one table occupied and a couple people in line, but he didn't recognize any of them—and slipped inside. A chime tinkled, and Josh looked up from making a sandwich.

"Bro!" he shouted. "What are you doing here? You just missed your family. Back early from In—, er, from camping?"

"Yeah, and not for long," answered Dan. "What time is it, anyway? And what's the date?"

Josh pointed to the clock on the wall that showed 1:10 and said "Tuesday," as the customer in the front of the line said, "Man, you really have been out in the woods."

"Out in the woods with no soap, looks like," said Josh. "And I bet you're hungry, and I know you're broke, so I'll treat you. One of your healthy bean sprout things?"

Dan looked at his grimy hands and noticed his reflection in the glass counter: smeared face and tangled hair. "I'll go clean up in the restroom. A bagel sandwich would be great, and forget the sprouts. Scrambled eggs, bacon, and cheese. Real Outl—I mean, American food. Can I wait in the Jeepster?"

"Hey, man, I'm a little in a hurry here," said the customer.

Josh tossed Dan the Jeepster keys and turned back to the bagel he was working on, saying, "I'll make yours next, Dan. Jeepster's around the corner. I'm off in twenty minutes."

JOSH GOT into the driver's seat and handed Dan his lunch—he'd even brought a bag of chips—and said, "You eat, I'll drive and talk." Josh reported that after he and Alice popped back into New York they'd gotten right to work contacting Graciela and arranging a rendezvous in Mexico City to pass off Breaklock. "Thank God she made the trip in from her dinky little village. She seemed pretty excited to get Breaklock, and to see you again too, dude." Josh looked at Dan a moment with raised eyebrows. "Otherwise it's just been normal life, except putting in a lot of overtime to pay for changing our plane tickets. Well, I guess one other exciting thing, Alice and me are still hooking up, you know, dating, whatever."

Josh parked on the narrow shady lane that bordered one side of the Goth Woods. Dan swallowed the last bite of lunch and smiled. Food in his belly, his best friend beside him, the whole computer simulation feeling was gone. Dan crumpled his lunch bag and tossed it into the debris pile in back. "Outland definitely does some things right," he said, licking his fingers. "That's cool about you and Alice."

"It's funny, you know, about Inland and Outland," said Josh, looking out the side window. "I don't think either Alice or me can tell yet if we're really a couple, or if that just happened because of the craziness of Inland. It's kind of hard to fit the two places together."

"I was thinking the same thing a few minutes ago," said Dan. Suddenly he really hoped Josh and Alice would stay together, but he didn't think he should mention it.

Josh shrugged. "So the real action's with you. Did Graciela make it? You showed up looking like you came straight from a war."

"Well, yeah." Dan summarized everything that had happened since Josh left.

When he finished, Josh had slid down in his seat. "Dude!" he said, running his hand through his hair. "Inland sucks! And especially that Skriker dude sucks. Why don't you come back home? I mean, I know you can't, your friends are there and you'd have to be a real coward to not go back ..." Josh slid down another inch.

"Josh—" Dan started.

"Don't say it," said Josh, sitting up straighter. "I'm coming back with you. You've got the whole gate-time thing figured out, when we've fixed Inland you can send me back so I won't even miss any of my shifts."

"You are *not* coming back with me," retorted Dan. "I've had all sorts of weapons training there that you've never had, you can't help in a battle. I wouldn't have even come see you today if I thought you'd have such a crazy idea. But you know why I came to see you? Because it makes me feel better knowing I've got my good friend here."

"To come back to?" asked Josh. "Are you ever going to really come back?"

Dan shrugged. "Or you can visit Inland when it's safe. You're still on for Best Man when Maggie and I get married. And Alice Maid of Honor."

After a minute of silence, Josh said, "What about your parents?"

"What about them?"

"And Theo. It was nice seeing them today. I'd forgotten how cool they are."

"So they're cool." A big reason he'd started seeing Dr. Green in the first place was because even though his family was basically nice, everything felt empty. Sometimes he told Green that he almost wished his parents had been jerks because it would be easier to understand why he was unhappy, and easier to move out. Although he'd moved out pretty decisively ... "Why are we talking about my parents?"

"You gonna see them before you leave? Dude, that Skriker

thing means you may not see them ever again, or, or anyone here." Josh was looking out the side window again.

Dan spoke fast to tamp down that feeling in his stomach that had started to uncoil as Josh spoke. "I'm not going to see them now. I'll go crazy if I don't hurry back and, and get to the end of the battle. I'll see them when things calm down. The Gates of Inland, remember? The whole point of finding First Changing Beast is so people can go back and forth more easily, and that includes me."

Josh peered through the windshield into the Goth Woods and said, "Two words: Green. Goblin."

"What? Where?"

"Naw, I guess it was someone else," said Josh, leaning back again. "But maybe you should go look for him. Because if I can't help you in Inland, I bet he can. That whole charm about someone fixing things if they love Maggie and Sister too? Maybe it doesn't just mean love like the way you love Maggie. Maybe it could be love the way the Goblin loves Maggie. Don't get jealous, he's gay, but you know better than me they've always been good friends and they understand each other. Like friends do, right?" Josh looked at Dan. "And if anyone could love Sister, it would be the Goblin, 'cause he's a total weirdo. Kinda like you but worse."

"Wow," said Dan. "That's good thinking. That could work. I don't know when or why, but Maggie told the Goblin about Inland and I wonder why he hasn't already asked to go there, the way he's into art and alternative stuff. I bet he'd come if I explain it. Goblin to the goblin world! But what time is it?"

Josh checked his watch, "4:30."

"Damn. No time to look for him then. I've gotta get back to Green's office and catch him after his last patient."

They were silent on the drive. When Josh pulled over in

front of Green's office, he said "For you, Mags, and Graciela, two words: Stay. Alive."

Dan couldn't think of anything to say. He laughed, leaned over the console, and bear-hugged his friend.

IT HAD ALWAYS BEEN hard to schedule an appointment in the evening, so Dan figured Dr. Green wrapped up around 5:00. He buzzed the outer door and was relieved when Dr. Green buzzed him in without checking to see who it was. An older woman was waiting in the most comfortable chair. She glanced at him and then dropped her eyes to the magazine she was reading and ignored him, which was normal waiting room etiquette. He'd have to bide time through her session. Dan took a chair close to the cabinet with Native American artifacts and gourd rattles. The Rattleman. He smiled.

As Dan sat there, the feeling he had been trying to suppress climbed out of his belly and poked at his brain until he had to acknowledge it: sadness. Maybe it was because he was scared of Skriker and the war, or maybe because he was in his therapist's waiting room, but he missed things about Outland. He missed talking things over with Dr. Green. If—no, *when* he freed First Changing Beast, Dr. Green would come back to Inland, but then he'd be Prince of the Fairies and even if Dan could visit him it wouldn't feel the same. And Dan wished he could take Theo camping, go birdwatching with his mother, and talk Tolkien with his father.

The clock on the wall said three minutes before five. That woman's session would probably begin at five. Suddenly Dan hated the idea of his first contact with Green after all this time being a momentary interruption of his welcoming someone else. Dan charged to the door and clicked the mechanism to leave it unlocked as he went out. The woman would probably tell Green that some crazy patient had just come in and left again. Fine. He'd cross the street and pace up and down like a crazy person so he could watch both office doors.

The back door opened. Dan knew it was prying to look at another patient, but he peeked anyway.

The Green Goblin! And not wearing his usual trench coat.

Dan shouted, "Hey, Goblin!" and ran over.

"People hardly ever call me that any more, Danny Boy," was the reply. "Mostly it's 'Dave' now. And mostly you're not this glad to see me."

"Uh, OK, sorry, uh, Dave. But actually I've got a favor to ask and at the same time I think it's something you'll like."

"Just had a really good session!" interrupted the Goblin. "Really good! And it's not like we fixed everything, but I feel OK. I hardly ever have seizures anymore, and the ones I have don't last as long. There's something special about Jack."

"Uhh." Why did the Goblin like using Green's first name and Dan liked 'Dr. Green'? At least Dan knew what was *really* special about their therapist and the Green Goblin didn't. "That's great, Dave." And it was, except why had the Goblin, who was much more messed up than Dan ever was, progressed faster than Dan in therapy? Maybe because Dan kept inter-rupting his treatment with trips to Inland?

"So what's the favor?"

Dan took a deep breath. "You know about Inland, right?"

The Goblin nodded. "Sure, Maggie's told me about it, and about how she's got a kind of evil twin there. How is Mags?"

"She's in an ongoing emergency." Dan sketched out the state of the battle and then described the charm cast by the Queen of the Fairies that whoever loved both Maggie and Sister would set them free. "So that's what I want to ask you, Dave. The Queen thinks I'm the one who can love Maggie and Sister both. Well, you know that I love Maggie, but I can't imagine me loving Sister. Especially at first when I thought it had to be romantic love like I feel for Maggie. But I was just talking to Josh and he had the idea that it could be some other kind of love, like a deep connection that isn't romantic."

"Josh must not be as stupid as he usually acts," said the Goblin.

"OK, whatever. Well, his other smart idea was that you might be able to love both of them. You already love Maggie, I know that because of how jealous I used to get. Maybe you'd connect with Sister if you met her."

"You calling me evil and crazy?"

"No! No! Sure, I did think that about you back in high school, but that was before I got together with Maggie, and before Inland. Maggie and Inland, after them I can't be rigid like I used to be. But you were never that way, and that's part of why Maggie likes you, er, loves you. You've always been able to see things from different angles and use that to make art. You've even helped me understand things about Inland with those poems you told me. You've got an affinity for Inland. You'd love it there."

After a moment of silence, the Goblin said, "That's the problem."

"What do you mean?"

"Loving it there. Didn't you know Mags already invited me?"

Dan shook his head.

"More than once. I almost went when she invited me back in high school, back then I thought there was nothing I wanted more than to get away from this world. But I was afraid I'd love it so much I'd never come back, or if I did come back, I couldn't stand living in this world anymore. Or it would be like an acid trip I couldn't control. And I'm not even tempted anymore, now I've met Roger."

"Your boyfriend."

"He's more than that. I'm painting better than I ever did. I've got a show in a gallery right now, and one of my big canvases even sold. I don't get so scared when I space out, because I've got Roger to anchor me. Roger wouldn't get Inland, and I'm not going to mess up what he and I have."

"It wouldn't have to mess it up," tried Dan. "I still come back, you could too."

The Goblin gestured at Dan's outfit. "I'm not so sure you fully come back. But it's not the same for you. You never had any trouble being in this world. I know you were unhappy here, but that's because you were too much in this world. The anchor you needed was to Inland, and now you've got that in Maggie."

Dan tried again, but all he could come up with was, "But, Inland is magic!"

"There's magic in this world. Roger and I are getting married."

Dan just stood there for a moment, and then held out his hand to shake the Goblin's. Then, to Dan's own astonishment, he yanked the Goblin close and hugged him.

"Yeah," said the Goblin when they'd stepped back. "But Mags is in danger." He poked his finger into Dan's chest and said, "You're in danger. So even though I won't go myself, I'll help you. While the front of my mind's been talking to you, the back of my mind's been working on loving Maggie and Sister. I've got two more poems for you, poems for the situation. The first goes:

Earth, water, fire, and air
Met together in a garden fair
Put in a basket bound with skin,
If you answer this riddle you'll never begin."

"Wow, did you write that?" asked Dan. It was weird, Mother Ferny had said the first part not long ago.

"Naw, it's from one of those hippie bands back in the '60s. Here's your other poem:

Praise life, it deserves praise, but the praise of life
That forgets the pain is a pebble
Rattled in a dry gourd."

"That sounds completely different," said Dan. "But thanks, I guess. How do I use them?"

"I don't know, man," answered the Goblin. "You'll figure it out." Then he capered away, chanting:

"Boys and girls, come out to play,
The moon doth shine as bright as day;
Leave your supper and leave your sleep,
And come with your playfellows into the street.
Come with a whoop or come with a call,
Come with ..."

There was more, but the Goblin's voice faded as he turned a corner.

Had a really great therapy session: *check*. 'Dave': *check*. But still the Green Goblin: *double-check*.

NOBODY ELSE HAD ENTERED through Green's front door, so that woman must be his last patient for the day. Even if he departed by the back, he'd check first to make sure the front door was locked. Dan pushed it open and sat in the comfortable chair.

Almost immediately, the door to the inner office opened and Dr. Green poked his head out.

Dan babbled, "Dr. Green, I know you're not expecting me, but can we have a session? It doesn't have to be a whole session, I know you probably want to go home now and we don't have an appointment, but it's important."

Dr. Green smiled and said, "I'm sure it is. Come on in."

Dan sat across from his therapist, as he had so many times in the past and as he hadn't for such a long time. There was the same painting on the wall that had reassured Dan during his first session, a view of a country lane that Dan had recognized as an actual place in Inland his first time there. Its glass frame had shattered the only time Dan had tried to get Dr. Green to talk about his connection to Inland; now Dan understood that was because of the curse that the Fairy King—Dr. Green's father—had cast on him. It didn't feel right knowing Green's ancestry when Green no longer knew it himself. And there sat Dr. Green as usual, in a comfortable slouch, expression curious and welcoming.

Dan opened his mouth to talk but choked on the first word. Before he knew it he was crying, and then sobbing. He took deep breaths to calm himself, grabbed Kleenex for his eyes, and sat back sniffling.

"Tell me," said Dr. Green.

Dan blew his nose and bought time by carefully placing the tissues in the wastebasket. He didn't even feel like too much of a wuss for crying because he figured he had good reasons. He told Dr. Green about the battle to which he had to return, and about Skriker's cry. "So it's me or Maggie or Graci, Nellie or Billy or Crackerbones. I love all of them except Crackerbones, so I hope it's him that dies, but that's a terrible thing to say. I'd rather have it be me than any of the others, but I don't want to die either." Dan took more deep breaths and rubbed his eyes.

"What else?" asked Dr. Green.

"Whaddya mean 'what else?' One of us is going to die, isn't that enough?"

"For most people, yes. But already in Inland you and your friends have faced death. You have rescued your friends, and they have rescued you. You have dealt death yourself. Something more is jolting you now."

Dan thought. "Is it because of the way Sister is turning Inland into Outland? Loosejaw told me they never used to have full-fledged battles. Gragguts talks about how she's making things more organized. But even though I hate those things, that can't be what's affecting me because I've known ever since my first trip to Inland that Sister was organizing things in an Outland way, and it's up to me to find First Changing Beast and stop her."

"Maybe it's not that Inland is changing," said Dr. Green.

"What then?" asked Dan.

Dr. Green just looked at him.

"You mean *I'm* changing?" Dan considered this. "It's because of Skriker's cry. It makes me choose which of the people I love I want to die. Thinking that way takes the fun out of Inland."

"Only if being serious cannot be fun."

That reminded Dan of Mother Ferny telling him not to put too thick a screen over his childhood. "Anyway," he said, "my choice of who I want to die isn't going to make any difference."

"You can't get off the hook that easily," replied Dr. Green. "You do not yet know that your choice will make no difference."

"So you're saying that I'm upset because I've become boring and serious in Inland as well as Outland, and that takes the fun out of life."

"No, *you're* saying that. I'm saying that you've always had trouble living both seriously and magically, but now you have to put them together or flounder, whichever land you live in."

Dan didn't speak for several minutes. An hour ago, if someone had told him Dr. Green would say that, Dan would have expected it to make him feel terrible, but somehow he felt a lot better. Finally he said, "There's definitely something in what you say, and I'm going to let it keep working in me. But is it OK if I change the subject now?"

"Of course."

The whole point of this trip to Inland was to ask Dr. Green about Minik Mingarria, but knowing that Dr. Green was Inland royalty when Green himself didn't know, it felt like whispering behind his back. Watching the painting for any sign of breakage, Dan said, "There's something I know about you."

"Oh?"

"Dr. Green, this may sound crazy, but back in Inland you're the Prince of the Fairies."

Dr. Green just looked at him. The painting was fine.

"The reason you don't know that, and you live in Outland, is because your father put a curse on you."

Dr. Green still just looked at him. Even though Green was good at the non-disclosing-therapist thing, Dan had been sure he'd show more reaction than that.

Finally Dr. Green spoke. "I guess it would be hard to tell me this thing."

"What do you mean? I just told you, you're Prince of the Fairies."

"It's all right. You can tell me when you feel more comfortable."

"You think I'm lying to you?" asked Dan, his voice rising. "Telling you that because I'm nervous telling you the truth?"

Now Dr. Green looked baffled. "Dan, between when you told me you know something about me and when you asked if I think you're lying, you haven't said a single word."

Oh. The curse must be stopping Green from even hearing about his life in Inland. Dan felt like crying again, but he said, "I'm sorry, Dr. Green. You're right, I'll tell you when I'm more comfortable. There's something else though, the main reason I came here today." He told Dr. Green about Minik Mingarria: that it was Sister's truename, that somehow she was able to use it to control First Changing Beast, that FCB had told him that whoever understood its twofold meaning could wield it against Sister, that the dragon who understood the Old Tongue had translated it as "painful, injurer," so that was one meaning, but Dan had no idea what the second meaning was. "And that's what I'm hoping you can help me with," Dan finished. "I feel like the other meaning is buried inside me. How do I find it?"

Dr. Green leaned forward, chin in hand, and said, "You say she controls First Changing Beast with her truename? Isn't it usually the other way around?"

"For sure."

"I think that's a clue to the twofold meaning. People who have had very troubled childhoods—and from what you've told me, Sister more than qualifies—often have trouble telling which feelings are their own and which feelings are someone else's. They may project feelings they don't like into someone else so they don't have to own them, or experience other's feelings as though they were their own."

"That makes a lot of sense about Sister," said Dan. "It fits with the way a lot of times she appears not as herself but in the form of someone in my mind, like Principal Snyder or the Rattleman I imagined. And in Inland, where magic is real, that kind of boundary loss could also mean Sister's truename can work on First Changing Beast instead of her—like when she says it to him, it's his truename as well as hers." Dan's face had been bright with excitement, but now he frowned. "It feels right, but I'm not sure how it shows me the twofold meaning of Minik Mingarria. I'm supposed to be a painful injurer too? I don't like that."

"I'm sure that whether you like it or not has nothing to do with whether it is true," said Dr. Green. "Bringing serious and magical together, remember? All the same, I'm not sure that's the answer."

"Then what is the answer?"

Dr. Green smiled. "Like usual, I don't know. As you said, the answer is inside you. But boundary loss is only a problem when it's too big. When boundary loss is small it isn't a loss but a gain, and we call it empathy. I think you will realize the twofold meaning of Minik Mingarria when you gaze into Sister's eyes."

7

MADE MAKELESS

*G*raciela jumped back. "Were you even gone? If that's a return gate it formed before the one you left through even faded."

"Yes, he was gone, and long enough to wash his face and comb his hair," said Maggie. She took Dan's face in her hands and kissed him. "How did it go?"

"Learned ... a lot," answered Dan. "None of it urgent, I'll tell you after—" he gestured at the gathering battle. "Except about Minik Mingarria: Green thinks I'll figure out the other meaning when I gaze into Sister's eyes. Not something I'm looking forward to."

The bulbeggars growled, and the People from the Sea halted. Their company wasn't huge; by Dan's quick count fewer than fifty. But they were taller and stronger than goblins or dwarves, and had better armor. Gragguts's goblins were assembling behind them.

Dan ran across the ridge to check on Nellie and the noggles.

The center of the lake roiled, and Dan saw noggles splashing back to the creek, and other noggles floating lifelessly. It looked like the water women had surprised them and driven them back. So far so good.

The red raven perched on a dead tree near the People from the Sea. So far none of its companions had appeared, and there was no other sign of Sister. "So Maggie, can you feel Sister yet?" asked Dan.

"You have only been gone seconds, remember? I feel nothing different."

"Maybe Billy or Mother Ferny will know if she's coming. I'll go see." Dan waved to Maggie and Graciela and ran inside. Billy and Mother Ferny were murmuring together by the stove.

"Billy! Mother Ferny!" shouted Dan. "Sorry to interrupt, but I wanted to ask if you know where Sister is. Maggie can't feel her anywhere, but one of her red ravens is already here."

Billy held up one hand to stop Dan and with his other hand clasped Mother Ferny's. They continued murmuring, and then broke apart looking tired.

"Thank you, Dan," said Billy. "We feel her near, and she feels us and is uneasy. As long as Mother Ferny and I remain in the hall, she fears our power to resist her."

"What about our warriors? Can't she use magic to kill them?"

"Everything we have learned about her tells us that her power dissipates as she uses it. After a while she needs to replenish the blood of First Changing Beast in her veins. If she weakens herself killing our warriors, she fears we may capture her just as your Auki friends captured her. And she is right to fear this. So she waits and hopes for her soldiers to clear the way so that she can attack us at full strength."

"Who would win then?"

Billy and Mother Ferny looked at each other.

"That we will learn when the time comes," answered Billy.

Dan ran outside. In the back of his mind he was thinking that Billy was safe from Skriker's call as long as he stayed inside with Mother Ferny, but he didn't know if that was good or bad. Very good that Billy was safe, but that meant the danger was even greater for Maggie, Graciela, Nellie, Dan—and Crackerbones.

"Where is Crackerbones?" cried Dan. "If he's War Chief, he needs to come up with something fast!" The People from the Sea were marching toward the outnumbered Gatemoodle warriors on the road. The Gatemoodle warriors facing the valley were evenly matched by Gragguts's troops, so none could be spared to reinforce the road.

"He ducked into a tunnel as soon as you left for Outland," answered Maggie.

Then two things happened at once: The People from the Sea charged, and a great roar went up from the troops on both sides of the valley. Dan jerked his gaze away from the People's onslaught and searched for what caused the other sound. Everything was in an uproar that was hard to make sense of, but gradually he realized that dwarves and good goblins were attacking enemy troops from the rear. He saw a figure that gestured orders from a distant hillock; she was too far to make out her features, but he recognized the familiar gesture of hand to face.

"Loosejaw!" shouted Dan. "Go, Loosejaw!"

The enemy troops turned to engage their new attackers. Dan expected the troops guarding Gatemoodle to charge down the valley and trap the enemy like a pincer, but suddenly

Crackerbones was back, bellowing, "To the road! The road!" Most of the goblins peeled away and followed him. Drula directed a skeleton crew of dwarves to protective positions and led the rest behind Crackerbones.

None too soon. The People from the Sea were driving forward as a wedge on the road, supported by goblins harrying from the side. Already they were almost to the foot of the hill on which Dan stood with Maggie and Graciela. Wherever the Gatemoodle troops faced only goblins, they more than held their own, but they were unable to win against the height and armor of the People from the Sea. Even the bulbeggars were driven back. Some of the People began laughing and chanting stupid words like blood and honor as they swung their axes.

Then Crackerbones and Drula were upon them! Surrounded by their best warriors they crushed the goblins on the People's left flank and crashed into the People themselves. The bulbeggars drove back the goblins on the other side. Laughter and chanting ceased. The People from the Sea formed a circle to defend against the new attack.

"I have one more big spiderweb in the stable," said Graciela, her eyes starting to blacken. "Mother Ferny said to save it in case they have another giant, but should I use it on the People?"

That question was answered immediately by a bellow in the direction of the valley battle. They did have another giant. Maggie and Graciela ran off discussing tactics for her magpies to elude enemy magpies and web the giant.

Dan hated being confined to the ridge top by his promise to Crackerbones while all the fighting was down below. He hated it even more when he saw four of Gragguts's goblins cut two dwarves away from their troop. He hated it yet more again when he recognized Lammer and Tanly. He hardly knew them, and all the other warriors must be just as deserving—but the pair of dwarves wouldn't be able to fend off those goblin swords much longer. Crackerbones was nowhere in sight, and Dan charged down the hillside. The goblins were intent on the surrounded dwarves so Dan got within a few feet without being noticed and shouted, "Hey!" One goblin turned and Dan shot him point blank. Startled, the other goblins didn't know which way to turn, and Lammer and Tanly quickly slew two. Dan's arrow took down the last.

"Hee-ro indeed," panted Lammer.

Tanly laughed briefly. "Thank you, even if you only saved us so that we can tell you the tale of Jake and the Sunflower Stalk."

Lammer said, "Perhaps we should begin now, for in my bones I sense today is fell for me, although you have delayed my reckoning: Long ago, when the world was new and mortals were true, Jake climbed the Sunflower Stalk."

"Clumb," said Dan.

"Beanstalk," said Tanly.

Lammer grinned. "Ah well, no time to clear this up now." He and Tanly raised their swords and charged back to the battle, crying "For Jake!"

Dan longed to fight by their side, but he didn't want to be more untrue to his promise to Crackerbones than he already had. He ran back up the ridge, wondering what happened when Jake reached the trolls.

Dan ran to see how Nellie was doing. The lake still roiled. Three noggles had made it past the water women and almost reached the near end of the dam, in range of Dan's bow. Finally, Dan could do something useful. He drew an arrow, but for some reason the noggles turned and ran back to the middle of the dam. Dan thought about slip-sliding down the bank and pursuing, but the blood and honor chant started up again behind him. He figured Nellie could handle the noggles anyway. Dan ran back to overlook the road and groaned.

It was another company of People from the Sea, as numerous as the first, running to join their countrymen. Gragguts was there too, rallying his goblins. Crackerbones and Drula had driven the first group of People back, but fortune changed swiftly, and the best that the Gatemoodle troops could manage was a controlled retreat. Soon they had reached the base of the hill and begun backing toward the hall, many fewer than they had been.

Dan looked around for Maggie and Graciela and was glad that he couldn't see them; anyplace was probably safer than here. Now he had more chances to be useful than he wanted. His first arrow bounced off armor, his second felled his target, and then the melee was too near for shooting. Dan drew his sword. He wished Crackerbones would order a retreat into the hall. They were all going to die here. Dan gulped and prepared to charge.

Then something checked him—at first he didn't know what. He hesitated and listened. A great hound was baying, sounding both near and far away. More bulbeggars? But even their leader Boe did not have a voice that deep. Horns Dan heard, and song, distant as a dream. The ground quivered, and suddenly the horns and song rang clearly:

Bones of life and bones of sorrow!
Death today for life tomorrow!

From a hole in the side of the ridge where no hole had been before burst a great red slavering hound that would have left the Baskervilles quivering beneath their beds. Right behind rode the

King of the Fairies and twenty warriors, a skeleton army on swift horses with wild eyes and wildly blowing manes. Their heralds blew on trumpets carved from massive horns of some lord among bulls. Then hound and horn grew silent and were replaced by the more terrifying sound of metal armor clattering against bare bone. Straight to the battle rode the fairy army and clove through the People from the Sea, slaying as they went. The People broke and ran, and the fairies turned their horses and pursued.

"The King of the Fairies has things well in hand here," shouted Crackerbones, voice hoarse but still strong. "To the others to lend what help we may!" He rallied the remnants of the Gatemoodle defenders. Drula was there too, and they all ran or limped toward the valley.

Time to check on the others. Dan spotted Maggie and Graciela at the north side of the ridge, gesturing at her flock of birds. They seemed fine; whatever had happened with the giant, it was nowhere in sight.

Dan meant to run to the lake to check on Nellie and the noggles, but before he even turned he heard Crackerbones shout. Gragguts had intercepted him as Crackerbones helped his weakest goblins at the back of the line, and now the brothers faced each other alone.

"It is time, Crackerbones," said the heavier goblin. "Now at last our swords meet and you learn that mine is sharper."

Crackerbones was silent except for his blade ringing against that of Gragguts. Gragguts was stronger, and his blows forced Crackerbones back, but Crackerbones was quicker and hopped from side to side, keeping his brother off balance. Dan had seen Crackerbones defeat a bigger opponent before, Matamucho of the Mukis, so he wasn't surprised when Crackerbones scored first blood. It was only a slight wound to the arm, but Dan was confident that the Gatekeeper goblin would strike more deeply soon.

Then another thought stung Dan like a wasp. *Maybe it would be better for Crackerbones to die.* That would take care of Skriker's curse. Dan wouldn't have to worry about Maggie and Graciela, or Billy or Nellie Longarms, or himself.

The goblins had broken apart. They leaned on their swords, breathing heavily. Gragguts's cheek had been sliced from mouth to ear; Crackerbones was still unmarked. They raised swords and attacked again, but now Crackerbones was driving Gragguts back. Dan smiled, ashamed of his thought from a moment ago.

Then he saw movement off to the side. One of the fallen goblins with Gragguts's insignia had been playing possum, and now he sneaked toward the fight on hands and knees, knife in his mouth.

"Look out behind you, Crackerbones!" shouted Dan.

Crackerbones dropped, rolled, and leapt up a few feet away, calling as he did so, "Now, Dan! Now is time for an archer on the hill!"

Dan nocked an arrow to bowstring and drew. There was no time to think, but wasps are fast.

"You do not yet know that your choice will make no difference." Dr. Green's words. *It would look like an accident. I can shoot Crackerbones and everyone will understand it was an accident. And then no more worry about Skriker. Maggie will be safe. And Graciela. And Billy and Nellie. And me. Crackerbones is usually a jerk, anyway. He says he'll eat me if I don't find First Changing Beast soon.*

Dan tried to aim, but the fighters were in constant motion. Crackerbones was in front of his bow for a moment, but then it was Gragguts, and then the sneak. As sword rang against sword,

Crackerbones danced to the uphill position to try to gain an advantage. That put him closest to Dan. Finally there came a moment of separation between the fighters—half a moment really, but enough. Dan released the bowstring and his arrow flew swift and straight to its target. The sneaking goblin fell dead.

Crackerbones saluted Dan with his sword and turned back to Gragguts.

A scream came. From behind. From the lake.

Nellie Longarms was screaming.

Dan sprinted across the ridge. As he careened down the side he saw that Nellie had been roped and yanked from the water. Two noggles held her from opposite sides by cords around her waist, long enough that they could stay out of her reach. They were looping the ends through branches that formed the dam, tying Nellie down. A third noggle held a lasso, biding his time. Nellie thrashed and extended her arms not toward her enemies but toward the lake, reaching for water that she needed to touch or she would drown in air as surely as a human in the depths or a fish cast on shore. She bent forward at the waist and the noggle tossed his lasso over her shoulders and jerked, binding arms to torso.

Nellie's scream rent the air like a diving falcon, or like the rabbit it slays.

Where were her cousins? Were they deaf? Why didn't they come to her?

The lake splashed and churned in answer: her cousins battled other noggles.

Now all three ropes were tied fast. The noggles drew their swords.

The last six feet of the ridge side was sheer cliff. Dan hardly noticed; he leaped and landed running, pulling an arrow from his quiver. When he reached the dam he drew and shot without breaking stride. Whether it was Dan's heart or some magic in his fairy-made bow that guided the shaft, the nearest noggle fell dead. Dan already had another arrow nocked, but the other two noggles jumped into the lake.

Nellie cried out again, but quieter now, it was hard to hear her. She surged against the ropes, kicked her legs, and fell back panting.

It was a long run across the dam, but Dan was fast. Nellie wasn't calling out anymore, but he saw her still twitching; he figured he could make it. He threw down his bow and drew his sword to cut her bonds.

The two noggles flew out of the water and landed on the dam between Dan and Nellie.

Dan threw himself at them, screaming "Death" like one of the skeleton warriors. With a two-handed parry he knocked the sword from the grasp of one noggle, and on the backswing sliced off its head. He ducked a blow from the other noggle and came up swinging his sword, but this opponent was quick and parried Dan's blow. Dan roared at the wasted time, grabbed the fallen noggle's sword, and threw it. His enemy knocked it aside but that left him open for Dan's thrust to his heart.

Dan pulled his bloody sword out of the corpse and sliced one of the ropes holding Nellie down. Calling, "Nellie, Nellie!" he cut the other cords.

The battle had been brief, but not brief enough. Nellie lay still.

Dan picked her up and jumped off the dam, watching for any movement besides her golden hair swirling around her face as they sank in the cold water. When his lungs could stand it no longer he kicked for the surface and gasped for his own breath.

He held on to the side of the dam with one arm and cradled Nellie's head in the other.

Her eyelids flickered!

"Nellie! You're alive!" Dan was flooded with relief warm enough to banish the chill of the lake.

But Nellie shook her head, a tiny twitch but clear. "No, Dan Outlander. Nellie was in the dry too long."

"What are you talking about? You're in the water now! I've got you in the water! You're going to be OK."

One side of Nellie's mouth jerked up. "Now Nellie and Dan Outlander will never swim the long swim together."

She lay still.

The world fell dark and silent. There were no battle cries, horns, or drums from the direction of Gatemoodle. There was no turmoil in the lake. There was only Dan cradling Nellie Longarms.

Dan cursed himself. So many chances he had had to save Nellie, so many times he had failed! He had seen the noggles on this side of the dam running back to the middle; if he had gone down to kill them instead of turning to the People from the Sea, Nellie would be alive. He had checked on Maggie and Graciela; if he had checked on Nellie then instead of watching Cracker-bones with Gragguts, Nellie would be alive. He had had the chance to kill Crackerbones to fulfill Skriker's cry; if he had done that, Nellie might still be alive.

It was strange how light she was. Dan wondered if she had been that light in life, or if some substance had departed when she died. Her hair floated in the water, and one long arm drifted to her side. She had used those long arms to save him and Maggie and his friends more than once. But Dan knew now that his bond with Nellie had formed before then, even before she had given him his first kiss so that he could swim safely to her underwater home. It had formed when she first rose from a pool to try to capture Dan and Maggie. She had looked in Dan's eyes and invited him to swim with her, and beneath what seemed to be a threat to devour him it was an offer of wild freedom. Maggie had known and resented it, but Maggie truly had no cause for jealousy. There must be different kinds of love, because he knew Maggie loved the Moss Maidens but that didn't make her love him any less. Dan loved Maggie with all his heart, but he loved Nellie Longarms too.

Slowly Dan became aware that there was sound again in his world. But it wasn't from the battle by Gatemoodle, or the battle in the lake; it was Dan himself, shouting in grief.

Wait.

Maggie and the Moss Maidens.

Iralia was the Moss Maiden whom Maggie loved most of all.

Iralia who gave up her physical body to protect her forest.

By casting a Makeless Making, the spell that gave freedom to something else by surrendering a freedom of one's own.

Dan looked at Nellie's still face and said, "Listen, Inland." His voice quavered so he started over, and as he spoke his voice grew loud and firm. "Listen, Inland. I'm talking to you. That means all the land around, and all the water and all the air and animals and plants, like in our power tales that made the Gatemoodle ridge grow. It means Gatemoodle, and the Gatekeepers. It means Maggie and the Moss Maidens and the fairies. And it means the dwarves, and it even means dragons and goblins and giants and kobolds. And First Changing Beast, of course. And maybe more than anything it means Nellie Longarms. If I've forgotten anyone, I'm sorry, it means you too. I'm talking to all of you. I know I'm not a magician. The only magic I've had in my life is what I feel here, for Maggie and all the incredible things I never thought existed outside books. But if I'm really supposed to be here for some reason, then give me the power to do a Makeless Making. I don't care what freedom I give up, take anything you want, but bring Nellie Longarms back to life."

Nellie's arm moved and Dan's heart pounded, but it was only a wave lifting and lowering the long limb. Dan gently touched Nellie's eyelids, but she didn't respond.

The world shrank further; darkness covered even Nellie's face. There was nothing but icy water and Nellie's head upon Dan's arm, growing lighter; she was leaving, and as she lightened Dan grew heavier. Even if it didn't help, Dan couldn't let that go unspoken.

"Still talking to you, Inland. You see, Nellie and I are connected. That whole thing about our minds being linked because she helped me three times? Not sure I believe that's the reason. I bet our minds linked just because we like to help each other. She wouldn't have been here to die except for me asking her. I don't exactly feel guilty, though, because that's what friends do. And so I'm trying to return the favor, give something back.

"What I said about magic before maybe wasn't quite right. Tanly says my brother is an important part of the story, and the Green Goblin says there's magic in Outland too. If Outland has magic it's a different kind, much harder to notice, but if there's different kinds of love there can be different kinds of magic. So I'm including any Outland magic while I talk to you, Inland. That means I'm talking to Josh and Alice, and even to Mom and Dad and Theo. And the Green Goblin, of course."

Dan thought for a moment and then added, "The Green Goblin told me something to say about Sister, but he also said it was up to me to figure out when to use it. I think it fits right here right now:

Earth, Water, Fire, and Air
Met together in a garden fair
Put in a basket bound with skin
If you answer this riddle you'll never begin.

Now take what you want from me, and let Nellie live."

Perhaps a breeze had just started up, because Dan heard the lake lapping the dam. Light returned as though the first morning rays barely stroked the eastern sky. Then like a swift sunrise Dan heard her voice.

"Foolish Dan Outlander."

"Oh my God, Nellie, it worked!"

"What has Dan Outlander given up for Nellie?"

"I don't know. I don't feel any different at all, except so happy to see you!"

"Foolish Dan Outlander," scolded Nellie. But then she kissed him—and, after saying, "Because only one kiss would stop Dan's breath away from water," she kissed him again.

The world was back. Battle noise reached them from Gate-moodle. But the lake remained quiet. Dan looked around and the only noggles he saw were floating corpses.

Several strange faces rose above the waves and gazed at him. Dan recognized Lorelei, the green-skinned beauty. That ugly one must be Jenny Greenteeth—the long algae-covered fangs in her smile gave her away. And there were half a dozen others of all shapes and colors that seemed to shift like the liquid they swam in, so that every time Dan stared at one, she looked different than she had looked a moment before. They sang wordlessly, or else in a language Dan had never heard that conjured for him better than English a dark stormy sea and a sparking laughing river. Then they sang, "The waters thank you," and submerged.

"Perhaps Dan Outlander and Nellie will yet swim the long swim together," said Nellie. She undulated beneath the surface and was gone.

Dan climbed out of the water. He ran his hands over his body and said to himself, "I feel just the same. Well, no time to worry about what freedom I gave up. I'd better find out how the others are doing." He retrieved his bow and began to run.

8

THE END OF THE BATTLE

*D*an clambered up the hillside. The bottom was so steep he had to search for handholds and footholds, and even above that he needed to grab tussocks for balance. At least he wasn't an enemy facing armed defenders on high. As he reached the top he was surprised to discover Maggie and Graciela waiting. Maggie took his hand to help with the last step.

A smile flickered across her face. "We saw you with Nellie."

"The noggles tied her out of the water so she couldn't breathe," panted Dan. "I had to do something." He put his hands on his knees and gulped in air. When he stood back up, Maggie was looking at him with tilted head and creased brow. Graciela was in the background with her arms crossed. At least her eyes were back to normal.

"Something is different about you," said Maggie.

"Oh." Dan glanced down at himself. "I feel normal. But ..." He told them about rescuing Nellie, and about the Makeless Making.

When he finished, Maggie looked pale and held her arms limp by her sides. "Oh, Danny, that was nobly done, but—*what have you done?* I am glad that Nellie lives, but—what have you lost?"

It was the first moment since Dan saw the noggles subduing Nellie that action had slowed down enough for him to reflect. "I don't know. But I don't think I could have done it differently even if I did know. Not after everything Nellie has done for us. She's been there since the beginning."

Maggie gave a single nod. "I bet Mother Ferny will know." The three of them started toward the entrance to the hall. "I was feeling happy because my father finally did something right, showing up when he did. Now I do not feel happy any more. At least the battle seems to be ending."

But when they stepped inside, Billy and Mother Ferny did not look like the danger had passed. They still stood beside the stove, holding hands and murmuring. The only sign that they had noticed Dan, Maggie, and Graciela was that Billy made a pushing-away gesture with his free hand.

"What are they doing?" whispered Graciela.

"Bolstering the power of the hall against Sister," answered Dan. "She must be coming!" He pulled the others toward the door, Maggie protesting that she still could not feel Sister.

Suddenly, Mother Ferny dropped Billy's hand, sniffed loudly, turned toward Dan, and screeched, "What recipe is this?"

"That is for later, Mother," said Billy. He took her hand again and jerked it, and she turned her face from Dan and resumed murmuring.

"What was that all about?" asked Graciela.

Dan groaned but answered only, "We need to see what's happening." As they ran back outside, he heard Maggie explaining that on their first trip to Inland, Mother Ferny had said Dan was still raw, and that he needed to cook before he could help them. On their next trip she had deemed him adequately done.

Sister was nowhere to be seen. The single red raven perched unmoving in its dead tree. And it was as Maggie had said: the battle was winding down. In the valley to the west, Loosejaw was directing her troops as they surrounded a batch of kobolds who had laid down their weapons; most of the enemy goblins seemed to have been killed or have run away. Soon Loosejaw marched toward the hall and the road with all her troops that were not needed to guard the captives.

The King of the Fairies and his skeleton army held the road. The bulbeggars and the great hound of the fairies roamed beside them. Many People from the Sea lay dead. Those who remained were crouched behind a shield wall, and behind them, facing outward to complete a defensive circle, was a band of the burliest goblins. Gragguts was there, so Dan darted his eyes around until he spotted Crackerbones; the duel between brothers had been inconclusive. Crackerbones stood with Drula and many Gatemoodle warriors at the foot of the hill, behind the fairies. Dan figured they would stage a final attack when Loosejaw's reinforcements joined them. Only one thing worried him.

"The People and Gragguts are way outnumbered. Why don't they surrender?"

"Some idiotic fight-to-the-death credo?" wondered Graciela.

"Either that or they expect Sister to show."

The red raven fell from its branch, then soared high. It turned and slowly flapped away, around the bend.

Graciela sighed. "It's leaving."

But the raven floated back into view. With it came the sound of hooves and an unidentifiable creaking.

A frost-white horse cantered around the bend. Sister rode it, clad in robes as white as the horse, with a red cape, red gloves, and a red metal circlet holding her golden hair. A small red vessel was strapped to her breast by silver chains. The creaking sound came from a litter and the half-dozen malkins who supported it. Sister halted just behind what remained of her army, and the malkins lowered the litter beside her. They pulled open the curtains.

"Weird," said Dan.

Mrs. Westerley stepped out, dressed in white and red just like her biological daughter, except that she wore no circlet.

Dan shook his head and said. "That can't be good. But according to Dr. Green I need to look into Sister's eyes to figure out the other meaning of Minik Mingarria. Which also can't be good, but I'd better try."

"Aren't you forgetting something?" asked Maggie.

"Oh. Right." Dan leaned in to kiss her.

Maggie pushed him away. "No, silly. We need to truename each other so that Sister cannot."

"Oh. Right!"

"And we have to be sure to break the truenaming as soon as we're away from her, lest it grow so strong that like the last time we cannot."

Dan turned to Graciela. "At first we're going to enjoy the truenaming and won't want to break it. If it goes on too long it'll feel like torture, but we won't have the willpower to break it. So it's best for us to break it right after Sister is gone. If we dither about breaking it, slap us. Even cut us if you have to. Pain brings back our willpower."

Dan and Maggie looked at each other, and in the same

moment the one said, "Maggie Magpie," while the other said, "Círdan James Hillman."

Dan fell into the pellucid pool that he remembered from the other time. And like the other time, someone swam beside him, someone who might have been Maggie, but might have been himself. The other time he had swum down and down until he emerged through the light that shone from the bottom of the pool. But that way took too long. The other figure plunged past him, headed deeper, but he grabbed its hand and pointed to the surface. They kicked up and broke into the air.

They were back on Gatemoodle ridge. Nothing had changed except that Dan and Maggie were clasping each other in a tight embrace.

Sister's voice carried from below. Dan tried to shake off the truenaming's false assurance that everything was fine, and listened. "Good job, Father. You have delayed me. Now I must waste my powers getting past you to Johnny Quickfoot and the witch." She raised her eyes to Dan and Maggie, and smiled. "Hello, my sister. Hello, Daniel. You were planning to approach me? No matter, I will join you where you are."

The King spoke in his voice like echoes in a tomb. "Begone, Sally. Your army is defeated. Only out of mercy have we not yet slain those who remain. Begone! How do you imagine passing me to gain the hall?"

"Gladly will I show you! The trees of the Marrowland you control. The trees around Gate Moot Hall are controlled by Johnny and the witch. But these"—she gestured at the shrubbery beside the road—"and these"—she gestured at the trees on the hillside above. "These are free."

Sister called out in a voice like a hammer crushing metal, "Minik zuhaixka!"

The dragon had translated *Minik* as *pain*, and now the bushes and trees moaned, creaked, and popped like old joints forced to climb stairs. Branches twitched and then swayed as though buffeted by a great storm, but there was no wind. Sharp cracks sounded, and for a moment Dan worried that Sister had somehow imported guns into Inland, but it was branches snapping and falling to the ground. When it was as loud as armies shooting at each other, Dan put his hands over Maggie's ears and she put hers over his. Goblins, dwarves, and People from the Sea dropped their weapons and crouched, shielding their ears. The fairy hound and the bulbeggars howled. Only the skeleton fairies and their steeds, Sister, and her magnificent white horse, were untroubled.

Mrs. Westerley pushed the curtains of the litter against the sides of her head, and somehow Dan could hear her cry out, "What are you doing, dearie?"

"I am sorry, Mother," said Sister. "This will give you peace." She gestured, and Mrs. Westerley smiled and released the curtains.

The noise crescendoed and stopped. All around, splintered sticks, broken branches, and shattered trunks lay where thickets and groves had stood.

"Bautu minik zuhaixka!"

A new sound began, of rustling, bumping, and creaking. The wood piles twitched and jerked as though shaken by earth tremors, but the earth was still. Branches rose, fell, twisted, and snapped. Shapeless debris fell into shapes of arms, legs, and fingers, of torsos and heads. Sections spun, rushed together, and snapped into place.

A malkin army arose. As one they looked at their hands, recognized that in their moment of creation they were weaponless, and bent to select blades and clubs of broken wood. They faced Gatemoodle and called in one voice like branches grating together in a high wind, "We come!"

Loosejaw's forces were still approaching when the shrubs and trees near them collapsed and reformed as malkins, so they were the first to engage this new enemy. The malkins jerked and twitched as they fought, swinging and stabbing off-target and leaving their bodies unguarded, so at first the goblins had an easy time of it. But more and more shattered wood became malkins, and their stick arms did not tire like flesh muscles. Soon Loosejaw drew her band close and it was all they could do to fight their way through the malkins to join the rest of the Gatemoodle army at the foot of the hill. Drula led a band of her dwarves to help, but soon they were fully occupied just holding their own against malkins surging down the road.

"What is wrong with the fairies?" asked Graciela.

"They have trouble with malkins," said Dan and Maggie at the same time.

Dan smiled and shook his head. "Truenaming makes us think alike. You tell her, Maggie; I will clamp my jaw."

Maggie continued, "It is because the fairies are akin to the marrow of the land, but the malkins are a monstrous false creation."

The fairy horses skittered and sidestepped when malkins approached. The fairies themselves became almost as clumsy as the malkins, thrusts of spear and sword going wide twice for every one that connected. Only the King and his steed were impervious to the malkins, and wherever he rode he left a swath of lifeless wood. The fairy hound and the bulbeggars joined him, taking doglike pleasure in breaking and shaking sticks.

But more malkins came and poured around the King and his dogs. The People from the Sea broke their shield wall and attacked as Gragguts and his goblins followed right behind. A group of malkins skittered to the left and began flanking the defenders, heading for the valley approach to the hall.

Sister sat smiling on her horse. She leaned and said something to Mrs. Westerley, who nodded and climbed back into her litter. Sister put her hand to the red vessel and then back to her reins. She walked her horse after her advancing army, and malkins bore her mother behind her.

Graciela shook Dan and Maggie by their shoulders. "What is wrong with you?" she snapped. "We can't stand here doing nothing. Back to the hall!"

"Oh, right," said Dan. They backed to the doorway but did not go in.

Somehow, Crackerbones, Drula, and the Fairy King worked out a plan in the heat of the battle. The fairies and bulbeggars held the road where it reached the top of the ridge, where the attack was heaviest. Dwarves and goblins ran to take positions along the side of the hall, blocking the malkins who charged up from the valley.

For a while, having the high ground and simply being better fighters than malkins was enough. But only for a while. Malkins came, and were cut down; more malkins came, and more were cut down. Even when the ridge side looked like a tornado had passed through a woodland leaving a carpet of matchsticks, more malkins came. And here and there, fallen dwarves, goblins, and fairies lay among the debris. When the defenders were backed up almost to Gatemoodle itself, Sister rode to the top of the ridge and laughed.

"We're losing, we're gonna lose," said Dan. He saw the terror in Graciela's eyes and realized that only the calmness that came in the early stages of mutual truenaming kept him from feeling the same panic. "I could stop this if I could truename Sister, but

I can't get close enough to look into her eyes and learn the other meaning of Minik Mingarria. Too much fighting in between."

An aisle opened between the fighters and Dan dashed for it, but immediately he was blocked again by dwarves and malkins. Dan jumped back, shook his head, and said, "Remember the unicorn, Maggie?" Once with Maggie, once with other friends, Dan had seen unicorns destroy malkins.

"I wish we had unicorns now," replied Maggie.

"Oh! How about deer?" asked Graciela, holding up the horn made from an antler of the blue deer that had been Maggie's father. "The aluxob said for the right person to blow it at a time of need. And if this isn't a time of need ..."

"You're brilliant, Graciela!" said Dan. "Do it!"

Graciela put the horn to her lips and blew, but the sound that came out was like a weak buzz from a broken kazoo, barely loud enough to hear over the shouts, groans, and stick shattering that surrounded them. Graciela frowned and reversed the horn but this time when she blew it was no better than puffing through a straw.

"It must be for you," said Graciela, handing the horn to Maggie. "You're his daughter, after all."

Maggie blew, and blew again, but Dan could hear nothing above the roar of the battle. She handed the horn to Dan.

"It just must not be the right time," said Dan. "No reason I'd be the right person if his own daughter isn't."

"Unless it's because you can love Sister as well as Maggie," said Graciela.

"But I don't want to love Sister," said Dan, at the same moment that Maggie said, "But I don't want him to love Sister."

Graciela slapped Dan, and on the backswing slapped Maggie. "Damn your truenaming!" she cried. "Blow the horn!"

Dan blew, and from the horn came an impossible note. It

was sweet as the fluting of a wood thrush but loud as a waterfall down a sylvan precipice; it was gentle as the footstep of a fawn and yet as harsh as bucks clashing antlers in a battle for dominance.

All fell silent. No weapons clashed; no one shouted or called out in pain. Everyone listened to that note.

And when the note faded, they heard bugling from the mountainside north of Gatemoodle, bugling wilder than any human- or dwarf-made horn. A great blue stag stepped from beneath the pines, lifted his head, and loosed his strange call once again.

Down the mountainside he charged, gathering speed as he came, and crashed like an avalanche into the malkins. With his great antlers he tossed stick men left and right; with flashing hooves he trampled his enemy into kindling.

The malkins began to flee but Sister held up her hand and like robots they turned to face the blue deer. The Fairy King rallied his cavalry and charged the malkins from the other side, and whether they absorbed something magical from the deer or were simply inspired by hope, their clumsiness vanished and they struck with deadly accuracy. Crackerbones and Drula fell upon those of Gragguts's goblins and People from the Sea still standing and drove them down the hill.

The way to Sister lay clear.

"Now, Maggie!" said Dan. They strode forward. Sister looked up and he met her gaze, but he saw nothing but the cruelty and anger that he already knew.

"Why stare at me so, little mortal?" said Sister with curled lip. "You hope to hide in your truenaming and sneer at my defeat? You hope to gloat at me while I despair? But I am not defeated and I do not despair!

"Faithful goblins, to me! Men, to me!"

Gragguts's goblins and the People from the Sea backed toward Sister, fighting for their lives. Sister raised her hands and the air crackled. Right in front of Dan, Drula swung her axe at one of the People—and her axe bounced off the air in front of him. All around the same thing happened. Sister's army let their arms drop to their sides, surrounded by a faint reddish cone of protection.

A group of malkins ran toward Sister but she shook her head and flicked her fingers at them. They stopped, and Dan was sure that the look on their faces must be what branches feel like when they sense a high wind about to crack them. The malkins fled into the valley where the blue deer was chasing down their kin.

"To safety, Gragguts, and take the People," said Sister. "Protection will follow you."

"Nay, brother!" shouted Crackerbones. "Let us finish now what we could not finish before. Come out and face me; the others will stand aside!"

Gragguts made a rude gesture, turned away from his brother, and led his troops down the road. The King and his fairy warriors rode on either side to make sure no one strayed out of the redness or attempted a sneak attack. Dan saw the fairies occasionally prod with their spears, but the cone turned them aside.

Now only Sister remained, and behind her six malkins waiting beside her mother's litter. Again Sister touched the vessel she carried and fidgeted with it before shifting her hand back to her reins.

A dwarf raised her ax and charged at Sister. Drula shouted "No!" but at the same instant Sister clicked her tongue. The dwarf dropped her ax and crumpled, blood coursing from her nose.

"Let no one else attack her," came Billy's voice. Dan turned and saw him standing beside Mother Ferny on the front stoop.

"We have set the hall's protection on all of you," said Mother Ferny, "but it will fail the moment you take the offensive."

Sister rode her horse two steps closer to the hall and said, "So Johnny and the Fern Woman emerge from their lair at last." She raised her voice and called out, "Are these your leaders, oh, you goblins? Oh you dwarves? The cowards Quickfoot and Ferny who lurk behind thick walls while you fight for them? Would you not rather join me? We could—"

"Shut up, Sister," snarled Crackerbones. "We all know they were preparing the hall for your arrival."

Sister frowned at the interruption, but then smiled again and again rode two steps forward. "A kind reception, then? I will thank you for it. But you, Crackerbones, need not perpetuate this rift with your brother. I could use you well. I do believe that if you had been my general you would have better coordinated my attack. Join me and I will put you above Gragguts."

Crackerbones spat. "You think yourself powerful enough for the hall's reception? Then ride on."

Sister rode two steps forward. She spotted Graciela and pointed at her. "Daniel even brought the Mexican bitch? Maggie, my sister, do you not yet know what is going on? Let them have each other. Come with me!"

"No one brought me!" called Graciela. "I am here by my choice, to be with my friends. I will always be with those who oppose you and the People from the Sea!"

Dan and Maggie looked at each other and took each other's hands. Whatever nerves or confusion Sister's words might otherwise have brought just flowed off the truenaming.

Sister laughed and rode another step forward.

"Think hard and choose well, Sister," said Billy. "Gate-moodle returns what it is brought: good will to those of good will, defeat to those who wish to defeat. Think you that you are strong enough to break these ancient spells? For if you fail, the hall will have you and hold you."

Sister leaned forward and stroked her horse's muzzle. "I know your plan, Johnny. You wish me to ride away, even though you know I would return sooner than you like with an army better ordered and organized, an army that waited to attack until all its forces are gathered." She snorted. "Gragguts was too eager to delay, but even now the frost giants are marching. I will speak to him about patience." She looked at Crackerbones again. "Are you sure you do not wish to be my Commander?"

Crackerbones spat again.

Sister laughed. "Never mind then. But as I said, I know your plan. You expect my sister and her pathetic boyfriend to free First Changing Beast before I return. Believe me, that will not happen. Even if they do find him he will be a hull, a husk, not worth the effort. I need only one more visit to make his power permanently mine.

"You hope that I am too tired to overcome you and take the hall now. You hope, but you do not know: I see the doubt and fear in your eyes."

"Perhaps you see only the reflection of your own doubt, Sister," said Billy.

Sister sat up straight in her saddle and stretched. "I admit I am tired. To wait for another time is tempting. But ... I think not. Begone from my path, Gatekeepers, for I wield the Unlight."

Sister reached into the red vessel and lifted skyward what it had held: a dull gray lump that looked like nothing, yet in its nothingness lay its power. From the lump emanated a dull gray light that spread in all directions, and whatever it touched was bleached of color, and whoever it touched despaired.

But Billy Portman and Mother Ferny had not spent the hours of battle in Gatemoodle for naught. From the timbers of the old building a white light shone, and it too spread, and when it reached the grayness of the Unlight it splintered like sunlight though a prism into all the hues of the spectrum. To whatever it touched it gave back the rightful colors only brighter: fresh greens for leaves and grasses, rain-washed blue for the sky, scarlet for path-side flowers and bloody wounds.

Dan grinned and looked back at Sister to watch her disappointment and defeat, but she merely laughed. "A pretty show!" she cried. "But only a brief one. I shall bring the Unlight to the heart of the hall and blanch the rainbow, and all who oppose me shall fall at my feet and despair!"

Suddenly a wild bugle split the air. Dan had forgotten about the great blue stag. It bounded in front of Billy and Mother Ferny, faced Sister, and snorted. Her white horse reared and bucked, and Sister fell from its back. Dan hoped for the fall to break her but she landed on her feet. The stag scraped its hoof on paving stones and charged. But rather than crashing into Sister he stopped with his antlers grazing her body, and then with a twist and pull used one tine to wrest the Unlight stone from her hand. He stomped on it where it landed, once, twice, thrice, and the Unlight was gone.

But Sister did not flinch. She raised her hands to the sky as her white robe and scarlet cape billowed and her golden hair floated, and she shrieked, "Come to me, my children of the air!"

A dozen red ravens plummeted out of nowhere. Straight for the stag they flew, chattering and croaking. Red feathers covered blue hair. Wings buffeted the stag's eyes, claws raked its back, and beaks ripped its side. The ravens rose, revealing rivulets of blood flowing through blue hair. Down swooped the ravens again, and the stag toppled to its knees.

Then Dan heard the last voice he expected: "What are you doing, dearie?" Mrs. Westerley had climbed out of her litter. "Why are you letting them hurt that lovely deer? Make them stop!" Mrs. Westerley ran into the flock more quickly than Dan had ever seen her move, and wrapped herself over the stag's head and neck.

Sister shrieked again, but a different shriek than the one that had summoned the ravens. Dan stared straight into her eyes, and he saw her face collapse like straw felled by a sickle blade. She looked like the dry gourd with the pebble rattling in it from the Goblin's poem. It was only an instant before her usual regal, angry expression returned, but it was enough.

Dan knew the twofold meaning of her truename.

"Minik—" he began.

Sister was swift. In the fraction of a second that it took his lips and tongue to form the next word, she focused on him, and she knew, and hate and fear suffused her face.

"—Mingarria!"

But Sister had vanished, along with Mrs. Westerley and her white horse.

The malkin litter-bearers collapsed into piles of sticks.

The red ravens flapped across the valley and over the hills, trailing mournful calls.

9

WHAT WAS LOST

*W*here had Sister gone? If she attacked First Changing Beast again, they had to pursue her fast.

But the magnificent blue stag lay wounded in front of them. Maggie and Graciela already knelt beside him. Dan joined them and asked, "Will he be OK?"

Raven beaks had jabbed holes all over the blue pelt; raven claws had torn swatches of flopping skin. Graciela stroked a patch that the birds had missed and the skin twitched, but the stag lay unmoving.

Maggie curled her fingers into the thick curly fur on the beast's forehead. It opened its eyes and looked at her. Maggie brushed tears away, smiled, and choked.

"Now then, now then." It was Mother Ferny with a jar of oily looking liquid. "I brewed a great batch of healing potions for our people. None of it will be quite right for this fellow, but it will help some. Drink, great one. Drink." The stag shifted its gaze to Mother Ferny and opened its mouth enough for her to pour in some liquid. The stag blinked, looked at Maggie and Dan, made a sound halfway between a snort and a sigh, and staggered to his feet.

"Now it is a matter of time in his own groves," said Mother Ferny.

Billy came out of the house with a golden apple and said, "In no way is this adequate thanks, but it is the finest of my supply from Outland. Eat now before you journey."

"Why does he have to go at all?" wailed Maggie as the deer crunched his apple. She touched his antlers. "Why do you have to go?"

"He needs time—" began Mother Ferny, but then she broke off, stared at Dan, and sniffed as though trying to catch a faint aroma, before shaking her head and repeating, "He needs time in his own groves. I am sorry."

Before Dan had a chance to worry about Mother Ferny's weird sniffing, Maggie stomped down the road shouting, "Father! Oh hell. Other father! Fairy King! Where are you? Get up here!"

As the deer swallowed his last bites, Maggie reappeared with the Fairy King treading beside her. He had cast back his hood, revealing the rotting flesh covering his bones, his decaying visage even more livid than usual. He stopped several strides short of the stag, who scraped a hoof against the ground once and snorted.

"Why did you stop, King?" asked Maggie. "He saved you from the malkins—*he* saved *you*, even after what you did to him. Make amends!"

The King's step showed none of his usual fairy grace as he approached the deer. "I do not make a habit of allowing even my blood to speak to me so," he said, "but I am conscious of owing a great debt, and of having done a great wrong. You have shamed me by giving succor I did not deserve. I humble myself before you." The King knelt and bowed his head.

The great stag tilted back his head and bugled, and though his sound was much weaker than before, it was still shocking at close range.

The King said, "No. Nevermore will I or any of my people hunt blue deer. Henceforth our Marrowland is sanctuary for you." Head still bowed, he rose and began to walk away.

"That is not what I meant!" cried Maggie.

The King paused and looked at her.

"Change him back! Change him back! He was human, he was the only parent who was ever nice to me, and you did this to him. Take off the spell!"

Slowly, as though he faced a hostile dog, the King approached the stag. The stag did not move. The King lifted his arm and his sleeve slipped back from his decaying flesh. Still the stag did not move. *What will Mr. Westerley look like?* wondered Dan. The King placed his bone fingers in the hair that Maggie's living fingers had so recently entwined. Dan braced himself for one of the weird Inland body transformations.

Nothing happened.

The King pulled back his hand. "He does not wish to become again what he was before."

"What?" cried Maggie.

"He chooses the life of a deer. Now I understand why he has been gentle with me. He chooses the freedom of forest and meadow. I could force him to change as I did once before, but I do not think anyone wishes for me to impose such an injustice."

Maggie sobbed, ran to the stag, and laid her head against his.

"He must go so that he may heal," whispered Mother Ferny.

Maggie stepped back, sniffling. The stag stretched out his neck and licked her on the nose. Then he hobbled toward the woods.

A white doe stepped from the edge of the trees, nuzzled the stag, and then walked beside him so that he could lean on her. Her whiteness was lovelier than simple albinism; her glossy fur glinted and emanated its own pale radiance, reminding Dan of moonlight on a misty eve. Just as the pair reached the shadows of the trees, the doe turned and gazed at Dan with deep brown knowing eyes. Then doe and stag disappeared.

Dan glanced at where Mrs. Westerley had stood a few minutes earlier. He had a thought that he decided would be unkind to voice.

But Graciela went ahead and said it: "I can see why he decided to remain a deer."

DAN COULDN'T TELL if the thin keening sound was all around him or in his head. Maggie stood slumped over with limp arms, and he knew he should comfort her, but somehow he felt like he was the one who needed to be comforted.

Graciela took him by the hand and led him to Maggie, saying, "I think the truenaming makes you stupid."

Truenaming! Dan had forgotten it in the uproar. That's why he felt so bad: he was feeling Maggie's feelings. He hugged Maggie and she put her arms lightly on his back.

"Now break the truenaming," said Graciela.

Dan looked at Maggie looking at Dan.

Graciela said, "Two words: I'll. Slap. You."

Dan didn't care about the slap, but Graciela channeling Josh made him laugh. Maybe he should have brought Josh back with him after all. He whispered in Maggie's ear, "I release you, Maggie Magpie."

Almost instantly she responded, "And I release you, Círdan James Hillman," but Dan discovered himself already on the ground, slumped with the misery of being only Maggie's slave and not her master.

He still heard the keening, and as his head cleared he realized it was coming from all around him. Dwarves and goblins were mourning friends and comrades among the fallen. Those who still breathed they escorted into the hall for Mother Ferny's ministrations. Those who breathed no more were carried to where the ridge north of Gatemoodle joined the trees. Dan stood and saw Drula, her sword arm in a sling, speaking intently while Crackerbones listened. The goblin nodded, and he and Drula directed their people to lay dwarf and goblin in the same pile.

"So something good grows even from Sister's war," said Billy Portman. "It will be known as the Mound of Two Kindreds. But how are my Outland friends? In need of Mother's medicine?"

"Just exhausted," answered Dan. Then he cried out, "Oh, no!"

Ratskin, tear-stained face no longer creased with giggles, was laying Wormhair on the funeral pile. And the day had been fell not for Lammer but for Tanly; the dwarf followed his goblin friend to lay Tanly's corpse beside Wormhair.

Dan felt all the adrenaline drain from his body, and he almost slumped back to the ground. "Now they'll never tell us about Jake and the Sunflower Stalk. I know that's stupid and unimportant, but it's all so sad. All this death, and Maggie—your Outland Dad ..." Dan took Maggie's hand.

Maggie laughed in a machine-gun rhythm. "Is it not the

same old story, now in Inland as in Outland? Father feels cooped up by domestic life, leaves the family to run wild?" Her laughter went up and up in pitch, and Dan squeezed her hand. Maggie stopped abruptly. "I did not have him before, so this is no loss. Next to Ratskin's loss, and Lammer's and all the others, my father is nothing. We have a job to do, defeating Sister. I have a job to do, tracking her."

Dan nodded. "If she has gone to First Changing Beast, we need to follow right away." No matter that he was almost too sad and tired to stand and Maggie was feeling ... he remembered the keening in his head.

Maggie let go of Dan, closed her eyes, and breathed deeply but raggedly. After a moment she frowned, clenched her hands, and stilled her breathing. Then she looked at the others and shook her head. "I cannot locate her."

Dan looked over his shoulder as though Sister might be nearby. "What has happened so that you can't sense her anymore?"

Maggie lowered her head and stamped her foot. "I have a sense of her far away but I cannot say how far or what direction. It is because I am tired. It is because I am upset. It is because I am so worthless all my parents hate me. At least I am good at something. Most children are lucky if they get two parents to hate them. I managed four!"

"Maggie—" began Dan.

"I'm so worthless my mother made me cut up my stuffed bunny."

Maggie had told Dan that back on their first trip to Inland. He had no idea why she dredged up that sad memory now, but it gave him an idea to try to cheer her up. "You were never worthless. Even back then your brother loved you, that must have been the rabbit he made specially for you." When the

Queen of the Fairies had told them the history of Maggie being switched for Sister, and all the sorrow it brought, she mentioned that Maggie's brother had made a toy rabbit and rattle for her.

"No wonder Mother hated it," shouted Maggie. "She wanted to destroy any sign of me being loved. She tried to smash the rattle too, but she was drunk and dropped it and I hid it where it's still safe."

"See, Maggie, you did good—"

"Stop!" she interrupted. "I know I am ridiculous, but stop trying to make things sound better than they were!"

Billy took her arm. "Come, all of you. A little food, and then to bed. Even if Sister bleeds First Changing Beast at this very moment, in your weariness you are no match for her."

As Billy led them inside, Dan found himself thinking a selfish thought. It was pretty clear that Maggie's Outland father —the blue deer—wasn't going to be loving Maggie and Sister both. That sure hadn't been love between the deer and Sister, and it wasn't clear that the deer loved Maggie either. So it looked like the Fairy Queen had been right: if anyone were going to love both Maggie and Sister, it would have to be Dan. Which as far as Dan was concerned was definite proof that the charm was not going to be fulfilled. They would have to defeat Sister some other way.

The great hall had been transformed into a hospital ward. Injured folk lay on cots and blankets, and Mother Ferny wended her way among them dispersing medicines, assisted by goblin and dwarf healers. No fairies were in sight; Dan knew some had been killed and some injured, but the fairies must be tending to their own in their pavilion. Dan and his friends joined the line in front of the stove where they ladled thin soup from a huge pot. Their upstairs room was still commandeered for the injured, and now all the corners were full too, so they grabbed blankets and took their soup outside. They settled on the ridge overlooking the lake. It was pretty in the gentle evening haze, and early fireflies began to flicker, but Dan hardly noticed even when fireflies made a glowing crown on Maggie's hair.

They ate silently. After they placed their bowls aside, Maggie said, "I am sorry for my outburst earlier. Even though I am too tired to talk, I need to know one thing: what did you learn? What is the twofold meaning of Minik Mingarria?"

"It won't surprise you at all, because you've empathized with Sister's suffering all along," said Dan. "The dragon told us those were words in the Old Tongue for hurt and pain. When I saw Sister control First Changing Beast with Minik Mingarria, it obviously caused him hurt and pain, so that was the first meaning: the hurt she makes others feel. Just now when Sister's ravens were maiming the blue deer—her own biological father —and then Mrs. Westerley—her biological mother, the deer's ex-wife—begged her to stop, then for just a moment Sister's arrogant expression fell away and I saw the second meaning of Minik Mingarria in her face: her own hurt and pain."

They sat silently for a moment, and then Dan said, "But here's something I don't understand: the Green Goblin told me this poem to help me figure out Sister.

> Praise life, it deserves praise, but the praise of life
> That forgets the pain is a pebble
> Rattled in a dry gourd.

And that helped me, because her face looked exactly like a dried up gourd with a stone rattling inside. But even though I'm no kind of poem-meister, even I know those lines don't mean pain rattles like that; they mean praise that ignores pain is false and useless like that pebble."

"Look," said Graciela, gesturing forward. Dan saw the lovely rippling lake. "Listen," she said, gesturing behind them. Dan heard dwarves and goblins moaning from Gatemoodle. He gazed at Graciela, her thick black hair matted with sweat, her face dirty, but determination in the set of her mouth and the spark of her eyes. He looked at Maggie, frowning in grief and exhaustion beneath her living crown of fireflies.

"Thank you," he said, because it seemed like the thing to say. But as they rolled themselves in their blankets and dropped into sleep like rocks into a pool, Dan was still confused: Did Graciela and the Green Goblin mean he should see Sister as though she wore a firefly crown?

DAN WOKE first and studied the lake in the dawn light. It was still except for circles where feeding fish broke the surface. There was no sign of Nellie and her cousins, and although they could stay underwater indefinitely, Dan was pretty sure that he would feel her if she were still around. They must have gone back to wherever they came from, knowing that their work was done for now. Dan felt a mixture of sadness that Nellie was gone, and huge relief that she was alive. He wondered again what he had given up in the Makeless Making. He didn't feel any different at all, and if it weren't for Mother Ferny's weird sniffing, he'd think he really hadn't given anything up. Maybe he hadn't! Maybe Nellie hadn't been dead in the first place and had recovered naturally. That was probably it. Ignorant mortals couldn't do spells like Makeless Making anyway.

Dan's eyes left the lake and turned to the two women

sleeping beside him, Maggie's lush body and Graciela's thinner one wrapped in blankets. The last few days had been way too manic to even think about romance or sex. Dan wished he could have a few days, at least a few hours, of alone time with Maggie before they charged off after Sister. Even rumpled in sleep and creased by war and disappointment in her fathers, Maggie glowed with unearthly beauty. Graciela was plainer—duh, all women were plainer—but suddenly Dan had the sense that that didn't matter at all. One side of Graci's mouth twitched into a dream smile while Dan watched.

Maggie's firefly crown had departed during the night. Now a dragonfly hummed up from the lake and hovered in front of Dan. Dan had always thought dragonflies the most perfectly named of creatures: they were insects, sure, but they were dragons in spirit and beauty. An early ray of sunlight caught it and it iridesced blue, green, and then blue again, as though its creator god had not yet made up her mind. Dan watched the apparition zoom to the side, circle, and light upon Graciela.

Maggie sighed and stretched and the dragonfly darted away.

"Hey, Mags, good morning," said Dan.

"Sun and lake, grass and ridge, the world around is good. But still I cannot sense Sister."

Dan didn't want to say anything because he didn't want to make Maggie feel worse, but this was bad. If they couldn't follow Sister, he didn't know any other sure way to locate First Changing Beast, and if he couldn't reach her to truename her first, she might capture all of FCB's power.

They woke Graciela and went to the hall. The valley and roadway were empty of the fallen, and no troops were to be seen. The only evidence that the previous day had actually happened was the Mound of the Two Kindreds, already clothed in young pale green grass, and in the valley a tent pavilion with the banner of the Marrowland flapping in the breeze. When they entered the hall they saw that all the injured dwarves and goblins were gone. Fir Darrig had disappeared too, and there was no sign of Boe or any of the other Bulbeggars. Dan was reminded of the way the dwarves left Bag End after the Unexpected Party as though they hadn't even been there. It was like the old days, with just Billy, Mother Ferny, and Crackerbones talking around a table.

It was comforting, and Dan indulged the fantasy that the battle, Nellie dying, the Makeless Making—none of it had happened. But then the table grew silent and Mother Ferny started her sniffing again. She strode over to Dan and he cringed because he was pretty sure what would happen next. Yup: she pinched his cheek, hard.

"Still cooked!" she screeched. "Still medium rare, but now missing a crucial ingredient! What has happened? What have you done?"

Dan explained about saving Nellie with a Makeless Making.

He had never seen Mother Ferny taken aback before, but now she grabbed a chair for support and then slumped into the seat. "Makeless Making by a mortal!" she muttered. "I only believe it because I smell it."

"By a mortal fool," snarled Crackerbones. "Your timely arrow aided me yesterday and I thank you for that, but still you are a fool. Your quest is for the aid of all of us and so is more important than Nellie Longarms or any of us alone. What if you lost something that renders you unfit to finish the quest? What have you lost?"

The world wasn't good old Gatemoodle, grandfatherish Billy, and an exciting quest to find FCB. The world was selfishness, cruelty, grim death, and ... "Crackerbones, you monster, you're lucky to be alive!" Dan snarled. "I saved you from Skriker's call, and because of that Nellie was picked, Nellie was suffocated and everyone else who heard Skriker is safe. You think I'm going to let Nellie die in favor of you? I wish I'd let them kill you."

Crackerbones pulled a knife and bounded over the table, but just as fast Maggie and Graciela stepped between him and Dan.

"Sit, Cracker," said Billy. "You have both spoken hard words, but hard words after a hard battle are no surprise and need not be heeded. Let us not criticize Dan's choice with Nellie, for to love and help the whole it is necessary to love and help the parts. It was bravely done. But your question is needful: what has been lost? Mother?"

Like the old witch testing to see if Hansel was ready to eat, Mother Ferny poked, prodded, and pinched Dan, sniffing all the time. Finally she squeezed her nose and said, "I cannot tell. I must brew a brew of finding." She went to the shelves and banged around, grabbing ingredients.

Dan sat in a fog of anger and sadness, which seeped away only to be replaced by an even nastier fog of anxiety: what if Maggie could never locate Sister? And ... what had he lost from the Makeless Making? The Gatekeepers' reactions pretty much put the lie to his fantasy that it wasn't a big deal.

Muffled by the fog, Dan heard Graciela say, "Well, I have a question: where is everyone?"

Billy and Crackerbones explained that Mother Ferny's potions had healed the wounded dwarves and goblins enough that they could return to their tunnels to finish recuperating. The tunnels were safe because during the battle, dwarf engineers had sealed off the passages that led to Gragguts's domain. That was why Loosejaw's band had been free to turn the tide during the battle in the valley. As for the captured kobolds and goblins, they had all been released.

"Released?" protested Graciela. "Doesn't that mean they can just attack again?"

Billy rubbed his eyes, and even Crackerbones looked pensive. "We do not keep prisoners," Crackerbones said. "To live in bondage is no life. But ... perhaps Sister is changing this. Never before Sister have we had organized campaigns and ongoing war. In the old days, released prisoners would go about their lives and their captors would go about theirs. Perhaps we must adjust ..."

A frown rippled across Billy's face and was gone. "We put much on your shoulders, Dan and Maggie. I doubt we will have to make such an ... adjustment, if First Changing Beast is free. Maggie, where is Sister? I know you should rest and recover before the next phase, but it is when Sister approaches First Changing Beast that you will have your opportunity."

"Alas!" said Maggie. "My need to rest and recover is greater than you know or I imagined, for I am too sick at heart to sense Sister."

"Done!" called Mother Ferny. "A quicker brew than I expected, for the toadwort was aged perfectly, and this has been a good year for henheather. Drink!"

She handed Dan a small wooden bowl carved with twining foliage. The liquid inside was colorless and—whew!—flavorless. But as soon as Dan swallowed it he felt exposed and embarrassed as though he were lying naked on a doctor's examination table, and frightened of what horrible disease or lack the doctor would diagnose.

"Now we give it time to work," said Mother Ferny.

"How long will that be?" asked Dan.

"Until it is done, of course." Mother Ferny bustled away.

Great. Now it was like being alone in the cold examination room, wearing one of those stupid flimsy robes that tie in the back and you know your butt will hang out if you move around much, waiting you don't know how long for the doctor to show up. Dan went and sat beside Maggie, but he still felt alone; even though he was in the conversation, it seemed like he was just hearing nurses murmuring out in the hall. Probably about how he was really a bad case.

"I hope it doesn't take too long," said Dan.

"I know," said Maggie. "I am nervous too, but it will probably be all right."

"What do you think I lost?"

Maggie shrugged. "I too can feel that something is different about you, but it is only a glimmer I cannot grasp. Maybe ..."

"Maybe what?"

"Oh, I do not know. Let us think of something good. Let us think of how you saved Nellie Longarms."

Mother Ferny called out, "Time!" She came over and put one hand over Dan's heart and the other on his forehead and began to mutter and hum, hum and mutter. It took forever. Finally she stepped back, put her hands on her hips, and frowned.

"What? What?" asked Dan.

"I cannot understand it all. Mortal Makeless Making is unique and therefore mysterious. You have lost something to do with travel. Somewhere you can no longer go. But I cannot tell where."

"Are the Shadowlands closed to him?" asked Crackerbones. "That would sink all chance of him freeing First Changing Beast." The goblin glowered at Dan.

"Perhaps, perhaps," muttered Mother Ferny.

"Can the brew be strengthened, Mother?" asked Billy.

"The herbs and makings were strong. But I believe an attribute was missing that waits nearby: a touch of fairy magic. Someone invite the King."

Dan was thoroughly shaken up by Mother Ferny's investigations and he didn't want to go see old Rotface anyway. He wasn't at all surprised when Maggie shook her head and slumped back in her chair too. But for some reason none of the Gatekeepers stirred. Finally, Graciela sighed and said, "I don't know what's going on here, but I'll get him. He's pretty disgusting, but I kind of like the rest of them. They look like they're ready to join one of our Dia de los Muertos celebrations. But he's a king, I can't just boss him. What's the protocol for inviting a fairy king?"

"For this occasion no great protocol is needed," said Billy. He went to the shelf that Dan remembered from long ago was covered with raw materials for making gate-opening amulets, and selected a piece of straight, polished bone with a faint carving of two heads looking in opposite directions. "We cannot cook these into amulets these days without First Changing Beast, but the bone King will recognize this. Give it to him with the compliments of Billy Portman."

Graciela took the bone and hurried out. A short time later the door swung open and revealed the Fairy King. He was still clad in his stained battle garments, but on his skull he wore a silver crown studded with emeralds. He paused on the threshold and said, "Greetings to you, Johnny Quickfoot. And greetings to the witch and goblin. May I enter Gate Moot Hall?"

The Gatekeepers all stood. "Enter and be welcome," said Billy—or Johnny.

As Graciela followed the King, she made eye contact with Dan and Maggie, pointed at the King, pointed at her own face, and mouthed the words "Dia de los Muertos."

It was true. Rotten skin, decaying muscle, dangling liga-
ments—all were gone, leaving a visage of clean white bone.
Dan almost laughed. Not long ago a skull face would have
frightened him, but by comparison with what went before, the
King looked charming.

Mother Ferny was saying, "Be welcome indeed, for you have
come at our request."

"But before anything else," said Crackerbones, "we wish to
thank you. Your timely aid turned the battle."

The King bowed his head. "And in the same stead I wish to
thank you. For it has become clear to me that whatever our
differences, your battle and my battle are the same. It is I who
brought into our world Sally Wandil who is your scourge. It was
little and late, my joining the battle before your hall."

"Yet timely too was your delaying her in a Marrowland trap
so that she was tardy joining the battle."

The King laughed. "I fear that Sally is too clever for my
traps. It was the fat mortal she travels with whom was caught.
For some reason Sally bears so much affection for that one that
she would not leave until she managed to free her."

"Because she is her mother!" shouted Maggie.

The King turned to her and said, "Maggie, first daughter of
mine. It was your visit, you and your mortal friends ..." He
trailed off, looking at Graciela, and then said, "The mortal girl
looks so different I almost did not recognize her when she
sought me in my tent—"

"Because this is a different girl," said Maggie, rolling her
eyes. "That was Alice. This is Graciela."

"Ah well," sighed the King. "I have never made a study of
mortals, for they stray into the Marrowland rarely, and more
rarely still have cause to seek the King. Only mortal
changelings do I know, and they grow more and more like our

fairy kin as they dwell among us. Just as you took on mortal qualities as you dwelt among them. I fear that this has sundered our minds so that you can never fully comprehend me and the Old Ways, just as I can never fully understand your passions and sympathies. Nevertheless, as I began to say, your visit started a breeze in my mind that blew like the gale of Arnil sweeping away the webs of the Great Spiders to help us defeat them.

"How it went so wrong I do not know. Perhaps I shall never understand. But I do understand that in switching you and Sally I wronged you both. For this I apologize."

Without turning her gaze from the King, Maggie reached out and squeezed Dan's hand. Her face took on the rose tint of an early dawn. She bit her lip and nodded once.

The King turned to the Gatekeepers and said, "Now, Fern-witch, what is your request?"

"The mortal boy performed a Makeless Making," replied Mother Ferny. She held up her hand when the King began to protest and said, "I know, I know, it is impossible, but it is true nonetheless. Noggles had pulled from the lake one of the wild water spirits who was helping us, and the boy brought her back to life. We must learn what freedom he surrendered in return, but with my brew of finding I only discover that he has lost the ability to travel ... somewhere. We must know what door is closed to him."

"I would help you if I could, but you know as well as I that your witch magic is not my fairy magic. The very hall in which we stand is like foreign soil to me. I have no herbs or ingredients to strengthen any potion you create."

"Of course, of course," said Mother Ferny. "But in these strange days when Sister, your Sally, tries to twist our world, perhaps we can kink it to a better shape. I need your fairy mind to entangle my primal magic with light. Let me hold your hand, bony though it be, as I stir!"

"Oh God, how long will that take?" asked Dan, not knowing if he wanted it to be fast or slow. Mother Ferny didn't answer, but at least there were other important things to take his mind off it. He was still holding Maggie's hand, and he whispered, "Wow, Maggie, he kind of apologized. I mean, he didn't exactly come across as a loving father, but maybe it makes things a little better? How do you feel?" He held his breath and waited, because it was hard to talk about her parents in ways that didn't make Maggie feel worse.

"I feel ... I feel ... I feel Sister! I know where she is! Billy and Crackerbones, listen! But how strange."

"What is it? Is she in the Shadowlands? Is she with FCB?" asked Dan.

Maggie shook her head. "Remember the great forest?" Of course Dan remembered it. He and Maggie had been just at the edge of it on their last trip to Inland when they sought the country where the Old Tongue once was spoken, but on an earlier trip they had walked through the forest for many days. Maggie continued, "Remember on that first trip we saw a path turning off with a sign saying it led to the Castle of the Mad Prince?"

"Sure, and I remember we totally avoided that path."

"Sister is in the Castle of the Mad Prince."

"Well, I guess that explains why the Prince is mad," said Graciela.

Dan laughed. "I don't like the sound of chasing her there, though. One good thing about the catch-her-in-the-Shadow- lands plan is she'll most likely be alone, but a castle is bound to be well guarded. Although if I get in shouting distance I can truename her and make her call off the guards and take us to

FCB. Oh my god, Billy, that reminds me I haven't even told you I figured out the twofold meaning of Minik Mingarria."

Dan explained it to Billy and Crackerbones, and then burst out with, "Hey! It doesn't have to be me! You know her truename now, and I'll tell a bunch of other people too, and then we can go with a small army and whoever gets through can truename her."

But Billy shook his head. "I wish it were so, but the twofold meaning was smelted into your mind like copper with tin in your moment of realization. Only you have the true bronze understanding. But it is well done, well done indeed, that you puzzled it out."

"Yeah, I figured that sounded too easy." Dan frowned. "So what's your advice? Go after her now, or wait till she takes to the Shadowlands?"

"I say wait," said Crackerbones. "The castle will be thick with malkins and who knows what else. You may be slain before you ever speak her truename."

"Although her creatures are more likely to capture Dan and Maggie and bring them to Sister than to slay them, and travel in the Shadowlands is much more treacherous than the great forest," said Billy. "Yet waiting will give you time to rest and rebuild your strength. On balance, I agree with Crackerbones."

"As do I," said the King. Dan jumped; he hadn't noticed the King return from the stove. Mother Ferny was there too, with the cup. Dan was staring at the cup so he hardly paid attention to the King adding, "She will be recuperating also, and while she does she will be sure to have many protections around not only herself but her mother as well."

Mother Ferny offered the cup silently. Dan swirled the liquid around. The King's participation really had added threads of light. He held it to his lips, looked at Maggie and

Graciela, and swallowed. This time it tasted like medicine. Dan felt like he was naked in front of a roomful of doctors while the professor demonstrated on his body the symptoms of a weird incurable tropical disease.

"Again we must wait," said Mother Ferny.

Great. So he was still the demonstration patient, but the professor wasn't there yet. All the residents and interns stared at him with worried expressions, mumbled to each other, and took furtive notes.

"And while you wait, I will take my leave," said the King. "I and my warriors are needed in the Marrowland."

"You leave me just like that, Father?" began Maggie.

The King bowed to her. "Here and now is not the time for us to talk. You know the conditions we already spoke of."

Those were the conditions that the King had laid on them when they first met him in the Marrowland: he would permit Dan and Maggie to wed if they freed First Changing Beast. But Dan hardly noticed the King's comment, or Mother Ferny thanking him, or the door closing behind him.

Dan turned to Maggie and asked, "Maggie, what did you start to say after my first drink of brew? You sensed something about what I have lost."

"Oh, I do not know, but I worry that it will affect us both."

"Maybe it's what Crackerbones said, that I can't enter the Shadowlands anymore. That would affect us both because we couldn't find FCB there together. But we would figure something out."

"Yes, we would."

"I hate the Shadowlands anyway."

"I hate them too. If we can find First Changing Beast some other way it would be a blessing never to go there again."

"So maybe this will work out all right. Maybe I lost a freedom I never really wanted."

Maggie smiled at him but she was having trouble meeting his eyes.

Finally Mother Ferny came back. Again she placed her hands on Dan's chest and forehead, again she muttered and hummed, but not for as long. She stepped back with an expression that you never want to see on your doctor's face.

"What was lost?" asked Billy.

"He has but three moons," replied Mother Ferny.

"Three moons until what?"

"Until he must leave Inland, never to return."

10

THE MOUND OF THE DEAD

"*N*o, no, No, NO, *NO!*" shouted Dan.

"No, no, No, NO, *NO!*" echoed Maggie as though they were still truenamed.

They ran outside together, past the stricken faces of the Gatekeepers. Even Crackerbones looked sad. Billy reached his arm toward them as they went by, then let it drop.

The door closed behind, and Inland was before them. Dan felt the warm air kiss his face. Already where Sister had shattered the groves new shoots arose, their pale leaves whispering and winking. A cluster of butterflies lifted from the roadway, broke apart, whirled and rejoined, wings singing a song of many colors. A golden-threaded breeze wove the fluting of an unknown bird around them. A horse nickered and Dan saw the last of the fairies about to ride into an impossibly small hole in the side of the ridge. The fairy looked at him, and as he did so living flesh formed on his hand and skull, and he became an eerily handsome man yet not-man, skin a faint green, features a little too sharp. The fairy saluted and entered the hill, and the hill closed.

"I'll leave Inland too," whispered Maggie. "I'll stay with you."

Maggie. Warmer than the breeze, fresher than new growth, sweeter than birdsong, fairer than the fairies. They hugged, and then hugged harder. Maggie would come with him. At least he wouldn't lose Maggie. Except …

"No, no, no, Maggie. You are part of Inland. We already know Outland makes you sicken and wither. Even if that weren't true, your happiness is here."

"Then I'll do a Makeless Making to break yours!"

"That would probably just ruin things for us another way. Besides, Mother Ferny told us one Makeless Making can't undo another, remember?"

"There must be something they can do." Maggie took Dan's hand and they strode back inside.

"We are sorry, children," said Billy.

"Don't be sorry," said Dan. "Do something. Fix it so I can stay!"

Billy looked down. Crackerbones frowned. Mother Ferny sighed and said, "We are truly sorry. But you have heard me say that even the strongest magic weavers refuse Makeless Making because of the cost. Now you understand the cost."

"I didn't understand!" shouted Dan. "I wish I hadn't done it! I take it back!"

"Even if you could, I doubt that you would," said Billy gently. "It was a deed brave and good, saving Nellie Longarms."

Dan sagged into a chair. After he-knew-not-how-long, he looked up and saw the Gatekeepers staring at him. They still looked sad, but there was something else in their expressions, too. Tension?

The Gatekeepers were worried he would forsake his quest.

And why not? Dan's life was ruined, why shouldn't theirs be ruined too? The Gates were closing for him anyway, why should he give a damn what happened to Inland, and Billy, and all the rest of them? Let Sister win.

Dan groaned. "Don't worry. I'll still do the stupid quest. Just have to hurry, I guess."

The Gatekeepers relaxed. Billy gave his Grandpa smile, which was kind of annoying, actually.

"And while we do it, we'll be looking for some magic that will repair things for Dan ... and me," said Maggie.

"Guys." It was Graciela. Dan had forgotten she was there. "Guys, I have an idea."

What idea could this Outlander have?

"You're getting married, right?" said Graciela.

"Not any more, I guess," said Dan. Maggie clutched his hand.

"Yes, you are, it's more important now than ever," said Graciela. "I'm surprised you didn't think of it already. Maybe it's more obvious to me because I'm Latina. It's not as easy as it used to be, but back in the US of Outland A, it still helps with visas and citizenship. Maybe if you get married they'll give you a magic visa."

Dan jumped up. "Graciela, you're brilliant! What about it, Gatekeepers? Billy?"

Billy raised his bushy eyebrows and whispered to Mother Ferny. She ran her hands through her hair and whispered back. Billy smiled. Not as big a smile as Dan wanted, but a smile.

"We have not heard of it happening," said Mother Ferny.

"But that does not mean it cannot happen," said Billy. "Perhaps a wedding will work such magic."

"How do we find out?" asked Dan.

"Weddings between mortal and fae are under the law of the Fairy King. You must ask him."

"But we just saw the last of them leave," said Dan. "Wait. Kintravel! You can kintravel us to your father, Maggie."

Maggie's eyes were wet. "No, I cannot, remember? Father has forbidden kintravel in the Marrowland, in order to keep Sister out. We could reach the outskirts but would have many days of travel ahead of us."

"And Sister will not delay long before she feeds on First Changing Beast again," said Crackerbones.

Dan leapt up and sprinted outside shouting, "Hey, King! Fairy King! King, come back!" He ran to where the fairies had gone into the hill, but it was covered with grass and flowers, no entrance or even blemish to be seen. Dan dropped to his knees and scrabbled at the ground, ripping plants up by their roots, throwing turf aside, finally breaking his nails on rock. The hole he had made was hardly big enough for a badger, let alone a Fairy King.

AFTER SUPPER, Dan and Maggie stepped outside to find the moon. Dan probably had to leave forever the third time it returned to its current phase, so he'd better know what it was. The sun had just dropped behind the western ridge, but the sky was empty except for one star bright enough to shine in the twilight. Dan didn't feel like making a wish—or rather, his wish was so obvious and important that he didn't want to play with a star.

"Moonrise after sunset means the moon is waning," said Dan. "We might have to wait a long time for it to rise. Or I guess it could be full and rise soon. Full moons rise right when the sun goes down, and the sun wouldn't be down yet except that those mountains hide it."

"I am a fairy and I love the moon, but I could never keep those phases straight when I was an American girl and I still cannot," said Maggie.

"Yeah, I only know because it's one of my dad's quirks. It's come in handy here in Inland, though."

There wasn't anything else to say. Dan and Maggie had spent the day talking about the curse and fear and sadness, and about their hope that Graciela was right, and about not knowing how to reach the Fairy King to find out. There wasn't anything else to say.

Darkness deepened. Frogs began calling from the lake, a moth floated by, and fireflies reached out to each other with brief flashes. None flew to Maggie or crowned her.

The east grew lighter rather than darker. Moonbeams shot between the trees, skittered across the lake, and silvered Maggie's hair, but the moon would need to rise above the woods before they could learn its shape. An owl hooted from the shore, almost as if it were urging the moon to hurry. Finally it was all in view, an unbroken orb.

"Full," whispered Dan. He had learned what he had come outside to learn, but somehow he didn't want to leave, and Maggie seemed to feel the same way. They held hands and watched as the lake caught silver fire that jumped into Maggie's hair and eyes.

The owl rose from its lakeside perch, silhouetted against the bright water. It turned and flapped closer. Dan knew it could see them in Maggie's illumination, but it wasn't frightened. In fact, when it reached them it circled three times before flapping over Gatemoodle and dropping from sight.

"Let's follow," whispered Maggie.

They walked around the hall. The owl had landed on the tree closest to the Mound of the Two Kindreds. It hooted once more and flew into the woods.

The mound glowed in the moonlight. Beautiful pale green, and yet ... Dan looked at the moon fire in Maggie's hair, soft and pure, then back at the mound. Its glow looked slimy, like the skin of an old mushroom that collapses in on itself.

Dan and Maggie approached the mound, but when they got close enough that the glow lapped at their feet Maggie took his hand and pulled for him to stop.

"I must not go closer," she said.

"But that owl must have been a sign."

"I must not go closer. Do you not know that the fairies are the dead? But that form is not for me. Not yet. Not for at least three full moons."

She released Dan's hand and stepped back. Now he knew why the mound called to him: the fairies are the dead ... the dead are in the mound ... fairies are in the mound ... a way to reach the Fairy King. Dan took another step, and another, and reached the foot of the slope. The green glow covered his shins. Dan looked back at Maggie, who stood with her arms crossed over her breasts, looking down. The moon fire was gone from her hair, and Dan's courage left him.

"Let's go back to the hall," he said.

"I'll seek out the Fairy King for you," said Graciela the next morning. "Like I said the other time, I'm used to him from Day of the Dead. Maggie can kintravel me close and kintravel back to you, and I'll find him."

Dan checked around the breakfast table and was glad to see

nobody looking enthusiastic. "Thanks, Graciela, but it's not a good idea," he said. "Without Maggie leading the whole time, I'd never have found the Marrowland."

"But—" began Graciela.

Mother Ferny interrupted her. "Dan is right, Graciela. You showed your courage and power with your spiderwork, but seeking the fairies alone would be foolhardy."

Graciela slouched into her chair and pouted, and then leaned forward again. "Then let me help you when you go after Sister in the Shadowlands, Dan and Maggie. She's my real target anyway. And you need my help to break the spell if you truename each other."

Strangely, it was because the feelings were no longer there that Dan suddenly recognized a bunch of feelings he'd had for Graciela. Sister had been hinting that Dan and Graciela would betray Maggie and become lovers ever since she'd first met Graciela. She'd said it again just now at the end of the battle. Just messing with their minds, Dan had always figured, but, well, there was truth to it. Josh had been turned on to Graciela first, and Dan hadn't seen it, but the more time he'd spent with her, the more he'd realized how smart and strong she was. And sexy. They'd kissed after defeating Sister in the Natural History Museum, but instantly jumped apart protesting that the kiss was just a crisis stress reaction. He'd never known if Graci was interested in him. Yet somewhere inside him where Dan hadn't wanted to look, he'd wanted to kiss her again. But not anymore. He didn't want Graciela with them in the Shadowlands. He only wanted Maggie.

Maggie handled it. She ran around the table, hugged Graciela, and said, "It has to be just Dan and me. He will focus my attention as I try to follow Sister. Anyone else, no matter how willing, would distract me. The truenaming ... it will be the third time, I think we can remember to break it."

Graciela locked eyes with Dan, paused, and then said, "OK. I'm useless here." She broke eye contact and finished with, "Send me home, Dan."

"You are far from useless, Graciela," said Billy.

"Indeed," added Crackerbones. "Although we have repelled one attack, we don't know for sure that rat Gragguts won't attack again while these two are chasing after Sister."

"And if they do attack, I will find your Spiderwork a great help in the defense," said Mother Ferny.

Dan was relieved by the Gatekeepers' input. He had hated seeing Graciela so distressed, but now she smiled.

"Besides," added Maggie, "I still want you to be a Maid of Honor, and if you stay here we won't have to chase you all over Outland when the time comes."

DAN PEERED around the corner of the hall at the Mound of the Two Kindreds. In the daylight it was just an ordinary grassy mound. A robin hopped about the top and cocked its eye, trying to discover worms lurking below. Dan knew he should come back to the mound alone that night. But he hoped that instead Sister would enter the Shadowlands so they would have to pursue her today.

But Maggie did not feel Sister moving from the Castle of the Mad Prince.

DAN EASED OUT OF BED. The moon had risen hours before, but

Maggie had been restless and Dan didn't want to leave until she was fully asleep or she might feel like she had to accompany him. He adjusted the blanket over her shoulder, carried his boots down the ladder, and sat on the floor to slip them on.

Dan looked up to see two pairs of eyes glittering back at him, and he jumped before he made out that they belonged to Billy and Crackerbones. Weird that two people who seemed so different could have such similar eyes, hardly blinking, almost orange in the glow of embers from the stove.

"Have care to whom you speak in the depths," said Billy.

"Uhh, thanks." What the hell did that mean? Right now Billy didn't look like someone you could ask questions, so Dan grabbed his cloak from its peg and hurried outside.

The bright moon was directly overhead, and an answering glow spilled out several yards from the mound. Dan walked to the base of the mound, the glow covering his knees. Now what? He circled the mound widdershins, but saw no entrance. He circled again, clockwise this time, but there wasn't even an indentation.

Dan sighed and climbed to the top. After scanning for openings and seeing none, he walked to the very center. The glow reached highest here, almost to his shoulders. It felt unwholesome against his skin and Dan brushed his hands together expecting to feel a film, but they were dry. Almost too slowly to notice, the glow rose until it reached Dan's neck, then his chin, and then his mouth. In anxiety that he wouldn't be able to breathe, Dan tried to run, but his feet were stuck tight. The glow wasn't rising; Dan was sinking. He held his breath as long as he could while green covered his nose and then engulfed him, but finally he had to gasp in a new breath. To his enormous relief, it was just sweet, grassy smelling air. Then the bottom dropped out.

Dan landed on his feet in utter darkness. How could he have been so stupid that he didn't bring a torch? A bunch of dwarves and goblins were buried in this mound, was he standing on corpses? Dan tried not to panic. Billy had seemed to know where he was going, and Billy would have told him if he needed to bring light. Although Billy with those glittering eyes hardly seemed like Billy. Dan took deep, slow breaths, almost laughing when it turned out to be fresh, cool air with no scent of decay.

So dimly at first that Dan worried he was imagining it, light began to grow, the same green that glowed outside. Soon Dan could see that he stood in a dome-shaped chamber. The stone floor was totally empty, no corpses anywhere—that was good. But there was no sign of the opening that he had dropped through, and no exits in the walls—not so good. Just to make sure, Dan walked around the chamber fingering the cool stone, lingering to examine rough spots. No exits.

Suddenly Dan noticed a hole in the floor. The light shone brightest there, and Dan was sure he couldn't have missed it during his exploration, which could only mean it had just appeared. Dan knelt and peered down. A stone staircase descended out of sight. It was silent as a—Dan didn't want to think the t-word that usually completes that phrase.

Only one thing to do. Quiet though he wanted to be, Dan's foot clumped on the first step. It was like that all the way down, as though the stairs wanted him to be heard. He didn't like the idea of something else stirring unnoticed during his passage so he paused frequently to listen. Nothing.

After a dozen steps, an alcove appeared in the wall. It was big enough that Dan could have stood in it, and looked like it was meant to display a statue, but it was empty. After another dozen steps Dan came to another alcove, and after that they appeared regularly on both sides, always empty. The feeling grew more and more on Dan that they should have something in them, and he stopped more and more often to listen for anything besides him breaking the silence.

He grew so accustomed to the alcoves being empty that he almost didn't notice when one wasn't. Dan backed up and looked. A goblin slouched against the back of the alcove, and Dan became acutely aware that he had forgotten not only a torch but any kind of weapon. At least the goblin was small, and as Dan looked closer he realized he didn't need to worry. The goblin's eyes were shut and an arrow pierced its chest, an arrow with the green and black fletching the fairies used. Dan used arrows the fairies had given him. Dan leaned in and studied the goblin's face. It was the one he had slain as it sneaked up on Crackerbones. Dan felt sad, and he opened his mouth to say, "Sorry, bud."

The goblin opened his eyes.

Dan lunged back and struck the wall behind him so hard that he knocked his breath away before the words came out.

The goblin just lay there, blinking. Then it pointed at the arrow, pointed at Dan, and pointed at his mouth.

A dead goblin wanted Dan to talk to him. Dan was totally freaked out and feeling a jumble of other things too as he struggled to get his breath back. Sad about the whole stupid war, angry at Sister for causing it, guilty about killing the goblin, scared the goblin would be mad, angry at the goblin for making him feel guilty and scared, because after all the goblin would have stabbed Crackerbones if Dan hadn't killed it. Curious if the goblin saw all these complications and accepted its own responsibility for being dead. Dan would ask him, if he ever got his breath back.

But then he remembered Billy: "Have care to whom you speak in the depths."

Dan backed down the steps, shaking his head. The goblin flapped its hands at him to come back, but Dan turned and hurried away. He sped past each alcove in terror that a cadaver would gaze at him, reach for him, but all were vacant.

Gradually the angle of the stairway lessened, and then Dan was walking in a level passage. As it widened Dan knew he was reaching the end. He hurried on; for better or for worse, he would soon know what was here.

The passage ended in a small rectangular chamber, just high enough for Dan to stand straight. At the far end was a stone ledge like a bench. Between Dan and the bench was a depression, and in the depression lay the dwarf Tanly and the goblin Wormhair. Their faces were calm, and their swords and shields rested across their breasts.

"We meet again, Dan," said a voice.

After what happened with the goblin in the alcove, Dan was afraid these corpses would speak, but he had been staring at them and their mouths didn't move. Slowly he raised his eyes. On the bench sat Tanly and Wormhair. Dan glanced back down, and now where their bodies had rested lay only skeletons.

Even though Tanly and Wormhair looked completely solid, without any ectoplasmic transparency, Dan asked, "Are you ghosts?"

Wormhair laughed. "Do you not come seeking the fairies? Do you not know that the fairies are the dead?"

"Then you *are* ghosts. Fairies are ghosts."

Wormhair laughed again. "Your stiff mind bumps against a fantasy that Outlanders use to scare themselves."

"Why must the dead be fearsome?" added Tanly.

"Speaking of that, where are all the other dead?" asked Dan. "Every alcove but one was empty, and only you two here. I'm glad it's you, I'm so sorry you died, but still ..."

"Do you know any of the others who died?" asked Tanly. "Do you remember them, do you have wishes for them?"

Dan shook his head, and when they didn't add anything he said, "You mean you're figments of my imagination."

Dwarf and goblin both laughed, and Tanly said, "We would be insulted by that, but we know it is hard for Outlanders to understand."

"Tanly, we do not have much time," said Wormhair.

"You are right. Listen, Dan. Our brief friendship was built on a story, so I will tell you a story."

"Jake and the Sunflower Stalk?" asked Dan.

Tanly shook her head. "I think not. Here is the tale more timely. Listen.

"Long ago, when the world was new and mortals were true, a maiden and her man wandered into a forest that became a forest not of the mortal world but of this world. There a grammarye took the man and spun him away, and when the maiden sought him she was told that now he was prisoner of a troll who dwelt East of the Sun and West of the Moon."

"Wait a minute," said Dan. "My mother used to tell me this one. I mostly forgot it but I remember that her boyfriend was a bear or something in the daytime and a man only at night, and she wasn't supposed to peek at night but she did and that's why he was taken away."

"Typical Outland effort to make everything rational," replied Wormhair. "Why blame the girl? Grammarye's reasons are not reasons for a mortal mind."

"What I am telling is the true story, not the Outland fairy tale," said Tanly. "May I continue?"

Dan nodded.

"The maiden thought that either the east wind or west wind might know the way. First she sought out the east wind in his castle, and asked him if he knew how to travel East of the Sun and West of the Moon. The east wind moaned around his battlements and said he did not know, but he gave her a golden apple. As the maiden traveled west, the south wind smiled on her and ruffled her hair, so she asked him if he knew the way East of the Sun and West of the Moon. He did not know, but he gave her a golden comb. Her heart falling, the maiden came to the forest home of the west wind. The west wind rattled branches and bent boughs, but he did not know the way East of the Sun and West of the Moon. He had nothing to give her but advice: 'Ask the north wind. The north wind will know.'

"So the maiden took the trail that led north, but all the air had fallen still: neither east, nor south, nor west wind blew, and the north wind was not there. The maiden began to fear for herself as she traveled north and the cold bit more and more deeply. At last the north wind woke from his nap, and took pity on her, and carried her East of the Sun and West of the Moon."

"Tanly," said Wormhair. "Tanly, we must go."

"But there is much more about how the maiden outwitted the troll and won back her man," said Tanly.

"Nevertheless, we must go."

"I don't understand any of this," said Dan. "I don't understand why you used the little time you had to tell me that story. Why can't you Inland people tell things to me straight?"

"Farewell, Dan," said Wormhair.

"Remember Jake and the Sunflower Stalk," said Tanly.

Dan was alone in the chamber.

❄

A ROBIN SANG its repetitive song. Dan watched it fly down from its perch and land near him in the grass. The robin cocked its eye, stabbed with its beak, and came up with a twisting worm that shook dew from the grass as it wriggled.

Dan was covered with dew himself and he shivered, grateful as beams from the early sun struck him. He was lying on top of the mound. Sprouting beside him was a young sunflower stalk.

11

THE MAD PRINCE

The moon passed through its waning gibbous phase and shrank to almost a half moon, and still Sister did not enter the Shadowlands. Six days gone out of the three months, and Dan and Maggie had made no progress on their quests. Six days gone and they had no idea how to reach the Fairy King to learn if Dan could stay in Inland after their wedding.

If not for those worries, it would have been idyllic. Cracker-bones was off somewhere conferring with Drula and organizing his troops in case of another attack, and Billy and Mother Ferny were preoccupied bolstering the magic in Gatemoodle's walls, and Graciela spent most of her time trying to improve at spider-work, so Dan and Maggie were on their own. They explored the countryside, marveling at how quickly the land healed after Sister's destruction. They splashed up the mountain stream until they came to a beaver pond where they laughed to see the plump animals and thanked them again for building the dam. They picnicked by the lake, and spent hours skinny-dipping and lying in the sun to dry off. And they made love joyously and fearfully, wondering if soon they would never make love again.

DAN AND MAGGIE ROLLED APART. Waves splashed against the shore in a breeze that brought the perfect amount of coolness to gentle the early afternoon sun.

"The more I think about what happened in the mound, the less sense it makes," said Dan. "They were dead but looked the way they looked when they were alive. They said they weren't ghosts. They said that whole 'the fairies are the dead' thing, sort of implying they were fairies, but they didn't look like fairies. They said that out of everyone buried there I only saw them and the goblin I killed because I only had wishes and memories about them, but also said they weren't figments of my imagination. Anyway, fairies obviously aren't figments of my imagination—you're the realest thing in my life!" He stroked her hair.

Maggie leaned on her elbow, looking at Dan, and tweaked his nose. "You mean you don't have wishes and memories of me?"

Dan laughed. "I started having wishes for you way back when we were in high school, and now I have wishes that you keep fulfilling, and wonderful memories. But I didn't create you."

Maggie kissed him. "But you did create me. And I created you. Not entirely, of course, but think how different we are now than we would be if we had never gotten together."

They thought about that in silence, and the silence turned into lovemaking, and the lovemaking turned into a long swim. As they lay drying in the sun again, Dan said, "It's weird that

Billy and Mother Ferny couldn't explain it any better than Tanly and Wormhair. At first I thought they were too caught up in strengthening Gatemoodle, but now I think it's just something Inlanders can't put into Outland language.

"Like when I asked Billy why Tanly and Wormhair couldn't just give me some clear idea what was going on instead of telling me East of the Sun and West of the Moon. He said he didn't think I'd come to Inland because I wanted everything to be just the same as in Outland. Total conversation stopper."

"The Gatekeepers are wise but they are also worried, and I think they are frustrated that they cannot give us more help," said Maggie.

"I've been trying to remember that fairy tale the way Mom used to tell it, see if that would be a clue, but I was really young and I just don't remember. But you know, Dad used to joke about it. He said it was easy to figure out what was East of the Sun and West of the Moon."

"Then what is the answer?"

"He never told me. Aagh! He said he'd tell me if I couldn't figure it out when I got older, but then we just forgot the whole thing. It was probably just a dopey Dad joke anyway, I bet he never knew.

"Hey! Maybe that sunflower stalk has grown into the clouds and we can climb it to the land that is East of the Sun and West of the Moon. Let's go see."

Dan and Maggie pulled on their clothes and headed for the mound. The stalk had indeed grown fast and was already a little taller than Dan, but nowhere near the clouds. It was more like a regular sunflower that was maturing super-fast, so that it already had a big brilliant bloom aimed at the sun.

❄

THE NEXT MORNING Maggie was jumpy. She insisted they go look at the sunflower stalk even before breakfast and coffee. It was no taller but had aged so much overnight that some of its leaves had turned brown and rattled when the breeze touched them. The yellow petals had all fallen, replaced by a mature head of dark seeds.

"Harvest it," said Maggie.

Dan was already reaching for his knife. "Yes. In memory of Tanly and Wormhair." He sliced the stem just beneath the seed-head and carried it cautiously, although none of the seeds were loose yet.

When they entered the hall, Billy had biscuits, butter, and jam on the table and was pouring dark coffee into their cups. He took one look at Maggie and said, "Is she on the move?"

"I think so," replied Maggie. "She is not yet in the Shadowlands, but she is preparing."

"Eat," said Billy. "I will take care of the rest."

Dan's bow and arrows and their packs with clothes and water bottles had been prepared days ago. Now Billy bustled about adding foodstuffs. Mother Ferny and Crackerbones joined them at the table and ate without speaking, although Dan thought they kept eyeing him weirdly. Finally, Mother Ferny said, "Well?"

Dan swallowed his last bite. "Well what?"

"Your moment approaches, Dan," said Billy. "The moment for which we brought you to Inland. Your chance to complete your quest."

"You are about to find First Changing Beast," said Mother Ferny. "How will you free him?"

"Uhh—" Days ago Billy had said they all needed to ponder how to free First Changing Beast. Dan had been so preoccupied he hadn't given it a thought.

Crackerbones broke into laughter, but the expression on his face was nasty. "All this time looking for him, and no idea what to do at the moment of truth? Oh, ho ho ho hee hee!"

"Well what's the big deal?" protested Dan. "I have Breaklock. I'll make us a gate back to Inland."

"That will not be enough," said Billy. He locked eyes with Mother Ferny, and then continued, "We have an idea, but we hoped to hear something else from you, Dan, to confirm it. It was your unawareness that human love is part of the web of the world, after we raised Gatemoodle with power songs, which started my thoughts on this path. That unawareness is a part of what has been closing the Gates of Inland, separating Outland farther from Inland. And so the land between grows farther and farther from both Outland and Inland. It is a distance too great for First Changing Beast to travel without help. The Beast is not in a trap within the Shadowlands. The Shadowlands is itself the trap that holds First Changing Beast."

Mother Ferny picked up the train of thought. "And so Dan, you with Breaklock must transport First Changing Beast. We have never understood why you are the one. But we thought about how human love is part of the web of life, how human love is necessary to the web of life, and we thought of how you love Maggie, and we remembered that the Queen of the Fairies cast a spell."

"A spell that whoever loved both Maggie the Inland Fairy and Sister the Outland mortal would free them both," said Billy. "And such a love would create a bonding link between Inland and Outland. And this could explain why you have the power to free First Changing Beast."

Crackerbones finished. "So how about it, Quest Boy? Any love for Sister?"

Dan looked at Maggie and Graciela who quickly looked

away; he thought he saw a small smile touch Graciela's mouth. There had to be some other solution. What did he understand about the Shadowlands? When he went there it was made partly out of reality and partly out of his mind. But what reality —Inland or Outland? He had fallen into the Shadowland from both places. And his mind too contained experiences from both Outland and Inland. Somehow the Shadowlands was made out of both worlds. Long ago Maggie had called it the land between, and Billy had just said the same thing.

"I will never be able to love Sister," said Dan. "That way is closed. But I think I know a different way to link Inland and Outland and free First Changing Beast. First Changing Beast must enter Outland and Inland both. So first I will make a gate and take him to Outland. From there, a gate to Inland where he belongs."

Billy bowed to Dan and said, "Whether with love for both women or not, we are certain you must proceed as you say, first to Outland and then to Inland. As to why it is you ... there must be something that we overlook."

Mother Ferny also bowed to Dan. Crackerbones crossed his arms and frowned.

THEN THEY SPENT the morning pacing. After a couple hours they ran to the privies. Who knew how long they would be in what part of the Shadowlands, and if bathroom spots would be easy to find? Dan felt like a child about to go on a long family car trip. The sun was almost directly overhead when Maggie froze and said, "Now!"

"Now is your hour, Dan and Maggie," said Billy. "Your last, best chance to free First Changing Beast. Your last, best chance to stop Sister. Your last, best chance to save Inland. Our hopes, and the hopes of all of Inland, go with you."

A bell began to ring, deep and at the same time bright, like when rain falls but the sun is still shining. Dan looked around, puzzled, because Gatemoodle had no bell, and then realized that the sound somehow came from the very walls. Billy and Mother Ferny embraced Dan and then Maggie. Even Cracker-bones hugged Maggie and shook Dan's hand in a solid grip. Lastly Graciela hugged them both.

Dan and Maggie clasped hands and closed their eyes, but Mother Ferny said, "Wait!"

They opened their eyes.

"Remember your twining rings," said Mother Ferny. Dan glanced at his. Maggie had made them and Mother Ferny had enchanted them so that if they were lost the rings would glow green as they came closer to each other. Dan didn't plan to lose Maggie on this trip. He held her hand tightly and they closed their eyes again.

This time it was Graciela who called out, "Wait!" She ran up and said, "You'll have to truename each other when you get close to Sister, and you've told us how hard it is to break the truenaming after. So here." She leaned forward and kissed Dan on the cheek. As he touched it, blushing, Graciela pushed her glasses up on her nose, grinned, and said, "When you need to break the truenaming, remember that."

"Uhh, thanks, I guess," said Dan, even though he had no idea how that was supposed to help.

"No matter," said Maggie. They clasped hands again, and Maggie concentrated on kintraveling to her changeling "sister." There were no more interruptions. The bonging and chiming rolled louder, and then all was silence.

DAN HAD REHEARSED this in his mind many times. As soon as the flickery falling feeling of traveling to the Shadowlands had passed and he felt his feet on the ground, before he could even focus his eyes, he shouted, "Minik Mingarria!" Then he looked around.

Sister was nowhere in sight.

Dan and Maggie stood in deep woods before a fork in a path. Nailed to a gray, weathered stake were splintered, moss-covered signboards. They had to scrape the moss away to make out the lettering. One direction read, "Woods Witch." The other read, "Castle of the Mad Prince."

"We've been here before," said Maggie.

"It's a little different. The trail to the witch split off before we got to the Mad Prince trail, and it said 'Gingerbread House,' not 'Woods Witch.' But yeah, it's the Forest of Gloom where we looked for FCB on our second trip. Why isn't Sister here?"

Maggie shrugged. "I am sorry. Perhaps because we are not truly kin I could get us no closer. Or perhaps she has prepared herself for us. But she is not far. That way." She pointed in the direction of the Mad Prince.

"I don't like the sound of that," said Dan. "But let's go."

The path, just wide enough that Dan and Maggie could walk side by side, hugged a steep slope on the left as it angled northeast. The huge trees gave way to smaller beeches and maples, although they were still huge by Outland standards. A jerky breeze kicked up in front of them, tossing fallen leaves at their faces, then subsiding. Where bare dirt showed, Dan studied for footprints, especially worrying about the scratchy marks of malkins, but there was no sign that anyone but them had ever walked there.

Maggie touched Dan's arm and pointed. He raised his eyes and saw that the trail was about to pass under a stone arch. It was covered with moss and lichens, and little saplings had taken root in cracks where mortar had fallen away, but it still stood firm, just high enough for them to walk under. Dan eased against one side, Maggie the other, and they peeked through.

On the other side the path joined a road paved with cobbles. They heard and saw no one so Dan ducked through and chanced a quick look. The road was empty in both directions. To the right it descended gently into the old forest. To the left it rose more steeply, along the side of the escarpment that Dan and Maggie had been following which now bent almost straight north. On the other side of the road the ground dropped away. As Dan looked, the breeze shifted to full east and rain spattered him. He ducked back to the shelter of the arch and Maggie.

"She is that way," said Maggie, pointing left.

Dan nodded. "The approach is much more defensible that way. I'm not sure why we don't see any of her malkins, but the road feels way too exposed. Let's see if we can make our way up this hill."

It was hard but not impossible. The great trees cast some of their roots along the surface, and these provided hand- and footholds. When they reached the top they paused for dried fruit and gulps of water and then headed north, paralleling the road. Occasional breaks in the foliage allowed them to look down on it, always empty.

In a low voice Dan told Maggie the worry that had been growing in him. "I know this is the shadowlands. It has the shifty, dreamlike feeling, like everything could suddenly switch. But it's weird that Sister was in the Castle of the Mad Prince in Inland, and now she's with the Mad Prince in the Shadowlands.

I thought she'd be with First Changing Beast and he'd be in that painted cave. I guess he could be here, but ... is it possible Sister has led you astray?"

Maggie took a moment before responding. "I have never tracked Sister before. I do not think she could trick me so, but I do not know for certain. I only know that I feel her presence strongly, in a place not far. And look!"

A gust of wind bent the branches, and before they sprang back, a stone turret showed through the opening. Dan and Maggie walked and slid down the eastern side of the escarpment until they had a better view, and then dove behind a tree trunk.

The turret was one of four rising from a dark gray castle that looked like it was only a few years away from crumbling into ruin. The farthest turret was partly collapsed and chunks of the battlements had fallen away here and there, but the lower wall still looked solid and impenetrable. The castle was built against the ridge that provided its north wall. A cliff dropped away on its eastern and southern sides. A river cascaded down the ridge not too far from Dan and Maggie and then flowed under a bridge on the southwest side before dropping down the cliff. The only approach was the road that looped up, fully exposed, to cross the bridge. On the other side the portcullis was down.

"I think I saw malkins up on the battlements," said Dan.

"I thought I saw them too, but now I am not so sure," said Maggie. "Look again."

Dan saw two stick people looking down between crenels, but as he watched they blurred and then came back into focus as though he had been adjusting binoculars, and they were merely shrubs that had taken root up there.

"Either I was confused or it's Shadowlands weirdness, but

they don't look dangerous," said Dan. "OK, but someone's definitely up there now!" Dan and Maggie hugged the tree trunk and exposed themselves as little as possible as they watched.

A figure had emerged from one of the farther turrets and was walking the battlement toward them. Too tall for a malkin and wearing a cape of scarlet and gold. On his head was a crown of the same gray as the castle. The east wind blew harder and brought a fresh shower of rain, but instead of taking shelter, the figure turned and faced into the storm, raised its arms, and began bellowing. Whatever he said could not be made out through the wind whining around the castle. The wind and rain ceased as suddenly as they had begun, and Dan and Maggie heard a high-pitched laugh trailing off in the silence. Then the figure turned back, strode to the nearest turret, and stepped inside.

"Mad Prince, check," said Dan. "Something about him looked familiar, though."

"To me also," mused Maggie.

"That's weird. How many people do we both know who could turn into a Mad Prince in the Shadowlands?"

"Could it be ...? No, I do not know."

"Who were you thinking?"

Maggie shook her head. "I do not know. But I feel Sister inside the castle."

"I was afraid of that," said Dan. "The only way in is up this road and anybody watching from the castle could see us there. It might be smarter to wait until night, but actually I'm more scared of what might show up after dark. What do you think?"

Maggie didn't need any time to consider. "After dark will be worse. Let us run up the road."

They scrambled down the ridge, paused in the bushes at its edge to look both directions, and when they saw that the road remained empty they began to sprint. The road curved left and then swooped steeply to the northeast. Dan ran crouched over, expecting arrows or rocks to land on his head at any moment. When he reached the bridge he saw that most of the center stones had fallen into the river rushing below, but he didn't even slow down and leaped over the gap. Maggie was much faster than he and already stood with her back against the wall beside the portcullis, not even breathing hard. Dan joined her, sucking in deep breaths.

"So far so good," said Maggie. "Now how do we get in?"

Dan looked through the bars of the portcullis, and seeing it empty, seized them and tried to lift. They budged not at all, and Dan's hands came away covered with rust. "It's so old I'm not sure even its proper mechanism could open it now," he said. Hoping to find a collapsed section, they walked the castle wall until it curved into the northern ridge, and then doubled back and followed it until its sudden drop-off to the east. All was solid. As if that weren't bad enough, the wind and rain started back up.

"Yuck," said Dan. "At least on the other side we'll be sheltered from the worst of this."

Maggie was in the lead, and when she reached the portcullis she called out, "Dan!" and stepped inside. Dan hurried up to see that the portcullis had vanished. He joined Maggie inside and they looked at each other and shrugged.

Dan pointed to holes in the stone ceiling. "Stay away from those," he whispered. "Those are for pouring down boiling oil." They edged along the wall, trying to be quiet, but a great uproar burst from one of the holes and Dan and Maggie jumped back. Black shapes swooped down, cawing, and zoomed out over the river.

"Just a pair of stupid rooks," said Dan, steadying himself.

The inner courtyard was overgrown with weeds and a few saplings. Nearby was a well with the rusty bucket chain hanging broken and empty. At the center of the courtyard stood a small keep. Dan thought he saw movement in the single window overlooking the door, but when he stared at it, all seemed still. They hurried forward but Dan darted aside to peer into the well before rejoining Maggie and climbing the three broken steps to the keep.

"What?" asked Maggie.

"That well gave me a ... feeling. I wanted to see what was there, you know, make sure nothing was lurking, like to come out after us." Actually, Dan hadn't been scared, he just said that because he couldn't quite identify his feeling but fear would have made sense. "But it seems fine, not very deep and it's even dry at the bottom."

They leaned all their weight against the keep door. It was heavy but it creaked and yielded.

"It's like a Harry Potter tent," said Dan.

The inside was much bigger than the outside, and fancier too. They stood in a wide hallway covered by tapestries that showed medieval hunting scenes. Several featured a king with a scarlet and gold cape, spearing a boar, firing arrows at a stag, or riding a tall stallion. Dan still had the uneasy sense that he had seen him before, so he studied the tapestries but always the king's face was hidden.

Doorways led in both directions, but Maggie pointed straight ahead. As they neared the end of the hall they saw that it opened into a larger room with a roaring fireplace straight across from them. Over the crackle of the fire they heard two voices in conversation.

"Why then did you leave me?" roared a deep voice.

"It was not I that left, milord." Another man's voice, quieter and not as deep. "'Twas you that left to come to this unearthly land."

"'Unearthly,' you say? But I say it is a land where a man is not weighed down with rules and regulations. A land where a man can eat when he wants, have sex when he wants, paint when he wants, and sleep when he wants. A land made for poets, not police! A land where a man can be free!"

"But you know what that old song says: 'Freedom's just another word for nothing left to lose—'"

"Quote me no Kristofferson and jape me no Janice!" roared the deep voice.

In the pause that followed, Dan whispered, "Who are Kristofferson and Janice?"

"No idea," Maggie whispered back.

The argument started up again. "Say again, why did you leave?" said the deep voice.

"Milord, if only you would come home with me, perchance all will be well."

"I wish to forgive you for leaving. But tell me, were you with another? Did you leave for a handsomer face and a stronger arm?"

"Of course not, lord. You are the only man I will ever love."

"Good, good. Then you will stay with me, now that you have returned? Nevermore to stray?"

"Milord. You are the only partner I desire. But to stay here is not good for either of us."

The voices ceased. After a minute they were replaced by sobbing, and then the deep voice said, "Gone again. Gone forever. Perhaps I will go mad."

Dan and Maggie looked at each other. "'Perhaps'?" mouthed Dan.

If the other man had left he had made no sound. Dan and

Maggie crept to the end of the passageway and peered into a great central hall. Light came from the fireplace and from many candles flickering in chandeliers and sconces. Tapestries showed more hunting scenes and scenes of battle. The long axis of the hall stretched from left to right. At the left end was the main entrance, closed by two great doors. At the right was a high dais, and upon that a throne, and upon the throne a man wearing an ugly gray crown, hunched over and looking at the floor.

"Why then did you leave me?" roared the man in a deep voice.

"It was not I that left, milord," came the quieter voice.

Dan looked around, bewildered because he couldn't see the other speaker.

"'Twas you that left to come to this unearthly land."

"'Unearthly,' you say?"

"Oh my god!" said Dan. It wasn't two men; the King was talking to himself. But Dan had spoken louder than he intended. The king broke off speaking and slowly raised his head to look at them.

"Oh my god!" repeated Dan, louder this time.

"It *is* he!" said Maggie.

Beneath the gold and scarlet cape, under the ugly gray crown, sat the Green Goblin. His eyes glowed when he saw Dan, and he grinned lopsidedly. "Roger, is that you?" he asked. "Roger! At last you return."

"I'm not Roger," replied Dan. Roger was the Goblin's partner back in Outland. "I'm Dan, remember?"

"And traveling with a wench!" continued the Mad Goblin King as though Dan had not spoken. "I would be jealous, but I know your loins will never turn in that direction. Come closer so I can embrace you."

"Not until you start making sense," said Dan. "This isn't some wench, this is your best friend Maggie, remember? Maggie Westerley? And I'm Dan Hillman. I talked to you not that long ago back in Outland."

"Come to the banquet board, Roger," said the King. "Bring your woman friend. We will feast your return."

"Oh, Dave," said Maggie, using his real name. She ran to him and kissed him on the cheek. "I really am Maggie. Do you truly not remember? All our fun times in the Goth Woods?"

The King staggered back onto his throne. He looked at Maggie, frowning, and said, "You thrive here?" Then he shook his head, looked away, and cried out, "No, I say no! All my friends have abandoned me, all alone I am. Was! For Roger has returned. Roger, come here."

Dan walked forward, held Maggie's hand, and said, "I'm sorry, but I am not Roger. He's a nice guy, but I'm not him. Remember how much you used to hate me and chase me out of the Goth Woods? Then we sort of got to be friends and you've given me all sorts of helpful strange ideas from time to time. I'm Dan Hillman, and you're the Green Goblin."

"Call me not a goblin! I am no goblin! I am King!"

"Of course you're not a real goblin, c'mon," pleaded Dan. "But you've always rocked that nickname."

"I remember you now," hissed the Goblin. "Last time we spoke you invited me through the portal of insanity." He turned to Maggie. "And you, you invited me before. Well here I am and here I am King. Goblin, you say? No goblins have I, but other servants and better." He gazed down the length of the hall and bellowed, spit dribbling down his chin. "Men! To me! Capture these two! Capture them and slay them!"

The big doors slammed open and malkins lurched into the

hall, five, ten, twenty. A small door behind the throne opened and more malkins scurried in.

The entrance they had come through remained malkin-free, and Dan and Maggie pelted for it, Maggie tugging Dan's hand to try to make him faster. Behind them came snicking creaking stick joints. Side doors flew open in front of them and Dan and Maggie sprinted past just as more malkins pushed through. One grabbed Dan's shirt and he heard it rip in the creature's hand. The front door was still ajar and they rushed into the courtyard just ahead of the grating pack.

Too late! A half-dozen malkins were reeling toward them from the portcullis entrance. Maggie had her knife out, but good as she was with a knife it would be little use against these hollow things. Dan pulled his unstrung bow from his pack and wielded it like a club. Luckily the fairies had built it from stronger wood than the malkins were made of and they went down with satisfying shattering sounds. Dan swung left and right and destroyed the first six, but by then a mob of malkins was coming through the entrance, and the others were pouring out of the keep behind them.

"That way!" said Dan, pointing to the well. His logical mind told him this was a stupid idea so he tried to shut it off and listen to his Shadowlands mind. They ran to the well and climbed onto its stone rim. "Hold me!" shouted Dan. Maggie threw her arms around him and he held her with one arm and jumped, grabbing the rusty chain with his other hand. Stick fingers grabbed and raked their skin but gravity was stronger. The chain groaned and grumbled and slowed their descent until it stuck with their feet about a yard from the bottom. Dan let go and they dropped and looked overhead.

Malkins leaned over the opening. More and more malkins, creaking and whining and blocking the sky. Then they seemed to sprout leaves, and their faces became knotholes, and their arms green branches, and the walls of the well fell away, and Dan and Maggie found themselves at the fork in the trail in the deep old forest. Stars twinkled in the narrow sky window directly above the trail. The moon had not yet risen.

As soon as Dan got his breath back, he said, "What in the world was that all about? Whatever it was we got away, but we never found Sister. How will we deal with all those malkins when we head back?"

But Maggie shook her head and pointed down the path to the Woods Witch and said, "She has moved. She is that way."

12

THE WOODS WITCH

*D*an and Maggie stared into a small, crackling campfire. They had backtracked a little way toward the Mad Prince's castle and then climbed to an open spot on the ridge. They wanted to take advantage since the breeze had shifted south. Now they wore dry clothes while their rain-drenched garments hung dripping on branches.

"We need a little time to recover, and I don't think we should walk in these woods after dark anyway," said Dan. "But what if Sister has FCB at the Woods Witch cottage?"

"Sister is feeling anger," said Maggie, "not the triumph and pride she would feel if she were draining First Changing Beast. The Shadowlands impede our search, so that even though I sensed Sister at the Mad Prince's castle she was not there. But the Shadowlands also impede Sister. The Shadowlands are both our worry and our hope."

"But how can it be impeding her?" asked Dan. "I thought she was expert at traveling here, that she could get to First Changing Beast whenever she wanted."

"I do not know how it is happening, but—" A wet knot in the firewood hissed and spat an ember into the air. "Just like that is her mood right now. If it changes, I will know."

"I wonder what was going on with the Green Goblin being the Mad Prince, anyway," said Dan. "I mean, I've been to the Shadowlands enough to know that a lot of unreal stuff happens here, so that wasn't really the Goblin. Was it? Real things get mixed in too. But when I was just back in Outland I invited the Goblin to Inland and he turned me down. I thought it would be totally up his alley, but he said that was the problem, that he would like it too much and that would mess up the good life he has with Roger."

"I told him about Inland when we were still in high school, after our very first trip," said Maggie. "I am sorry, I should have let you know, but that was before you and I got together, before you discovered I was a fairy and saved me, and after that I just did not think of it. But I knew our secret would be safe with the Goblin because if he has a madness, it is a madness that leads him to honor the madness of others. That was before he met Roger, before he started therapy with Dr. Green." Maggie laughed briefly. "Therapy with my brother. He said his life was a mess but he did not want to run away. I told him it would not be running away, it would be running to, but he was firm. He would not be here."

"But him knowing that singer we don't know—Janice Kristofferson or whatever—that's just like the Goblin, he knows all these strange artists."

Maggie shook her head. "I do not believe he was really here."

"OK, Billy said when I'm in the Shadowlands what happens comes partly from my mind. Since we're here together, it must be coming from both our minds. Maybe one of us heard about

Janice Kristofferson a long time ago and just forgot, like maybe she's one of those ancient singers my parents used to listen to. But why would we have it in our heads that the Green Goblin would be the Mad Prince?"

"We did both know that he feared traveling to Inland would do something to his mind," mused Maggie.

"And why would we make it that he went crazy because he felt his partner abandoned him? Is it because—" Dan fell silent. He didn't want to voice his thought: would he go crazy if he had to leave Inland and leave Maggie?

Luckily, instead of asking him to finish his sentence, Maggie kind of changed the subject and said, "I do not think we can understand everything about the Shadowlands. It was only late afternoon when we fled the malkins, but night had fallen when we popped out again on the trail." She shrugged.

But now Dan's thoughts were on their other quest. "If only we could figure out something about East of the Sun and West of the Moon that would help us learn from your father whether I can stay."

Maggie jerked.

"What's wrong?" asked Dan.

"Something made Sister very angry."

Overnight the wind had shifted from south to west and intensified. The "Woods Witch" signboard creaked and rattled. Last year's leaves rose in a vortex like a menacing genie.

"She's still down there, huh?" asked Dan.

Maggie nodded.

"I was afraid of that. You know one thing that bothers me? Why has the sign changed to call her 'Woods Witch' when it was Gingerbread House the time we were here so long ago? Does that change come from our minds, or Sister's, or what?"

A fresh gust took the vortex higher and then dropped it. Tattered leaves settled on Dan and Maggie and tangled in their hair. They brushed each other off and stepped onto the trail.

Immediately the wind ceased. The air was dead still and smelled faintly of mold. Despite the smell, Dan found himself breathing extra deeply because it seemed as though there wasn't quite enough oxygen, like someone had breathed the air already. But there were no other breathing creatures, not even the occasional squirrel or bird from the day before.

The path headed generally downhill, but it seemed in no hurry to get wherever it was going, wandering about for no apparent reason. Sometimes it even took them into patches of bramble or jumbled stones that made progress harder than it would be if they strayed to the side. The third time this happened, Maggie said, "Perhaps we should loop around these rocks and rejoin the trail; you can see it turns again just up there."

"No way," said Dan. "If I know anything about a place like this it's that we're safest if we stay on the trail."

"I bet you learned that when you used to play *World of Warcraft*, right?"

"And from *The Hobbit*. This place reminds me of Mirkwood."

Maggie sighed. "I wish Mother had read me that book, or at least had it in the house. But she never read me anything at all and we had no books."

"Yeah, that really sucks. Hey! I could bring you back a copy from Outland. Or ..." Dan stopped talking. What he just said reminded him he might have to leave Maggie forever, and that ruined the cheerful feeling he got from talking about *The*

Hobbit. He tried to get it back. "Anyway, when they're in Mirkwood they wander off the trail, and first giant spiders get them and then some elves."

"What is that?" asked Maggie.

"Elves? You know, like—"

"No, no, up in the tree!"

A dead branch stretched in front of them about ten feet off the ground, and in the middle of it, hunched over the trail, was a fat bird, black except for a white ruff and naked red neck and head.

"Vulture," said Dan.

"I do not like it," said Maggie. "Shoo!"

The vulture cocked its eye at them, bobbed its skinny neck, and croaked.

"You heard her!" shouted Dan. "Shoo!"

The vulture bobbed its head a few more times, croaking with each bob. It reminded Dan of laughter. Then it dropped at them, spread its wings and flapped barely in time to miss them, and disappeared in the foliage.

Maggie straightened her hair. "I was wishing there would be birds or animals here. But not like that."

"We could use some of your magpies about now," said Dan.

"None are in calling distance. They do not like this woods."

"I don't blame them," said Dan. The trees they now passed grew gnarlier, with twisted branches and knotholes like surprised eyes and hooting mouths. As the path wound lower, the ground became damper and mushrooms appeared. First were reddish buttons flecked with white that looked like strawberries, then larger ones with thick tan caps that looked like slices of bread.

"Hey, Maggie," said Dan, "you're always good at finding us

mushrooms to eat. How about those to supplement what Billy packed?"

Maggie wrinkled her nose, shook her head, and said, "Do not even touch them." Then she grabbed Dan's wrist and said, "I feel Sister, not far ahead."

They looked at each other, nodded, and whispered each other's truenames. The plunge into the pool, the ambiguous swimming companion beckoning to the light in the depths—Dan shook his head at all of them and swam for the surface. He emerged and found himself seated next to Maggie on a log beside the trail. Everything looked the same except that the light, always dim in these deep woods, was even dimmer.

Maggie smiled at him. "Do you feel, as I do, that the true-naming is becoming easier for us to manage?"

"Yes." But Maggie's eyes sparkled, her hair floated beguilingly, and her lips invited Dan to lean into them. He shook his head and checked down the path. "Especially if I don't look at you too much. Do you still feel Sister near?"

"Yes."

They stood and followed the path around two more turns and came to the edge of a clearing. From the long shadows cast by the trees Dan could tell that most of the day had passed while they were in the truenaming pool. On a stump warmed by a beam from the late afternoon sun curled a black cat the size of a beagle. Strawberry and bread mushrooms were scattered plentifully in the grass. And in the center of the clearing was a cottage.

"OK," said Dan. "If I know anything about fairy tales, I know that we don't take a single bite no matter how good it looks."

The aroma of freshly baked gingerbread wafted from the walls. Each plank was outlined with white icing. The window frames were chocolate cake, and the windows were made out of clear sugar. Somehow Dan could tell that just by looking, but he wanted to lick one to make sure. The roof was the world's two biggest chocolate chip cookies leaned against each other to make a peak. And that was only the part of the cottage visible from this side; judging by the tangled smells there was peach pie somewhere, and maybe cherry too.

Maggie giggled. "At least we can look."

They held hands, walked closer, and circled the cottage. It seemed to change before their eyes. Dan never located the peach or cherry pies, but there was key lime pie, and black forest cake, and chocolate bars studded with nuts, and cinnamon rolls, and cupcakes of every flavor with thick frosting …

The door creaked open behind them.

"Get ready," whispered Maggie.

But what was Dan supposed to say again? It was a good thing they had truenamed each other, because he couldn't remember Sister's truename, meaning they were at her mercy if she called out theirs. He knew it began with "M," but all he could think of was "Mmmmm."

"Nibble, nibble, nibble!" said the Woods Witch.

Dan and Maggie whirled.

It wasn't slender Sister.

It was squat Mrs. Westerley. Mrs. Westerley, accessorized with a long baggy black dress, a black cape, and a knobby walking stick. At least she didn't have a pointy black hat.

"Nibble, nibble, nibble!" she said again. "What children are these, nibbling at my house?"

"No, ma'am!" said Dan, as he and Maggie backed away. He held up his hands. "Look, fingers not sticky, no icing on mouth. We didn't take a bite. Ha!"

"With the mouth is not the only way to nibble," said the witch. She pointed to her head. "Curiosity killed the cat."

"Hey!" protested a voice.

Dan looked all around the clearing but he didn't see anyone else.

"I would prefer a different metaphor," said the same voice.

It was the black cat.

"Hee hee hee hee hee!" screeched the witch.

Dan caught Maggie's eye and with truenamed union knew she was thinking the same thing he was: Mrs. Westerley had always sounded exactly like a Shadowlands witch even back in Outland.

"Come inside, children," said the Woods Witch.

"Why should we?" asked Dan, even as he noticed he and Maggie had taken a step toward the buttered scone porch.

"Because your feet are under her spell," said the cat. Dan watched it stretch and yawn. Its sleek, soft fur invited stroking.

Then, like when you're in a weird but basically pleasant dream and suddenly realize that what's been going on over on the side is a monster, the cat flattened its ears and hissed through needle teeth. The sun dropped below the trees and the west wind turned cold in the darkness.

"I said 'inside,' children. Now!" Dan wasn't sure how much gin it would have taken to make the real Mrs. Westerley sound so mean. And it didn't matter what he wanted his feet to do; they marched him to the porch and up the three stairs.

There was no sweetness inside. The wall was of warped planks; more warped planks with a couple tattered rugs made the floor. The witch did have a black pointed hat after all, with a hatband of small animal skulls; it hung from a hook by the door. At one side was a small sink and next to it a wood-burning stove giving off way too much heat. In a corner nearby was a coatrack covered with blobby garments. In the center of the room was a rickety table with two chairs and a vase that Dan thought contained thistles, although it was hard to tell in the dim light. In the back wall was a doorway to another room, and beside it a piece of furniture that Dan couldn't make out at all.

"Here they are, I told you they would come, yes," croaked a voice that was neither witch nor cat. The witch lit two candles on the table and an oil lamp hanging from the ceiling, producing smoky flames that added to the stuffiness. Now Dan could see that one of the blobby garments was actually the vulture, perched on top of the rack. It clapped its bill at them and made its croaking laugh.

"Yes, good Piebald, I rely on you," said the witch.

Maggie tugged Dan and pointed to the piece of furniture in the back. There was enough light now to make out that it was a cage made of bones: long bones from arms and legs ran horizontally, crossed vertically by sharp rib bones. Dan wished they were made from deer or cows or something, but the magic latch made out of a human skull told him otherwise.

"Drop your packs and weapons by the door," said the Woods Witch. It was impossible to disobey. "Now step inside. Hee hee hee!"

Dan and Maggie walked into the cage and heard the skull snick shut behind them. They huddled together against the middle of the back wall, as far from the bones as they could get. The cage was empty except for a mouse that scurried into a crack in the corner. Oh, and above that a small spider with an eyeglasses pattern on its back was weaving a large web. Dan and Maggie scooted a little farther in the other direction.

The gaps between bones were wide enough to give a clear view of the rest of the room. The vulture dropped to the floor, half opening its wings to ease its descent, and then waddled to Dan's pack and tugged at a zipper with its beak. The cat bounded to Maggie's pack and shredded it. Soon the creatures had tossed the contents hither and yon.

"Nothing," said Piebald. "Not even anything good to eat." With one flap it bounded onto the table, and with a second flap resumed its perch on the coatrack.

"No information," hissed the cat. "No meaning." It hopped onto the empty chair; the Woods Witch had already seated herself in the other.

"Well clean it up, Pyewocket, clean it up," she said.

The cat hissed. The vulture bobbed its head and croaked.

The witch sighed and snapped her fingers. From the back room came a rustling sound, and then a broom popped into view, hopping on its bristles. It swept their ruined possessions out the door that had opened by itself.

"They left my bow and arrows," whispered Dan.

"And my knife," Maggie whispered back.

"If only we could get them, but I can't make my feet do what I want. You?"

Maggie shook her head.

"Even if you could," said Pyewocket, "the cage would stop you, and I would have your eyeballs out."

"I usually save eyeballs for dessert," said Piebald. "But at times they make tasty appetizers."

"Now, now," said the Woods Witch. "Don't be hasty. We must decide what to do with them."

"Supper and bones. Bones for the cage," said the vulture.

"The cage is complete," protested the witch.

"Prisoners can see out too easily," said Pyewocket. "Plenty of gaps to fill."

"Or we crunch the bones for marrow," suggested Piebald,

hunching its shoulders even higher as though it were shrugging. "Makes no difference to me."

The Woods Witch said something too quiet to hear.

"Did you say what I think you said?" asked Pyewocket.

"Yes. They remind me of my lost children."

The cat yowled and said, "Then you are dottier than I thought. Your children were both girls."

"And it is important to love my children," continued the witch.

"Yes, yes," said Pyewocket, its voice rising. "Love them the way they love your cottage. Nibble nibble!"

"Gobble, gobble," shouted Piebald. "You love them so much you could eat them up!"

"Like the others!" cried Pyewocket.

"Hee hee hee HEE HEE!" cackled the Woods Witch, standing and raising her arms. But when the creatures quieted she seemed to run out of steam and sat back down. "But I no longer have the same hunger," she said.

"We do!" said Pyewocket and Piebald together.

"Not since I met the right one," murmured the witch. "It wasn't her fault. Maybe it wasn't even the fault of the other."

The cat yowled again. Without leaving its perch, the vulture flapped its wings and puffed out the candles and lamp. All that could be seen were the cat's red eyes approaching the cage.

"Hush now!" said the witch in a firmer voice. The red eyes blinked and halted. The witch banged and bumped around and managed to relight the candles and lamp. "You must wait. I am going to make them dinner."

Pyewocket had almost reached the cage door. It twitched its tail and licked its lips, staring at Dan and Maggie, and then finally sat down.

"Make them dinner, yes, yes, as we wanted," said the vulture.

"Dinner *for* them, I meant," said the witch. She banged a pot on the stove and began slicing vegetables. Dan could smell onion.

"Really?" asked Pyewocket, without taking its eyes from Dan and Maggie. "Are you sure you meant it that way?"

The witch ignored the cat and began to croon.

"One was wrong and two was right,
One was bad and one was good.
Last came day and first came night.
Love them both the way you should.
Rattle fair and rattle black,
Rattle black and rattle fair,
Give her milk and pat her back.
Can she hope while I despair?"

Then she shook her finger at Pyewocket and said, "It was the wicked, wicked fairies."

Pyewocket yawned and said, "Often and often you chant about rattles. Never and never can you decide whether they scare you or calm you."

The witch shuddered and went back to cooking. After a while, Piebald stretched his long red neck to peer into the pot and asked, "A little poison there? Not too much, don't spoil the meat."

"Oh, hush," said the witch, glancing over her shoulder at Dan and Maggie. "I'm only adding tasty herbs."

Piebald gave his croaking, bobbing laugh.

"Done!" cried the Woods Witch. She splashed soup into two wooden bowls, grabbed two spoons, and whispered to the skull latch. The door swung open with a click. The witch set bowls and spoons on the floor in front of Dan and Maggie, said, "Enjoy, dearies," and left the cage, bone door closing behind her.

"Yeah, right," said Dan to Maggie. "I wouldn't trust her cooking even if I hadn't heard that ugly bird talk about poison."

"Oh, but I am famished!" said Maggie.

"I know, we haven't eaten since this morning," said Dan, "but we'd have to be a lot hungrier than this to risk witch soup."

Maggie moaned, licked her lips, and held her hands over her stomach. Puzzled, Dan took her hand to restrain her, and then it struck him too: a wave of hunger as though he hadn't eaten in a week. The soup smelled delicious, like the finest chef had perfectly melded exquisite ingredients. Still ...

Something scampered across Dan's foot. He looked to see the mouse run to the bowl in front of him, lean its front paws on the rim, and sip the soup. The mouse looked at Maggie and him and twitched its whiskers.

"It's not poison!" said Dan. He grabbed a spoon and dipped it in, and Maggie reached for the second bowl. With a squeak so loud it was almost a shriek the mouse ran under the second bowl, braced his back against it, and stood on his hind legs, spilling the soup.

Pyewocket yelled, squeezed between bones, and pounced at the mouse, landing in spilled soup. The mouse squealed and darted for its hole. Pyewocket leaped, but with a great effort of will Dan managed to bump him as he went by. The cat landed with his paw a hairsbreadth away from the mouse's tail. The mouse still had a yard to cover before it reached its hole, but the spider had finished its big web, blocking the way except for a small opening near the floor. The mouse squeezed through and disappeared. Pyewocket skidded to a halt in front of the web.

Then, eyes flashing red, Pyewocket turned, growled, and crouched to spring at Dan.

"No, Pyewocket!" said the Woods Witch.

Pyewocket twitched his tail and crouched lower.

"If you hurt them, Pyewocket, I will punish you," said the witch.

"Grassy Ella comes!" called Piebald.

"What?" cried the witch.

"Grassy Ella comes! At midnight she will be here."

"Then we must flee," said the witch. "Grassy Ella hates us."

The Woods Witch hurried into the back room and began banging around. Pyewocket squeezed back out of the cage, tail twitching, washed soup from his paws in sink water, and licked them dry. The Woods Witch reemerged with a big cloth bag over her shoulder and the broom in her right hand. Without a word she snapped her fingers and the cottage door sprang open. She straddled the broom, Pyewocket hopped on in front of her, and they soared out. Piebald flapped heavily and followed them. The door slammed shut.

"Whew," said Dan. The spell had departed with the witch and he sprang to his feet. "Let's get the hell out of here." He grabbed bone bars and shook with all his strength. The cage was much stronger than it looked and the bars didn't even bend. Dan stepped back and smashed the bottom of his foot into the skull latch.

"Ow!" he cried. "Damn! That didn't do anything." He raised his foot again.

"Dan, it is all right," said Maggie, standing beside him.

"What?"

"Look how they fled. Grassy Ella is our friend. We only need wait until midnight."

"Oh. Right." Dan lowered his foot. "I just wish I knew how long that would be."

Maggie giggled. "There is much you do not know about me, Dan Outlander. I am a fairy. I know when midnight comes."

"Really? Cool! So ..."

"Only fifteen minutes."

Dan paced while Maggie sat and rested against the wall. After what felt like forever, Dan asked, "How long now?"

"It is three minutes before midnight."

Dan realized his time judgment was off, so he didn't trust when he thought three minutes had gone by. But when Maggie stood beside him frowning, he knew it was time to worry. "If she doesn't come, we could starve in here," he said, shaking the bars. He and Maggie walked around the cage pushing and pulling at bones, looking for a weak spot, to no avail.

Then they heard a thump on the porch. "Finally!" said Dan. He and Maggie hurried to the cage door.

The cottage door creaked open. But it wasn't Graciela who entered. It was an ugly vulture and an angry cat.

"Couldn't you get rid of her sooner?" croaked Piebald.

"She is not as weak and stupid as she seems," replied Pyewocket. "Especially when she thinks she is doing something good for her children. Ever since her mind started down that path of children and rattles she has not been the wicked witch we used to love. Good job, by the way, lying to her that Grassy Ella was coming."

Piebald flew up on the table and bobbed his head at Dan and Maggie. "But she is still useful. With her gone, they have freedom of movement. I cannot get through the bars to help you, but if we open their door we must be quick so they do not flee the cottage. Can you slay them alone?"

Pyewocket's tail was twitching like a metronome. "Maybe,

and maybe not. But I do not need to risk it. I have watched her mix the ingredients. My paws are too clumsy but your beak will do. Come."

Pyewocket stalked to some low shelves beside the sink, and Piebald hopped over to join them. As Pyewocket muttered instructions that Dan couldn't hear, Piebald grabbed a small bowl with his beak, laid it on the floor, and began opening jars. A lot of herbs and other stuff that Dan didn't want to think about got spilled, but a lot made it into the bowl.

"Doesn't it need water to finish?" asked Piebald.

"Not water. Liquid."

"Oh, gross," said Dan. Pyewocket was peeing into the bowl. A stench of herby cat pee filled the air, and Dan felt his feet sticking to the floor, his muscles weakening.

"That's right, hold still for us, boy and girl," said Pyewocket.

Piebald croak-laughed and then the two creatures advanced on the cage. Dan found that by straining with all his might he could shuffle backward, but that only got him to the wall.

"Danny!" said Maggie. "If we deepen the truenaming it should weaken the spell's power."

"But we might not be able to break the truenaming," said Dan. Pyewocket and Piebald were almost to the cage. "OK, let's do it, but how?" said Dan.

"Kiss me!"

Dan's mouth met Maggie's and bliss shot through him like a bolt of lightning. God, how much he loved this woman! Laughing, Dan and Maggie broke apart and jigged their feet just as the cage door opened. They leaped forward.

But even unenchanted this wasn't going to be easy. Piebald jumped into the air, buffeting their faces with his wings, and before Dan knew it he and Maggie had been driven back, the cage door closed, and both creatures stood inside staring at them. Pyewocket looked like he was smiling.

Piebald took a hop to the side and another hop toward them. Pyewocket circled at them from the other side. Dan and Maggie backed up until they almost bumped the spider web. Dan looked over his shoulder and saw the little spider in the middle. The eyeglasses on its back looked familiar.

"Maggie!" said Dan. "Grassy Ella!"

"Spiderwork!" answered Maggie.

Pyewocket squalled and pounced. In that exact moment, Dan and Maggie jumped headfirst into the spiderweb.

And landed on hard dirt, packs, bow, and arrows intact. Pyewocket and Piebald were nowhere to be seen. The moon was just bright enough that they could read the trail signs reading "Woods Witch" and "Castle of the Mad Prince."

Dan and Maggie laughed.

"Safe again and—" said Dan.

"Here again," finished Maggie.

They kissed, and Dan said, "I feel wonderful. I know it's the truenaming, but I don't care. This is all too hard. I don't care about East of the stupid sun—"

"And West of the silly moon," finished Maggie. "I feel like we should do something about Sister, but she's never where I feel her, and wouldn't it be nice to just run into the woods anyway?"

"Yeah. And the whole First Changing Beast thing, I think Josh would say Hakuna Potato."

They laughed until they had laughed themselves out, and then gazed around.

"The forest is so beautiful," said Maggie.

"Let's just find a quiet glade with no kings or witches, and stay there forever," said Dan."

They stood up, but then Dan cried, "Yowtch!" He felt a sharp prick in his arm, and now fire spread from elbow to fingertips. He looked and yelled, "The damn spider bit me!" He raised his hand to squash it, but the spider raised two legs and waved them back and forth, then twisted so Dan saw the eyeglasses on her back.

"Oh," said Dan. He lowered his hand, walked to the side of the trail, gently brushed the spider onto a leaf, and said, "Thank you, little friend."

Then he released Maggie from the truenaming, and she released him.

13

THE WAITING MOON

"I wish Graciela-spider had found a gentler way to startle me," said Dan, rubbing his swollen arm. Red streaks radiated from the bite mark.

"I am no Mother Ferny, but I can help," said Maggie. "I should have done so last night."

"We were both too tired," said Dan, but Maggie had already run into the woods. She soon returned with some moss and funny-shaped red leaves. She squeezed water from the moss onto the leaves, mashed them together, and tied them over the bite with a strip of pliable bark. The pain lessened immediately, and the swelling and red streaks gradually faded.

"And I brought these, for breakfast and more," said Maggie, holding out a mesh bag that she had filled with mushrooms.

"Sure, nice to have something besides nuts and dried fruit," said Dan.

"It is not only nice. It may be necessary. Sister is that way now." Maggie pointed uphill. The other time they had been here there had been nothing to eat up in the mountains. "She is even angrier, and she is moving away. Already I feel her more distant than when we awoke."

"Then let's go. We can eat mushrooms on the trail."

As they packed up, Dan noticed that the signpost carried a third weathered plank, pointing in the direction they were about to take. "That one wasn't there before, was it?" he asked.

Maggie shook her head. This plank was longer than the others, with enough room for a lengthy inscription, but so splintered and moss-eaten that only the last letters could be read: "—oon."

Even as they studied it, the planks indicating the Mad Prince and Woods Witch faded and fell away, and the forest disappeared all around them. Dan and Maggie stood on a rocky hilltop barren of vegetation except for a few short twisted evergreens and ankle-high plants with tiny leaves. Behind them the landscape rolled lower and lower until it faded into haze. In front of them the trail dropped into a wooded bowl with a small lake, and then reappeared switch-backing up a high ridge that hid whatever was beyond it.

Dan looked at the signpost with its now single plank creaking in the breeze from the north. "OK, that's gotta mean 'moon,'" he said, cupping his ear, "because I don't hear any bassoon."

Maggie shielded her eyes. "And I do not see a baboon."

Even those feeble attempts at humor felt good as they started down the trail and gray clouds scudded toward them. "Although no matter how high the next ridge is I don't think we'll reach the moon," said Dan. "But that reminds me to check the moon tonight. Even the crazy way things have been shifting around in the Shadowlands, the moon has seemed to follow its normal phases. It should be about at the last quarter, which means it will rise real late. And also means we have two and a half weeks left in the first of my last three months."

"Let us hurry," said Maggie.

It was tempting to stop by the lake in the little valley, partly because they both had the feeling that would be the last pleasant spot on this journey. But it was already late morning when they reached it, so they didn't pause long. After a snack and a drink of tooth-chilling mountain water, Dan stuffed his pack with as much dry wood as he could manage and they continued up the trail. Maggie darted from side to side harvesting mushrooms until the rising switchbacks pulled them out of the trees and into a land of ground-hugging plants with tiny white flowers. The gray clouds had blown past like a warning and the sun was hot on the south-facing wall that they climbed. Dan found himself sweating and wishing for a refreshing wind, but the mountain blocked the breeze from the north.

It was late afternoon when they finally topped the ridge and beheld the northern vista that awaited. In front of them to their left the ground dropped far below to a body of water so large they couldn't see the other side; an enormous lake, or perhaps an ocean. To the right the ground fell away into hazy valleys. The ridge they stood upon was a spur from a mighty mountain to their north. Its feet stretched to the ocean and its head seemed to reach for the moon. The path, only recognizable from a line of cairns, followed the ridge as it stretched eastward and then jogged left, north, toward the peak. Dan's eyes lost the cairns in the late afternoon haze, but if they kept on in the same direction the cairns would lead them into the snow and ice that reflected sun back from high above.

"I should have known better than to wish for a breeze," said Dan, hugging himself against the tongues of mountain air that licked them. "I wish I hadn't left my big bearskin robe back at Gatemoodle." Dan had received the robe in a Shadowlands ceremony, and it had helped them on many a cold night camping, but he'd expected this trip to take them into caves, not mountains.

"I am glad that the trail leads away from that sea," said Maggie. "I do not like that sea."

"Yeah, it's weird," said Dan. "Just geographically, it doesn't feel right. I don't think there's many places where snowy mountains rise right from the sea. Still—Shadowlands. At least down there it would be easier to find shelter. Where did Sister go?"

Maggie pointed uphill and said, "She followed the cairns. And I can see a spot sheltered from the north wind."

"Your eyes are better than mine. Let's hurry there before dark."

The first stars were flickering like points of ice when they finally reached the spot Maggie had seen. It was a small cove in a south-facing promontory that blocked the wind. A slender rivulet cascaded down the promontory and out the entrance to their shelter.

"This is good, Maggie," said Dan. He heaved his pack to the ground and shivered as the cold night air met his perspiration-soaked back. "It'll be nice to lighten this by burning some of the wood, but I wish we didn't have to yet because it's just going to be colder up above. I wish I brought my robe."

"Look, Dan!" Maggie stepped to the back of the cove and lifted what Dan had taken for a rock in the darkness. It was his bearskin robe.

"Wow!" said Dan. "I wish for a Thanksgiving dinner! I wish for Sister to come here and surrender! I wish for First Changing Beast to be free! I wish to be able to stay in Inland with you as long as I want!" He paused a beat, and when none of those things happened, said, "Oh well, I guess it wasn't my wish that brought the robe, it was just Shadowland weirdness. At least it did something nice for us for once. We can wrap ourselves in that and save the wood."

DAN WANTED to wake up before sunrise to check the moon, and it turned out to be easy to do, because even snuggled next to Maggie in the thick robe, he was so cold he only slept fitfully. Before he dropped off completely he was startled back to wakefulness by a whistle from the higher slopes. He didn't want to disturb Maggie so he lay quietly listening but heard nothing more. Sometime much later he thought he heard the whistle again, but it was a howl that brought him fully awake. Dan sat up and listened. The howl came once more, from far below in the direction of the ocean. It sounded like a wolf, although sort of weird and liquidish like it had water in its throat. Dan was pretty sure wolves wouldn't come up this high where there wasn't much for them to eat, so he turned his attention to the skies.

Dan had checked the constellations before they went to sleep, so he could tell by their positions now that it was only a couple hours till dawn. By his earlier count the moon should already be up. When it did peep above the eastern horizon a few minutes later it was only a sliver. It had skipped a couple days in the Shadowlands. "Only two days till the new moon," he muttered.

"What does the new moon look like?" asked Maggie, rubbing her eyes.

"Sorry I woke you," said Dan.

"It is all right. Angry Sister is no farther from us, but neither is she closer, so we should move early. What does the new moon look like?"

"It looks like nothing. It's called a new moon when there's no moon to see at all."

"Then that is a silly name," said Maggie. "It should be called the Waiting Moon."

The north wind buffeted them as soon as they stepped out of their sheltered cove. Dan would have offered Maggie the cloak, but they both knew that with her fairy blood she could tolerate cold much better than he. As they trudged uphill, the low-lying plants grew thinner and finally disappeared altogether, so that they trod on broken shingle. Feet left no marks, so the only way to know where the trail went was to follow the cairns. At first these were unremarkable rock piles about knee-high, but as they approached the snowline the cairns grew waist-high, then chest-high, and finally higher than Dan's head. At their bases were slabs much bigger than Dan would have been able to budge, let alone lift, and even the top stones were as big as his head.

By midmorning, Dan and Maggie were passing pockets of snow that hid inside rock shadows. Ahead of them the gray shingle ridge disappeared under a solid coat of white.

"I suppose it's too much to ask that the Shadowlands drop us some snowshoes like they did this coat," said Dan.

"Someone made this trail," said Maggie. "Perhaps they have cleared a path through the snow."

"Yeah, but who exactly was it that made the trail? Look at the size of these cairns."

Maggie didn't answer, and on they trudged. Distances were hard to judge in the clear mountain air, and the sun had climbed directly overhead by the time they reached the snow-line. Sure enough, there was a clear path through the snow, but when Dan saw it he wished they had to struggle through unbroken snow instead. He and Maggie slumped on the downwind side of the huge cairn nearby, and huddled under the bearskin cloak. Maggie passed out a few mushrooms.

"That path is wide enough to drive a small car through," said Dan. "Except there aren't any cars in Inland, so it must be made for giants."

Maggie nodded. "We have heard before that frost giants live in the mountains."

"Really it was obvious from the size of the cairns, but I didn't want to believe it," said Dan. "I don't think my bow and your knife will do us any good against giants. I don't suppose Sister has turned aside?"

"I fear not. But if she can pass safely, perhaps we can too." Maggie paused and squinted. "She has stopped moving."

Dan was about to ask what that could mean when they heard stones clatter on the path above them. He loosely nocked an arrow to bowstring and peered around the edge of the cairn. Nothing was in sight, but he heard another clatter, quiet but closer now.

"Could a giant be so stealthy?" he whispered. A huge dark shape loomed into view from around a bend, then a second and a third. Dan pulled his bowstring taut, but Maggie laughed and held his elbow.

"Look again, Danny," she whispered.

As Dan watched, the giant shapes resolved into shaggy cow-sized beasts casting huge shadows across the snow. They tromped down the trail, snuffled at Dan and Maggie, and began licking lichens off the rocks.

"This is crazy," said Dan, also laughing. "Those look like musk oxen."

"What are musk oxen? Why are they any crazier than any other mountain beast?"

"Because musk oxen live in the Arctic. No way have we been walking long enough to reach the arctic."

Still laughing, Maggie said, "I wish good old Josh were here. He would say—" Dan joined in to complete the sentence: "Two words: Shadow. Lands."

"If the giants didn't eat them, maybe they won't eat us," said Dan. "C'mon, let's catch Sister."

The trail was the same dry shingle they had been walking on before they reached the snowline. Dan knelt at trailside and ran his hand over the snow. The top was moist and heavy, but not crusted over.

"What are you doing?" asked Maggie.

"I don't know how long it would take snow to form a crust up here, but I'm guessing a day or two would do it. So this snow fell recently, and that means whoever cleared the trail did it recently and isn't very far away."

They walked faster after that, looking across the open expanses for any movement. The trail snaked northeast along the ridge top, angling toward the summit and away from the ocean far below to their left. At first the snow on either side was only an inch or two deep, but it got deeper as they got higher. Dan and Maggie rounded a bend and saw that the shingle trail ran into a waist-high ledge of ice. They hoisted themselves up and saw that the trail was now made of ice with gravel frozen into the top to provide traction.

Not far ahead was another ledge. As Dan and Maggie hauled themselves up that one, Maggie said, "I think we know what slowed Sister down."

"If we had any doubt we were on a giant's road, these steps

make it pretty clear," said Dan. He looked around, said, "Hey! What's that?" and pulled Maggie down beside him.

High on the slope to their right was a figure. Dan couldn't tell how far it was so he couldn't judge its size. "Is that a giant?"

Maggie shielded her eyes. "It is too small to be a giant. Whatever it is approaches fast." When it was a little closer, she added, "It is not even as big as we are."

Dan pulled an arrow from his quiver.

"Do not shoot," said Maggie. "He does not feel evil to me."

Dan nocked the arrow loosely and said, "OK, but I'll be ready just in case."

Now Dan could make out that it was a small man slaloming toward them on short skis. He was clad all in white, with a long white beard streaming behind him. With a final swoosh and a spray of snow he came to a halt in front of Dan and Maggie, hands held open in front of him to show no weapons.

He wasn't wearing small skis; he had schussed down to them on long, wide feet. And he wasn't wearing white clothes; he was covered in white fur.

Dan couldn't help himself. "Are you a yeti?" he asked.

The little guy ignored that question and aed his own. "Why did you ignore my whistles, why? I tried to warn you, warn you."

"That was you last night? Oh. Maggie, I heard two whistles in the night."

"Were you warning us about the giants?" asked Maggie. "Thank you, kind man. But we must go forward, giants or no."

"Not giants, not giants, giants are gone. The giants are not happy, no, the giants are gone."

Dan didn't like the sound of that. "What could scare the giants away?"

"Did Barbegazi say giants scared? Barbegazi said giants not

happy. It is man and fairy woman that should be scared, scared. Akhluts, akhluts."

"We hope you will help us understand, kind Barbegazi," said Maggie.

The furry little man put one hand on his hip, pointed to the ocean with the other and said, "The land contorts in pain, pain. No ocean belongs alongside Frostmane Peak. Two nights past we felt the earth groan, groan, and we awoke to behold a northern sea where valley should be. Giants have gone high, high, high and far. Do not worry about giants."

"We thought that ocean looked weird," said Dan. "We are sorry that your land is in pain, and I bet we know who did it—the woman we are pursuing. But if the giants are gone, doesn't that make us safer?"

"Akhluts, akhluts," answered Barbegazi. "Did you not hear them howl?"

"I heard a wolf in the night," said Dan. "Will wolves come way up here?"

"Sea wolves from northern waters. Sea wolves that walk on land when they choose, when they choose. Sea wolves that love snow and cold. Put away your sharp arrow. You will need it for akhlut, not Barbegazi. You will need many sharp arrows. And shelter, shelter." He pointed up the trail. "Twisted woman flees you. Barbegazi does not know why. Twisted woman spent the night in shelter but now has traveled on, on. By nightfall you must reach new ruin."

"New ruin?" asked Dan.

"Giants tore down their tower and tossed it about. You will see. Hurry, for it is not close, not close."

With that, the little man turned and began snowshoeing—snow*footing*, actually—up the slope, disappearing around a nearby shoulder of Frostmane Peak.

"You are the one whose mother read you fairy tales," said Maggie. "Have you ever heard of a barbegazi?"

Dan shook his head. "Or an akhlut, either, and I don't like the sound of them at all. Let's find that ruin."

It was a weary and precipitous climb. The incline steepened, and they had to clamber over more numerous giant ledge-steps. The wind was bitter against their exposed faces. The late afternoon sun began to fade and the trail took a left turn to circle a shoulder of the peak where a tall, narrow sea stack cast a cold shadow almost as dark as night. Before the trail looped back to the right it narrowed into a quarter-mile stretch with sheer cliff rising to their right and sheer drop-off to their left. Dan and Maggie hurried through this section, listening to breakers smashing into the mountain base far below. Dan thought he heard deeper howls mixed in with the howl of wind and the cries of seabirds.

"That must be the ruin," called Maggie.

Dan hurried to catch up and looked where the trail looped back eastward. They had almost reached a pass between Frostmane Peak and a nameless mountain north of it, and in the pass was a great jumble of stones, clearly unnatural. Their sides were smooth and straight, and a low section of wall remained standing.

The trail now took them away from the ocean and the boom of the waves, and in the silence it was easier to make out howls from below. Another howl answered from somewhere above, impossible to locate precisely as it echoed back and forth. Dan and Maggie panted up the final ascent to the pass, struggling to reach shelter before the akhlut found them. Another howl came, closer this time, just as they reached the first fallen stone.

It had been a tower fit for giants. It looked like its makers had smashed it at the base so that it toppled down the east side of the pass, where the jumble of stones extended into darkness. Sections of the circular base almost head-high to Dan remained at the top of the pass, and against the northern section of the circle a pile of stones had tumbled into a kind of small cave or rough chamber. There was no snow in front of it, and a few blackened sticks showed that it had been melted away.

"Sister slept here last night," said Maggie.

"She's no fool," said Dan. "It's defensible once we get a fire built, and it'll block the damn wind." He threw down his pack of wood.

A loud howl tore the air, ending in a watery gurgle. Dan spun to see a shape on the southern wall. As he put an arrow to his bowstring, a second shape leaped up beside it. It was so dark now that he couldn't make them out clearly. They were on four legs, but they were larger than wolves and their shape was wrong. That looked like a hump or spike on their backs, and their tails were much too big. Dan shuddered as they watched him and Maggie with eyes that glowed sea-blue in the darkness.

"Keep them off," said Maggie. "I will build the fire."

Her words were drowned out by howls as the two creatures bounded toward them. Dan had an arrow nocked for the second beast almost before the first arrow left his bow. Yelps and snarls replaced the howls. The creatures had been charging straight toward Dan, so even though it was too dark to tell for sure, he must have hit them in the face or chest, but it clearly wasn't fatal. The creatures backed up and began pacing side to side near the wall, howling and gurgling. Other howls responded from east and west.

"I have like twenty more arrows," said Dan, trying to keep

the anxiety out of his voice. "Not enough for all the beasts we hear. We need to rely on fire."

He heard a comforting crackle and glanced down to see that Maggie had a kindled a small blaze. "How large should I build it?" she asked.

The akhluts whimpered briefly and jumped away from them over the wall.

"Sea-wolves from the north. I don't think they've ever seen fire before Sister built one, and that makes it scare them that much more. Let's keep it small so we don't run out of wood. They seem to be nocturnal, so I hope we can escape in the morning."

The stone shelter was just large enough for Dan and Maggie to sit shoulder-to-shoulder behind the fire. There were a few big mushroom caps left but they had hardened until they were almost as tough as wood. Maggie tossed one on the fire and it quickly ignited. "More fuel if we need it," she said, setting the rest of the mushrooms aside and pulling out nuts and dried fruit for supper.

The cave narrowed behind them so that only one of them could lie down, but that was OK because they would need to take turns watching and keeping the fire burning. Dan volunteered for first watch. Before she lay down, Maggie said, "Such a dark night! If only we had light to better see our enemies. Where is the moon?"

"It will only be a sliver, and even that won't rise until just before the sun," answered Dan. "The moon will be no help tonight."

Nothing attacked during the first watch, but Dan could hear rustling as the akhluts moved around on the other side of the wall. He sat just in front of the fire so it wouldn't interfere with his night vision, and gradually he was able to make out the shapes of the jumbled stones. A few times he saw one of those strange big tails wave above the wall. It would have been bad enough if they had been regular wolves, but these things were monstrous. At least they didn't come any closer.

When Maggie woke Dan after her turn she reported that all remained quiet. Dan added a stick and resumed his spot in front of the fire. The wood was more than half gone, but at this rate they had more than enough to last through the night. It was hard staying awake in the thin mountain air after all the exertion of the day ...

Dan snapped back to alertness. *Idiot, drowsing off!* Something was different; something wasn't right. The fire still burned, but Dan got the feeling it should be bigger, so he reached for a stick to lay on it. Then he heard it again: a faint scrape on the rock overhead. Dan scooted farther back and grabbed his bow and arrow.

A great snarling shape dropped from above, blocking the stars. Dan fired at the same moment that Maggie darted past him and slashed at the thing. She leaped back behind the coals, holding her bloody dagger, and the shape roared and bounded away.

"It looked like a big fish," said Maggie, her face wan in the low firelight.

"That's crazy, but what else is new, and your night vision is much better than mine. Let's keep the fire a little bigger."

It was still a few hours before dawn, but neither of them could get back to sleep. They took turns trying, but quickly sat back up, fidgeting. The akhluts didn't come closer, but they began to howl. Dan figured they were angry that the night was going to end without Dan and Maggie for dinner.

"Hey!" said Dan. "Any chance these akhlut things have already eaten Sister?"

"I fear not," answered Maggie. "She has gone down the eastern slope."

"Oh, well, we need her to find First Changing Beast anyway. I wonder why she's stalling around up here."

"I do not think she wishes to," said Maggie. "She is angrier than ever, and I feel it is us that she is angry at. We cannot catch up to her, so she does not fear us, but somehow we are interfering with her plans."

"How could we be doing that?"

"I do not know. But if the Shadowlands are partly created by our minds, it must be something we are thinking of."

"Well, I'm mostly thinking about surviving the akhluts. And I'm thinking of catching Sister, and of hoping I can stay with you in Inland, and of East of the Sun and West of the Moon. None of which helps me understand."

"I am thinking of all the same things," said Maggie, "which must make our minds doubly strong, but I am not able to understand either how that interferes."

Finally the faintest stars could no longer be seen, and the brighter ones grew small. "Look!" called Maggie, pointing east. On that side the mountain dropped precipitously to forested lowlands, and a tiny fingernail-clipping moon had crept into view on a beam of sunlight. Quickly the sun rose and the moon vanished in its brightness.

"It is as though the moon traveled on a road cast by the sun," said Maggie.

"'Cast by the sun,'" mused Dan. "Sounds like 'east of the sun.' Except the moon rose first, so it's west of the sun ..." he trailed off, and then grabbed Maggie's hand.

"Maggie, you're brilliant!" he cried. "Something in our minds that's shaping the Shadowlands to interfere with Sister! When Tanly told me East of the Sun and West of the Moon, the girl first traveled to the east wind, then the west wind, and finally the north wind. Well, it was an east wind when we were in the Mad Prince's castle, it turned west when we went to the Woods Witch, and it's been freezing us from the north ever since we started climbing this mountain. We've been wishing so much that we could get a message to your father that we've trapped Sister in a Shadowlands version of East of the Sun and West of the Moon. And I bet when my father said it wasn't so hard to go there he was thinking of when the sun and moon are so close together!"

"Except you just pointed out that the moon rose west of the sun," protested Maggie.

"Tonight will be the new moon. The next day there will be a sliver of moon just like this morning, except it will be on the other side of the sun. When the sun is in the sky it'll be too bright for us to see the little moon, so we have to wait till the moment of sunset. The little space between them will be east of the sun and west of the moon!" Then Dan's voice fell. "Except I still don't know how to travel there."

"Do you still have the sunflower head from the Mound of Two Kindreds?"

"Sure, it seemed important somehow."

"It will be our message to my father. With your bow you will send it East of the Sun and West of the Moon."

"Then we need to double back on the trail so the mountain doesn't block our view west to the setting sun. We don't have to keep chasing Sister now that we know she can't get to FCB until we send our message. We just have to wait for it to get bright enough for the akhluts to leave and then get out of here."

Dan and Maggie let the fire die out as they ate breakfast. Then, in the full light of morning, they stepped out of the cave.

A monstrous creature stalked onto the trail they wanted to

take. They looked in the other direction and saw another of the creatures seated there, tongue hanging between long fangs.

Dan froze and said, "I see why you thought fish. Actually they're more orca."

"What is an orca?"

"Killer whale."

The strange big tails Dan had glimpsed were whale flukes. The hump on the back was a dorsal fin. Their skin was hairless, and they even had the black and white pattern of orcas. They had four legs, and they had wolf necks to allow them to turn their heads without having to shift their entire bodies like a sea creature, but otherwise they were orcas. Orcas made for land. Sea-wolves.

The akhlut to the east howled. The one to the west answered. A dozen more leaped over the wall in front of Dan and Maggie and began walking toward them.

Dan clenched his teeth and said, "I'm going to kill one and hope it gives the others second thoughts."

The akhlut straight in front was closest. An eye shot would be deadly, but if Dan's aim were off it might not do much damage. Instead he aimed just below the neck, hoping for a heart shot, and loosed the string. The arrow sank inches deep in the akhlut's chest, but instead of dying the thing screamed, leaped in the air, ran in a little circle, and then charged Dan. He shot two more arrows into its neck and chest and it finally collapsed and skidded to the ground inches from his feet. The other beasts growled and dropped back, but didn't run away.

"So much for nocturnal," said Dan. "When we send our message to your father we'd better add a request for help with these things. We'll have to spend the night here."

"Then it will truly be the Waiting Moon."

Dan and Maggie pushed the dead akhlut as far as they

dared and then ran back into the cave. The day dragged on and on. Twice more the akhluts attacked, and twice more Dan slew them, but his arrows were running low.

In the late afternoon he said, "We'd better light the fire. They fear that more than arrows."

"But we may not have enough to last through the night," said Maggie.

"That won't matter if we don't even last through the day. Let's make it small, just barely enough to scare them."

They sat by the little blaze as the sky darkened. The beautiful moonless sky full of stars stirred Dan's hopes that they had figured out East of the Sun and West of the Moon, but then he frowned because the idea seemed more and more tenuous. As if to underline his doubt, wispy clouds reached their fingers in from the east. Dan watched to see if they would thicken enough to obscure the stars, and if they would reach all the way to the western horizon.

He was almost grateful for the distraction when the first blue eyes appeared above the wall. Soon there was a ring of them watching, blinking, waiting. It was as though the akhluts knew Dan and Maggie didn't have enough fuel to last the night.

Neither Dan nor Maggie tried to sleep. It was halfway between midnight and dawn when Dan put the last stick on the fire and said, "That's it. I have a few more arrows for when they attack, and then my sword. Get your knife ready."

"We still have three woody mushroom caps to burn," said Maggie.

"Good," answered Dan, although that was only enough to buy them a few more minutes. Then he looked at them closer and felt a rush of relief. "I have an idea that might work," he said. He explained to Maggie, finishing with, "But I won't be able to aim straight, so we have to wait until they're too close for comfort."

Dan plunged an arrow through the center of each mushroom cap. Then they waited. It didn't take long until the fire was almost out. The akhluts crept close, closer, and closer still.

"Now!" said Dan.

Maggie ignited a mushroom cap in the embers and handed the flaming arrow to Dan. He aimed at the heart of the nearest akhlut and fired. As expected, the strangely weighted arrow flew erratically, and it lodged not in the creature's heart but its back. No matter. The beast went insane, screaming and snarling at its companions. Maggie handed Dan the other two flaming arrows, and two more akhluts went mad as the fire sent out the rank stench of burnt skin and blubber. Dan could see well enough from the flares in the beasts that he could shoot others with regular arrows. In a howling, yelping mass, the sea-wolves fled toward the sea.

Dan jumped up and down, whooping, and Maggie hugged him.

"Just one arrow left," said Dan.

"One is all you will need," replied Maggie.

THEY SPENT the day in the same spot in case the akhluts regained their courage away from the killings. They didn't talk much, because there wasn't much to say; either their idea would work, or, more likely, it wouldn't. The sun seemed like it wasn't moving at all, and Dan gritted his teeth as the clouds pursued and finally covered it.

"I don't suppose your fairy powers could clear those clouds away," he said.

Maggie touched his hand but didn't bother to speak.

When the cloud shadow yielded to the stronger darkness of encroaching evening they left the cave and walked until they could see the western ocean. Dan took the sunflower head from his pack. "I was already worried I wouldn't be able to shoot straight," he said. "You saw how my arrows with the mushroom heads wobbled. If I have to guess where the sun and moon are beneath the clouds…"

"For the clouds we can only use hope," said Maggie. "But as for shooting straight—give me the flower." Dan handed her the sunflower head and she cupped it in her hands and whispered to it before handing it back.

Dan stabbed his last arrow through the heart of the sunflower. The North Wind that earlier had tormented them puffed, gusted, and blew a hole in the western clouds. Dan saw the sun dip into the ocean and a pearly sliver appear just behind it. He aimed high and loosed his sunflower arrow. It arced higher and higher and then curved toward the earth, east of the sun and west of the moon.

The clouds flared red and the green ray flashed as the sun vanished.

Hooves clopped behind them.

"Greetings from your father, milady," said a voice.

14

SISTER'S SHADOWS

The fairy gazed down at the akhlut corpses and curled his lip. "Well it is that you slew these excrescences, milady. Far they are from where they should dwell."

"Thank you," answered Maggie. "Except it is not I who slew them, but my fiancé."

"Ah yes, the hopeful groom," said the fairy. At least his lip wasn't curled any more, but Dan could hear the curl in his voice. "Far he is too from where he should dwell." The fairy fell silent and stared at Dan.

Dan felt nauseated, maybe from burnt akhlut stench, but probably from his heart dropping into his stomach. "It's not you we want, anyway," he said. "I mean, not your opinion, we want to hear from the King."

"I am the voice of the King, and the King's opinion is mine." The fairy frowned. "However, our opinion does not sway the Old Ways. The King received your arrow and he sends this answer: If you wed, you have the Freedom of Outland."

Dan and Maggie sighed.

"*If* you wed," said the fairy. "For the King still requires you to free Formshifter if you would earn his daughter, and he deems this quest beyond you."

"Deem away, King!" said Dan with a laugh. "We are almost there."

But Maggie was frowning. "What I want to know is why my father is so moody about this," she said. "Not long ago he was friendly to Dan and me."

The fairy backed his horse and then turned it toward Maggie. The curl left his voice when he spoke to her. "Perhaps it is because he hoped for better for you, milady."

"There is no one better for me. Whether my father believes that or no, I do not care."

The fairy dipped his head, then yanked the reins and galloped back the way he had come. While still in plain view he turned to the side and vanished.

"Sorry about your dad's moodiness," said Dan. "Fine with me if we never see him again after the wedding. But this is good news! I won't have to leave once we get married."

"Tremendous news," said Maggie. "Who needs a father?" She hugged Dan and laid her head against his chest. Dan started to sink into the first peaceful moment in a long time, but Maggie gasped.

"Sister moves quickly. We must follow!"

"Should we truename each other first? Are we going to land right next to her?"

Everything went black before Maggie could answer. It was a good thing they were already hugging, because they had to hold on tighter and tighter so the wind didn't tear them apart. It felt like being in an airplane that had just hit major turbulence —except no airplane. Also no sound. Maggie's hair swirled and whipped around Dan's face, and there should have been a roaring gale, but everything was as silent as it was dark. Amid all the spinning Dan couldn't tell which way was up, and he steeled himself for a crash.

But the landing was gentle, really no landing at all. All sense of motion ceased, and Dan felt ground beneath his feet. Sound and sight gradually returned. First came a faint whistle that ebbed and flowed, and Dan felt steady dry wind against his face. Then the black faded to gray that revealed the shape of the land.

"What is this place?" asked Dan.

"It is the shadows in Sister's mind," answered Maggie.

The transition had jolted Sister from his thoughts but now Dan looked all around, Maggie's truename on the tip of his tongue. Sister was nowhere in sight, but Dan felt more anxious, not less.

The steady wind had picked up, whistling with a note just this side of fingernails on a blackboard. Worse than that, Dan felt it blowing from all directions at once: straight into his face, from the left and the right, and pushing against his back. But their clothes were still, and Maggie's hair was motionless. Dan reached out and touched it: soft and light like usual.

Maggie half-smiled. "I know," she said. "I feel it too, the unthinkable wind."

Everything was a shade of gray. It was impossible to tell if they were in a huge cavern or underneath a sky of unrelenting slate. They stood on a vast, flat plain with unobstructed views in all directions, but nowhere was there a hint of any color, not even brown or beige. Nowhere, that is, except Dan and Maggie themselves. They wore simple clothes of green and brown that had been muted in the world they came from, but seemed to glow here. Their twining rings flashed green when they moved their hands. Maggie's hair was a deep, rich brown, and best of all were her eyes, shining like emeralds that reflected a laughing summer sun.

"Your bow," said Maggie.

Dan hadn't noticed before since it hung at his back, but his fairy-made bow seemed to pulse with dark brown life. "And I have a full quiver of arrows!" said Dan. "I'd shot all of them at akhluts, and didn't have time to recover any before we fell here."

"Our minds are a small circle within Sister's now," said Maggie.

"It's like her Unlight, just not as strong," said Dan. "Makes me feel like looking for First Changing Beast is a thousand-page boring reading assignment."

The corners of Maggie's mouth turned up. "Then it is a good thing I did not go to college."

"Wait!" said Dan. "Wasn't it all just an empty landscape before?"

Maggie squeezed his hand and nodded. Scattered about the plain were bent, leering stone formations.

"Well, I guess weird rocks can't hurt us. We'd better get on with it," said Dan.

"Sister is straight ahead," said Maggie. "Not far, yet not near either."

As they stepped forward, the wind picked up another notch, and meeting the weird hoodoos it whined louder. Dan left inch-deep footprints in the soft dust of the plain, but none of it rose into the still yet windy air; none of it blew away. His skin prickled as though bitten by tiny gnats, but there were none to swat away.

At the same time that this Shadowland was creepy and uncomfortable, it was boring. Dan felt like they had been plod-ding along for ages but he knew it could only have been a few minutes when he sensed motion and jerked his head left to look. There was nothing to see except a few of the tortured hoodoos. When he looked forward again something seemed different, but what it was he couldn't tell. They trudged on, and then Dan thought something moved on the other side, but again he was unable to spot it. He watched Maggie out of the corner of his eye; she was looking around, too.

"The hoodoos are moving, aren't they?" asked Dan.

"What is a hoodoo?"

"Oh, sorry. It's a weird word for weird rock formations like those things."

"Hoodoo," mused Maggie. "A strange word but it has music in it. Not right for these skeletons of her dead thoughts."

"Skeletons of her dead thoughts," repeated Dan. He hadn't thought of them that way before, but it sounded right. "You know, I've seen real hoodoos, on vacation in Arizona and Utah, and they don't feel dead like these. They're pretty shades of red and brown in the sun, and some of them are almost like big strange animals." He noticed Maggie glance quickly to the side and he looked where she was looking. Nothing. "You sense movement too, don't you?"

"Yes, movement that I cannot catch no matter how quickly I look."

"But ... dead thoughts? How can dead thoughts move?"

Maggie shrugged. "What else are ghosts but dead thoughts that move? What else is despair?"

"There!" said Dan. "That one moved for sure!"

A little to their right and about thirty yards in front of them stood a dead hoodoo where none had stood before. Its midsection was gross and swollen. One arm seemed to beckon to them while another seemed to warn them away. On its top a large boulder balanced on a tiny round rock, looking like it was perpetually about to crash down. It made Dan dizzy, and he drew an arrow from his quiver.

"I'm going to kill it," he said.

"I do not think you can. Not with an arrow."

"I'm going to try."

Dan aimed for the swollen midsection and fired. His aim was true but the arrowhead merely shattered against the rock and the shaft turned to dust, leaving only fletching drifting down. Now the wind carried a new sound to them, far-off high-pitched laughter that grew to a shriek and stopped abruptly.

"I should have listened to you," said Dan.

They skirted left around the rock he had shot. Now the movement of the hoodoos became more obvious. Dan was almost never able to catch one in action, but if he looked to the side and then back in front, they would be in different positions, and if he looked back to the side, some of those would have moved too.

But something else bothered Dan more. He had vaguely been aware that his clothes and Maggie's were getting dusty, but then he realized that was impossible because none of the dust ever rose from the ground. He brushed his tunic and swatted at his trousers, and then brushed Maggie's back. No dust.

"Yes," said Maggie, "our colors have grown drabber."

"It must have started when I shot that rock," said Dan.

"No, it began before."

Dan figured Maggie was just trying to make him feel better, but he appreciated it. He smiled and said, "Well, I won't do it again. We better hurry, though."

But hurrying is just what was getting harder to do. Whereas previously the hoodoos had dotted the empty landscape like interlopers, now they were taking over. Soon Dan and Maggie had to wind their way through a rock forest where the pathways grew narrower and narrower. Dan twisted and contorted his body to avoid touching the rock, feeling silly because how could it hurt to touch a rock? He noticed Maggie working just as hard to avoid it, though.

Finally they could go no farther without climbing. There were plenty of footholds and projections to grab onto, and the formation was only ten or fifteen feet high, so it didn't look too difficult—except it meant touching the rock. Dan and Maggie looked at each other and then reached toward it simultaneously.

"Oh!" Maggie's voice was soft but sharp. "It feels evil."

To Dan it felt nasty, wet and clammy like the skin of a dead amphibian. He jerked back his hand and wiped it on his pants, then tapped the rock and looked at his hand. It felt dank but he could see that it was perfectly dry.

"Evil or not, it is our path," said Maggie. She shuddered and pulled herself onto an outcropping. Dan climbed beside her. The top was one of those balanced boulders, and Dan leaned against it with all his weight, but it didn't budge. He climbed onto it and then down the other side, Maggie right behind him. He couldn't resist wiping the nonexistent slime from his hands.

"Yuck," said Dan. "I hope we don't have to do that again."

But the way was only clear for a short time before Dan and Maggie again found themselves cringing and climbing the hoodoos. Twice more they dropped with relief back to the dusty ground, but the third time they could see no way down. They walked, crawled, and hopped along a corkscrewing platform of rock. Dan had a headache, and he saw frown lines that he had never seen before in Maggie's face. Worse than that, almost all the color had leached from their clothes. Worst of all, Dan felt lost. Not just lost in Sister's Shadowlands; he'd felt that as soon as they landed there, but it wasn't too bad because he was together with Maggie. Now he felt lost from Maggie, as though she was far, far away. Dan peered over, and of course she was only a few feet from him. Her hair was still filled with color, and her emerald eyes were flashing, and her twining ring was shining, but he could hardly feel her even when she turned the light of her eyes toward him.

"Dan," said Maggie. Her voice was hoarse, and she had to clear her throat to get the words out. "Danny, remember what Mother Ferny said. Look at your ring."

Dan's ring was as bright as Maggie's. "You made these rings to help us find each other when we kintraveled," he said.

"Yes. And Mother Ferny enchanted them so that they would help us find each other when we are lost."

With one mind, they reached out and clasped their ring hands together.

The hoodoos vanished, the incessant wind vanished, and Dan and Maggie stood on a dark and empty plain.

THEY SAT IN THE DUST, ate dried fruits and nuts, and washed them down with warm water. When Dan spoke he darted a look over his shoulder and lowered his voice. The absence of wind, so welcome at first, left a silence so deep that he felt like he was shouting for the whole world to hear.

"This isn't what I expected," he said. "It's hard to think clearly in this gray place, but we better figure things out. I thought that since our east of the sun and west of the moon preoccupation was shaping the Shadowlands, overriding Sister's desire to reach FCB, that once we'd dealt with that, Sister's thoughts would take over and we'd be sucked into her shadowlands. Then that should have landed us right with her and First Changing Beast. And yes, we've been sucked into her shadows, but she isn't here. Why can't we catch up with her? Is she making it hard on purpose? Is she already with FCB taking his power, and then she'll escape again?"

"It has been hard for my mind to work too," answered Maggie. "But look! Even our clothing has some of its color back, and Billy's good dried fruits are helping me too. I will try to feel Sister more clearly."

Maggie closed her eyes and slowed her breathing. Judging time in this place of permanent dimness was impossible, but after what felt like ages Maggie began to frown. The lines Dan had noticed in her face when they struggled over the rocks reappeared, incised more deeply. He reached to touch her but pulled his hand back when her mouth twitched into a smile. Then, slowly, her frown returned. Dan still hesitated, but when the luster began to leave Maggie's hair he touched her hand.

Maggie looked at him. Were her eyes paler? She blinked, and they were bright as ever. She shook her head and smiled.

"That is no place for fairy or human," she said.

"Were you with Sister? What happened?"

"Yes, I was with Sister. We are more sisters than I like." Maggie paused, then shook her head again and continued. "First I felt only her anger, relentless as the gray that surrounds us. That is familiar, that is how she usually feels. And I felt fear. That also is familiar in her, but now it is stronger. Much stronger. And other things are mixed in that I have not felt from her before. A tender feeling that she struggles against, a tender feeling for my mother. Oh, I mean *her* mother. No, damn it, I mean Mrs. Westerley! And she feels confusion, compounded from that and from First Changing Beast. He is stronger than she expected. He has found the strength to fight back. He has found hope."

"I bet he knows we're coming to rescue him!" said Dan. "Ever since the Gatekeepers gave me the quest to find him he's had an awareness of me that's made for brief encounters in the Shadowlands. He was even able to give me and Josh and Alice his message that Sister was using her truename against him. So now we're close and that's giving him strength to fight back!"

"Then let us hurry," said Maggie.

Onward they plodded. Dan kept watching out of the corners of his eyes for hoodoos or some other manifestation of misery, but it was always flat dust as far as he could see. He wished he could think of something to talk about, but his mind seemed to be growing dull again. He wished Maggie would come up with a topic, but maybe she was getting dull too.

"Why do you call First Changing Beast 'him'?" asked Maggie.

"What?"

"Why do you call First Changing Beast 'him'?"

"Uhh ..."

"You have told me before that you cannot tell what sex the Beast is. And you have told me that the Beast has appeared to you as a large woman. You said she was naked, so I do not think you got that sex wrong. So why do you refer to the Beast as 'him'?"

Dan flicked a glance at Maggie and looked away again before she could make eye contact. When he had wished for her to come up with a topic he hadn't meant a topic like this. He almost answered, "It's just easier to say 'him,'" but he knew that wasn't going to fly. The girls back at college who used to go on about the patriarchy would say he was imposing his toxic male view on First Changing Beast. And he wasn't even supposed to think of them as "girls"; he was supposed to think "women."

"Dan?"

It wasn't Maggie's angry voice. Dan risked another look, but she was just watching her feet. Suddenly Dan stopped.

"I don't understand, Maggie. I don't understand this. I don't think I understand anything. Remember when we first really talked, sitting on that log, and you laughed at me because I was so defensive I didn't even know the Green Goblin was gay? Now I'm friends with him and I can't even remember why being gay bothered me. But with First Changing Beast it's sort of the same but also completely different. How can someone be both sexes at once, or at different times, or no sex at all, or whatever he or she or they are? Back in college I kind of avoided conversations about this stuff because it made me feel guilty somehow. But now that stuff is in Inland too."

Maggie giggled, and Dan thought he saw sparks of green in the dust. "Those conversations don't just happen in college. You should have hung out with my gang in the Goth Woods." Then she took both Dan's hands and said, "But why do you let it confuse you so? You thought Outland with all its closed doors was so boring that you had to escape, and you learned to open gates to Inland. You sought me, and I am both human and fairy, and you saved me and have my love. You were chosen to free First Changing Beast so that gates between Inland and Outland remain open. So why shouldn't First Changing Beast have all the gates open inside her or him? You say now that stuff is in Inland too. But it has always been in Inland. And not only is it here, you are in the middle of it. You are the mover of it. Look at me. Look at where we stand. Look at yourself. You are the gate-opening hero!"

Dan looked at Maggie. He looked at the weird landscape. He looked at himself. And he said, "No. Remember on our very first trip to Inland, before we knew anything, when the Moss Maidens enraptured me? We saw that other mortal man who danced with them until he died, and that would have happened to me too, but you rescued me. And later the Gatekeepers told us that the guy who danced to death was the person they chose before me to free First Changing Beast. Ever since then you and I have been saving each other. It's working because we are doing it together. I am not the gate-opening hero. *We* are the gate-opening heroes.

"Uhh. Unless we keep standing here in the dust."

Maggie and Dan laughed, and this time he was sure he saw green sparks in the dust. They marched on toward Sister.

DAN FELT like something had clicked inside him that made him lighthearted despite the miserable landscape, and that made him feel that it was only right for them to find Sister and First Changing Beast quickly and finish the quest. But reality didn't go along with his feelings. Instead, the few sparks of green disappeared. The wind whispered grim thoughts and then whined and groaned about unfairness and failure. Dan's skin prickled and he had to concentrate on not scratching at bug bites because scratching bug bites makes them worse, and he knew there were no bugs anyway. Even so, Maggie caught him by the wrist and he saw that he had clawed at his arm almost hard enough to draw blood.

"We should drink a little," he said. But when he pulled out a water bottle it was empty. He scrabbled in his pack for the other ones, but they were empty too. He looked up to see Maggie holding out her dry bottles.

"How did that happen? I know we didn't drink it," said Dan.

Maggie shrugged and said, "Sister."

Dan put his pack back on and lifted his bow. Where before

it had glowed as though sap still coursed through it, now it was just a piece of dry wood. He was afraid that if they faced danger and he had to string it, it would snap. His clothes were fading too, and Maggie's. Even her hair was drab. Only their twining rings and Maggie's eyes remained vital.

"Well, let's go, I guess," he said. "Nothing else to do."

A woman's voice joined the wind again as they struggled onward. Not laughing this time, but wailing at the loneliness it hated, and shrieking that it wanted to be left alone. Dan pressed his hands over his ears but he could still hear her.

They could go back! It hadn't even occurred to Dan before. They had gotten here by Maggie kintraveling to Sister; they could get away by kintraveling to her Moss Maidens. Or if that didn't work he could use Breaklock and make a gate to ... who cares, wherever.

Maggie plodded beside him, slow and bowed. He had never seen her slumped like that, whether in weariness or despair. Dan knew he was slumped exactly the same. But their eyes and rings were still bright. Dan decided not to say anything until they faded too.

Maggie with her sharper vision was the first too notice. "Danny," she whispered. "Danny, even our rings begin to dim."

Dan cleared his throat, so parched it was hard to talk. "Shall we leave, Maggie?"

Maggie turned and looked behind them. "Walk all the way back?"

"No, no, we can just kintravel away. Or I can make a gate."

Still looking behind, Maggie said, "I cannot kintravel. I am too weary. Do you have the strength to make a gate?" Before Dan could answer, she continued, "But I do not think we will have another chance. If we leave, First Changing Beast will have no hope. Sister will defeat the Beast and take all its power.

She will conquer Gatemoodle and control the Gates of Inland. She will slay the Gatekeepers and in time she will be master of all." Maggie began to weep.

Dan had never let himself look so directly at what was at stake. Now he wanted to whine like the voice in the wind. He was just a regular kid. He'd come to Inland for excitement, and some danger was fine. Somehow it was even OK if he got killed, if his personal story got snuffed out. But it wasn't fair to have the whole world depending on him.

He couldn't stand thinking about that, but he could think about saving Maggie. "You're right, we can't both give up. But we don't both have to go on. I'll make a gate for you, Maggie. Where do you want to go? Gatemoodle? Moss Maidens?" Dan dropped his pack and reached in for Breaklock.

"What happened to 'we are the gate-opening heros'? Do you really think I would leave you here?"

Maggie plodded forward and Dan followed her. His eye was drawn to her ring as it swung back and forth on her hand, the only sign of life in the dead expanse. Something about it pricked at his mind and then faded. No, wait, it was Maggie's ring itself that was fading. Dan looked at his own ring. Fading, fading ... then he remembered.

"Maggie," he whispered. She walked on, unhearing, and Dan strained to make himself audible. "Maggie! I'm stupid. The shadowlands have made me stupid. Our rings saved us before when we put them together."

Maggie stopped and stretched her ring hand to Dan. He clasped it with his ring hand.

Nothing dramatic happened. They didn't drop to a safer spot like had happened when they connected rings on the rock platform. But things got a little better. Their rings glimmered back into life, not as bright as before, but like lovely moss under a full moon. Dan and Maggie smiled at each other and walked onward with newfound strength. They both wore their rings on their left hands, so keeping their ring hands together made for awkward walking, Dan reaching across his body with his left arm, but no way were they going to let go.

Onward. They could make it. Onward. Or could they? Onward. Maggie smiled at Dan, but her eyes were losing the fire at the heart of the green. Onward. Their rings too were fading again.

Maggie saw it first, of course. Maggie with her sharp eyes.

"Lightning," she said.

"Where?"

"Straight ahead. Thunder too."

Even a storm was welcome as a break in the monotony. They sped up. Soon Dan saw the low horizon flicker, and half a minute later came a faint thunder grumble. They let go of each other and began to run. The lightning flickered again, and thunder followed promptly. Soon they were close enough to see the lightning bolts, and the thunder boomed. They ran faster.

Then they saw the precipice right in front of them. Dan grabbed Maggie and tried to backpedal, and they fell and skidded. They dug their heels into the ground but the thick dust offered little resistance and they kept sliding. Dan had the sickening feeling of his feet and legs hanging over nothing when they finally stopped. They rolled onto their bellies and crawled back, choking as powder filled their mouths. Then they sat up and looked.

In the middle distance was the lightning storm, and in its midst figures struggled. Clouds roiled about and obscured them, whether rain clouds or clouds of dust Dan couldn't tell. But it was the only life they had seen besides each other, and somehow Dan knew it had to be Sister and First Changing Beast. They were almost there.

But between them, stretching endlessly in each direction, was a ravine as wide as a football field. Dan crept forward, looked over the edge, and jerked back. The walls were sheer and the bottom so deep that Dan couldn't see it.

"There." Maggie was pointing to the right. Dan looked and saw a narrow rock arch spanning the gap. They hurried to it and Maggie stepped right on, but Dan halted. It was only wide enough to walk single file. In the middle was a wider spot, a sort of island supported by a pillar rising from the immeasurable depths, but Dan didn't think he could make it even that far.

Maggie looked back and said, "Oh. Bothered by heights?"

"No more than everyone," replied Dan. "But yeah, a two-foot wide bridge and a jillion-foot drop, I'm bothered."

"It is easy for me to balance," said Maggie. "You know, fairy. If I go slowly and we hold ring hands, do you think you can make it? We can rest in the middle."

Dan breathed in and out deeply and nodded. He took Maggie's hand.

"It will be easiest if we walk steadily," she said. "If there were no drop-off you could easily walk on something this narrow without stumbling. Like they always say, just don't look down."

Dan nodded again and they started forward. Of course it was impossible not to look down because he had to watch where he put his feet, but to his surprise it was easier not being able see anything down there than it would have been if he could see what he would smash on if he fell. Before he knew it they were halfway to the island; OK, he was going to make it. Then the tumult of thunder and lightning that had been constant paused, and Dan heard the woman shrieking and wailing from below. This was the heart of her misery, and his heart was chilled. Thunder again obscured her voice, but Dan shivered and began to wobble.

Maggie squeezed his hand tightly. "Danny, I am with you," she said. "We are almost there. Steady, we are almost there."

Dan concentrated on her voice and made it the last few steps to the island. He lay flat, reveling in the feel of solid stone against his body. There was another lull in the storm, and the anguished voice wafted up from the chasm. Dan got up and stood next to Maggie.

"Not going to get any better waiting here," he said. "As soon as the thunder starts again and I can't hear her, let's go."

Immediately came the brightest flash and the loudest thunder they had yet heard. Maggie stepped onto the forward span and reached back for Dan. Thunder boomed louder and boomed again, louder yet. The rock arch quivered. Dan grabbed Maggie's hand and stepped onto the span. He felt the rock tremble beneath his feet and then settle down. They stepped forward. With a gigantic bolt of lightning and a deafening blast of thunder the world exploded into white silence. The span began to sway. Maggie shouted something at Dan but he could only see her mouth move. She pointed to the island and Dan released her hand and stepped for it. The span jerked and he began to fall; with all his strength and terror he converted his fall into a leap and struck the island with his torso, legs hanging down. He scrambled to the top as Maggie lightly leaped beside him.

The span to the far side continued to jerk and quiver. Just when it seemed like it was going to settle down, Dan heard a crack sharp enough to penetrate the rumble of thunder. Near the far side a chunk broke loose and plummeted to oblivion.

Like dominos, other chunks broke and tumbled away until only a short spar protruded from their island.

Dan and Maggie turned and saw the same thing happen on the other side.

They stood on a rock island, in the middle of a storm in the middle of nowhere, with the goal of their quest close and impossibly far.

Without speaking, Dan reached into his pack and pulled out Breaklock. Maggie nodded. They were beaten. It was over. It had never been easier to summon a feeling of holy dread. Dan spun Fuzzy Fat-Tail's foot around Breaklock.

Nothing happened. Had he gone clockwise in his despair? He did the ritual again, making sure his motion was widdershins.

Nothing happened. Not even the faintest glimmer of a gate. Nothing.

Maggie's eyes were as dim as the rings now. Moss under moonlight. Still pretty, but ephemeral, gone at the whim of cloud or leaf. And Dan understood. If even Maggie's eyes shut down, there could not be enough light for one of his glowing gates. They were in the shadowlands of Sister's mind, and in Sister's mind all gates were shut.

Maggie mouthed the word "Kintravel." Dan saw in her face that it would not work, but he nodded and took her hand. They closed their eyes. But when they opened them, they still sat on the rock island, trapped and hopeless.

"You've visited the Shadowlands more than I," said Maggie. "Do you think a person can truly die here, or is it like a dream where you wake up?"

Dan thought about how he had carried physical effects of the Shadowlands into the real world on past visits: injuries, a ceremonial face painting, even his bearskin robe. "I think you can really die here."

After a long pause, Maggie said, "Still, I am glad I am not Sister."

Dan gazed at the cold barren grayness that surrounded them, and said, "Yeah."

Maggie looked at Dan and Dan looked at Maggie. His mind wandered strange paths, always trying to leave Sisterness behind. Moss under moonlight. Dancing with the Moss Maidens under the moon. East of the sun and west of the moon. Gates he feared to open, gates he wished to open, gates that opened whether he wished it or not. First Changing Beast, him, her, or they. The Green Goblin. Dr. Green saying he needed to learn how to live seriously and magically at the same time. The beavers, and Mother Ferny telling him not to put his childhood too far away. The Green Goblin's song.

And in his crappy, gravelly voice, Dan began to sing.

"Boys and girls, come out to play,
The moon doth shine as bright as day;
Leave your supper and leave your sleep,
And come with your playfellows into the street.
Come with a whoop or come with a call,
Come with ..."

It actually helped a little. At least Dan felt a little better failing with a song on his lips. And their rings were a smidgen brighter, and Maggie smiled at him, and her eyes were a smidgen brighter too. Maybe if he knew the whole song it would really make things better, but that was all the Goblin had sung.

"Again," said Maggie. For the first time since the bridge fell,

Dan could hear her clearly. So he sang again.

> "Boys and girls, come out to play,
> The moon doth shine as bright as day;
> Leave your supper and leave your sleep,
> And come with your playfellows into the street.
> Come with a whoop or come with a call,
> Come with ..."

And in her voice like a sweet mountain brook, Maggie sang,

> "Come with a good will or not at all,
> Up the ladder and down the wall,
> A halfpenny loaf will serve us all.
> You find milk, and I'll find flour,
> And we'll have pudding in half an hour."

Maggie's eyes flashed with emerald fire. Their rings flared. They stood and sang the whole song through together.

Dan's spirits rose, and then he realized it wasn't just his spirits, he and Maggie were rising. They alit amid birdsong in a rainbow world. Only after Dan blinked did he realize that it was the usual Inland palette, looking heavenly in contrast to the horrible gray world they had left. They stood beneath pine boughs, and through the needles of a low-hanging branch they saw a wide glade. Within the glade rose a circle of ancient lichen-crusted standing stones; not huge monuments like at Stonehenge, but waist-high, bent and sharp like a mouthful of rotten fangs. In the center of the mouth two figures stood.

The thunderstorm was focused laser-like on the stone circle. But even through its booms Dan heard Sister's whipcrack voice: "Minik Mingarria!"

15
ON THE WAY

"*A*re we too late?" asked Maggie.

"I can truename her and make her release him. But first—" Dan lowered his voice to whisper, "Maggie Magpie."

"Círdan James Hillman," Maggie whispered back.

With so much tumult before them Dan barely noticed their dive into mutual truenaming. A shimmer of blue; deadened treble tones so that the roar of battle thrummed at him as though from a great distance; a brief twisting feeling; and he was back beside Maggie, pushing aside pine boughs to peer into the glade.

Maggie gasped and Dan gaped.

They heard lions roaring, men bellowing in rage and fear, men chanting of glory, women wailing and women singing songs of madness and joy, a great army of humans and animals. But only two figures stood there, and their mouths were locked in silent grimaces; it was as though the cries came from the sky, the earth, and the jagged standing stones. The two figures faced each other and circled just inside the arena formed by the ancient stone ring. If one stomped, the ground rippled and broke apart beneath the other; if one gestured, the air rippled and struck the other like a block of stone. Yet neither crumpled and neither fell. As the battle intensified, Dan saw vapors that formed, lost, and then formed again shapes part human and part animal, faces noble and beautiful but with horn and claw, scale and fur, writhing from the ground and twisting from the sky, gathering near the jagged stones, and from them sounded the cacophony of power and fear.

Yet none of that was what made Dan gape.

"I thought you said those were both First Changing Beast," said Maggie.

One of the figures was a giant lion man, sex no longer in doubt although he wore a loincloth: he had a deep chest, broad shoulders, thickly muscled arms, and a thick shaggy mane. The other figure should have been Sister, but she was nowhere to be seen; instead it was the huge, heavy woman that Dan had beheld before as the other avatar of First Changing Beast, now clad in an animal skin shift, powerful muscles clenching beneath her chocolate skin. The lion's mane shook in the air and sweat flew from the woman's braids as they blasted each other over and over.

"Why do they fight themselves?" asked Maggie.

"It has to be Sister making them do it," answered Dan. "So where is she? Do you sense her?"

"She is right here," said Maggie. "She must be hid behind one of the stones. Perhaps if we step into the greensward I will locate her."

It made Dan uneasy to leave the cover of the trees. He saw Maggie hesitate and knew she felt the same. Still, the First Changing Beasts were totally intent on each other, so if they just went a little way in it should be OK. Dan stepped forward, Maggie right beside him.

Maggie screamed. Dan heard no change in the uproar surrounding them, but Maggie clamped her hands over her ears, fell to her knees, and began rolling on the turf. Then Dan was struck with sympathetic agony from the truenaming. He was barely able to grab Maggie and drag her back under the pines. He gasped out, "What was that?"

Maggie stopped screaming, dropped her hands from her ears, and stood up, and a wracking pain left Dan's head. Maggie sobbed once and pointed at the figures. "Sister is nowhere else. Sister is there."

"You mean she's one of them? Disguising herself from us?" asked Dan.

And as they watched, the lion man and the great woman bent and shrank and expanded until each was replaced by the other. The wailing, bellowing, singing, and chanting grew even louder.

"I have to know which is really her," said Dan.

"Why?" asked Maggie. "Can you not simply truename both of them? The one who is really First Changing Beast has already been truenamed by Sister and will be unaffected by you."

"True," said Dan as he watched the two avatars of First Changing Beast dodge and shove each other around the ring. "But I'd rather just get in shouting distance behind the right one. For them both to hear me I'd have to get in the middle of the war. Could you tell which was her?"

Maggie shook her head. "Something was wrong. Something that hurt me and stopped me from fixing on her. This pine grove mutes the evil. But I will try again." She took a deep breath. "Please hold my hand. Perhaps if I just lean my head from beneath the boughs."

But Maggie screamed again and a sledge struck Dan in the head. The pain sapped his will but Maggie clenched his hand so hard that his knuckles popped and he was able to yank her under the trees by just falling backward. They hugged and Maggie sobbed against his chest.

"What's going on?" asked Dan.

"Sister is neither of them. Sister is both of them. Sister and First Changing Beast are one."

And before them the lion man and the great woman flickered, bulged, contorted, and shrank, and in their places stood Sister facing Sister, blond hair crackling with energy, red bolts flashing from their eyes, white capes flapping. The ground shook and the vapors screamed.

"Then I guess I do have to truename both of them," said Dan. "Then I'll make Sister release FCB, as long as I don't get squashed."

But Maggie held him back. "I am not sure that will work. Remember, it is not that one of them is Sister in disguise. Both are equally Sister and equally First Changing Beast."

"How does that even make sense?" protested Dan. "And how could it have happened? Some changey way for FCB to fight back? Now that he, I mean *it* has hope because we're close?"

"We never thought about how the Beast would deal with Sister. Maybe the Beast is trying to take her power just as she tries to take theirs. After all, we know that much of her power is stolen from them."

"Maybe that's it. She took so much of the Beast's power that truenaming it turned out to be truenaming herself as well."

"However that is, we must do something soon before they destroy each other," said Maggie.

"Right." Dan strode into the glade. At least with Maggie under the trees they didn't suffer from a mind meld with the Sisters or the FCBs or whatever they were, but sound battered his ears as though the very earth screamed and cursed. Dan didn't like the idea of getting inside the stone circle, or even trying to get past the weird wisps that streamed and chanted between the stones. He stayed a yard outside, ran to his right until he got behind the nearest Sister, and shouted, "Minik Mingarria!"

No reaction. Dan wasn't surprised, but he was scared. Those rock fangs enclosed the magic battle, and Dan was going to have to pass between them. By now ghostly shapes drifted in all the gaps between stones. Dan loped around the perimeter, past a woman whose torso coiled like a python, past a bulky creature studded with rhinoceros horns, past others that shifted too fast for him to make out. When he saw a small figure that from the rear looked fully human, Dan sped past it into the circle. It turned and clattered a curved ibis beak, but he was through.

The turf rippled and knocked Dan to his knees. He struggled to his feet only to be flattened by a pulse of air that struck with the force of an ocean breaker. From his back Dan saw the Sisters hurl light and air at each other. Dan started to shout the truename, but another quake jolted him against one of the standing stones, knocking his wind out.

The nearer Sister noticed Dan and a gentle smile touched her face. That one must be FCB! But no sooner had Dan seen her smile than a sneer erased it and she turned back to her opponent.

With a great gasp Dan was finally able to suck air back into his lungs. He ran toward where Sister fought Sister at the center of the circle, leapt to avoid a ridge of ground that bulged toward him, ducked beneath a pulse of air, and shouted as loudly as he could, "Minik Mingarria!"

Sudden silence. Both Sisters lowered their arms and gazed at Dan.

"Sister, I command you to release First Changing Beast!"

One of the Sisters tilted her head to the side. Both of them frowned and furrowed their brows. Then, as though Dan didn't exist, they turned back to each other. The cacophony of men and women and animals burst upon them like a thunderclap, they struck the ground, and Dan was thrown through the air and blacked out.

When he came to, he heard a voice say, "That way is closed."

Dan sat up and found himself outside the stone circle. However long he had been out, the battle was going on just as before.

"That way is closed."

It was one of the mist figures talking to him. It looked sort of like a crocodile and sort of like a man, except when it looked like a woman or a wolf. Dan averted his eyes before he answered.

"It can't be closed. Not completely. This has to work! One of them caught the other with her own truename, so I should be able to catch her the same way."

"The namer is the named. That way is closed."

Dan jumped up. What do crocodiles know anyway? Maybe the truename hadn't worked because he'd given Sister the wrong command. He tried to push the crocodile thing out of the way but his hands went right through it. Whatever. Dan ran through it feeling only warm mist, entered the stone circle, was knocked down, rolled and crawled until he was close enough, and shouted, "Minik Mingarria!"

Again the Sisters paused to look at him.

"Sister! I command you to separate and become Sister!"

It seemed to be working. The Sisters stood quietly and then seemed to flicker like a glitchy film. They bulged and shrank and shifted, and then they changed. But instead of Sister and FCB, two lion men stood in front of Dan. They faced each other and gestured, and the thunderclap of sound struck again. Dan ran but a wave of ground caught him just before he reached the stone circle and threw him outside.

The crocodile thing said, "Speaking to one you speak to the other. That way is closed."

Dan crawled to where Maggie waited under the pines. He started to tell her what had happened and what the croc thing had said, but she interrupted, "I saw. I heard."

"How?" asked Dan. "I mean, even fairy acuteness, how could you hear over that?" He almost had to shout over the wails and calls.

"Our mutual truenaming."

"Oh. Right." Dan should have known that, but another effect of mutual truenaming was that it made him stupid, like his brain cells had trouble focusing on anything besides how good it felt to be with Maggie. He started wondering if they would be able to break the truenaming.

"I also understood what was said because of my link with Sister," said Maggie. "A link of the Old Ways, a link of abuse."

"Can you figure out what to do, then?" asked Dan. "I don't want you to go out there again—it hurts too much—but do you understand them enough to know what to do?"

Maggie only paused briefly before answering. "We must figure out what they have in common. You must truename them and give a command that speaks to a shared desire."

"Not sure how that's gonna help. I mean, what do they

share? Fighting? Not sure they want to stop, and it won't help to make them fight more."

Maggie shook her head. "That is certainly not it. It must be a shared desire, and it must help First Changing Beast get free."

"But what can that be?" wondered Dan. "I'm sure FCB wants to be free, but if Sister shared that desire she would have released him just now when I commanded it. I think she's still holding on to take all his power."

"Look, Dan!"

Maggie pointed at the battle. For the first time, the combatants showed that the blows were taking effect. Manes and fur were matted and torn; one's arm hung loosely, and the other limped. The sight of those strong creatures weakened was frightening and pitiful. Dan thought he heard songs of lamentation mixed into the roars and chants.

"I don't want First Changing Beast to die," said Dan. "For itself, and for Inland." The quiet smile he'd seen from one of the Sisters flashed through his mind, and then the moment back in front of Gatemoodle when he'd seen pain on her face. "Crazy, but I might feel bad if Sister dies, too."

"I do not want either of them to die," said Maggie. "What is their common desire? You know more about the Beast than I do; what is the Beast's desire?"

"Besides getting free from Sister? Helping Inland?" Suddenly it was obvious to Dan. "It wants my quest to succeed! It wants to be free! It's trapped in this strange land and wants to get back where it belongs. Back home, back where it comes from."

"Then that is it," said Maggie. "Remember how as soon as you showed me that I was a changeling so long ago, I wanted to get to Inland where I am from, and find my birth parents? I am certain that Sister has the same desire to belong somewhere.

We have even had glimpses of her and Mrs. Westerley being kind to each other since you got them together."

It was true. Maggie's birth parents had turned out to be hateful to her, but Sister and Mrs. W seemed to be working out some kind of relationship. How ironic was that! But no time to think about it now.

"OK then," said Dan. "I truename them and tell them to go where they come from. A shared desire so the truenaming will catch, different places so they should separate."

"Will this free the Beast from the Shadowlands?" asked Maggie. "Will your quest be done?"

"I don't think so. If it could desire itself out of the Shadowlands it would have been outtahere long ago. I think it will be in a Shadowlands version of where it belongs."

Maggie's shoulders slumped. "Then all this awful trip will have been in vain. Sister will be somewhere else, so we will not be able to reach the Beast by kintraveling to her, and you will not be able to complete your quest, and sooner or later she will catch the Beast again. Still, you must hurry."

The lion men were moving slowly, broken and battered, but still landing blows like punch drunk heavyweights. The misty figures hovered statically between the stones, which now looked to Dan like the stumps of an old man's teeth. The air was filled with sobbing.

But an idea struck Dan and he flashed Maggie a smile. "Oh, I know where FCB will go, and I'll make us a gate there. If this whole crazy idea works, that is."

Dan took off running. The rhinoceros-horned thing floated between the closest stones but Dan didn't slow down. Instead of warm mist when he went through it was like being burned by flecks of ice, and Dan staggered. Perhaps Sister sensed Dan's presence and summoned the last of her strength to defeat him, or perhaps it was just bad timing, but the ground lurched and threw Dan on his back, and waves of air shoved him away from the lion men.

Then the mist figures converged on Dan. Human hands and feet, clacking bird beaks, smiling faces, snapping crocodile jaws, coiling python, drifting then streaming toward him. Dan kicked and hit at the bizarre menagerie, but only swung through icy mist. Then, even though he could not touch them, he felt them touching him: hands and paws and hooves and claws. Through their foggy bodies Dan saw Maggie running to save him but struck to her knees by the torture in her head that then became torture in his. How bitter to die so close to his goal!

But the mist creatures raised Dan and bore him to where the lion men battled and set him gently on his feet, and Dan choked out, "Minik Mingarria!"

As before, the din quieted and the battling figures paused and looked at him.

Dan took a deep breath and said, quietly yet firmly, "I command you both to go where you come from."

Wind moaned from the pine trees and brushed Dan's face. The lion men blinked out as though they had never been there, and the screaming pain left Dan's head. He wanted to thank the misty figures but they had wafted into nothingness. Dan turned to run to Maggie but she was already beside him.

"Are you OK?" they both asked, and replied, "Yes."

"Where is the Beast?" asked Maggie.

"The painted caves. That's where I've encountered the Beast most often. That's where people have legends about it. And the paintings are from ancient Cro-Magnon culture. I bet that's where First Changing Beast first came to exist, with the Old People."

Dan reached for his amulets but Maggie held his wrist and said, "Wait."

"What?"

Maggie blushed, looked down, and said, "The painted caves are where we almost died of truenaming sickness. I do not think Sister will be with the Beast any more so we should be safe from her truenaming me. Should we release each other now? I mean, before it is too late?" She shifted her weight from one foot to another.

Sheesh, it looked like Maggie was pretty far gone in the truenaming already. Dan didn't think it was claiming him yet, and he was a little uneasy about releasing Maggie, because what if his command hadn't worked after all and Sister was still with FCB when they went through the gate? Well, if so, they could always truename each other again right away.

But still. "But Maggie, this first phase of truenaming just feels so good, so close."

"I know. But Danny—please?"

Dan shrugged. "I relea—" something caught in his throat and he paused to clear it. "I re—" He choked and became quiet.

Maggie moaned, "We are too late."

Dan gritted his teeth. They had been stuck in mutual truenaming once before, each the other's slave, a mute agony where they could only cling to each other like scalded infants. That time they had been saved by Josh and Alice and a potion brewed by strange dwarves, but now they were alone.

Or were they? Wasn't there something that Graciela had said? Dan rubbed his arm where the Graciela-spider had bitten him but felt nothing there. But hadn't it been before the spider bite? Graciela had kissed him on the cheek! The second Dan remembered that, it felt like spider fangs stabbed his face and he blurted, "I release you, Maggie Magpie!"

"And I release you, Círdan James Hillman!"

"Thank God," said Dan. They sat on the turf laughing. Dan rubbed his face and asked, "Is it swollen?"

"You look fine," answered Maggie.

They laughed again, and then Dan said, "Do you think it's safe to truename each other again?"

"I do not know. Sister is quick and wants nothing more than to catch me herself when you have not truenamed me, so I am frightened. But each time it is harder to release each other. It is so seductive that I long for truenaming with you even though I know the danger."

"I feel exactly the same," said Dan. "With all this chaos it's almost impossible to think straight, but one thing I know is we can't afford to be locked in mutual truenaming in the Shadowlands with no one to help. That way lies insanity and paralysis. So no more mutual truenaming unless Sister is right there and we absolutely have to.

"But now let's not waste any more time."

Dan circled Fuzzy Fat-Tail's foot widdershins around Breaklock and a gate shimmered in front of them. For some reason it was snow white. Dan looked at Maggie and saw that she was puzzled too. They held hands and stepped through, wondering why it wasn't colored like all the other gates he had made.

IT WAS COLD.

Dan offered Maggie the bearskin robe, but she told him not to be silly. They both knew she was less affected by cold than he. But she did put on all the shirts she had packed, one on top of the other.

Then she asked the question Dan was asking himself: "Is this the right place?"

They stood about halfway up the side of a small hill. The hills that held the painted caves had been covered with dry brown grasses and a scattering of thorny bushes. The valley bottoms had been dry streambeds. This place was much damper. The grasses were mixed with unfamiliar plants and grew nearly waist high, dark green and patched with frost. The thorny bushes had been replaced by short evergreens, shaggy with moss. Mist wound between branches of the tamaracks that covered the valley floor, and Dan could hear a rushing stream hidden beneath.

Worst of all, there was no cave in sight.

But as Dan continued to gaze around he started to feel a little better. "Obviously my gate skills weren't top notch this time. I didn't land us right by the cave, and I have no idea what shadowland-y reason there is for the climate change. But if you imagine the vegetation like it was before, the landscape looks right, the same kind of low, steep hills. So I think we're close. I just wish I knew which way to go. I was so groggy and stupid from the truenaming last time that I don't have any clear memories. Do you?"

Maggie shook her head. She looked uneasy. Which was exactly how Dan felt.

"We'll just have to guess," he said. "Pick a direction and walk for a day. If we don't reach the caves we'll double back and go for another day. If I landed us farther from the caves than that I guess we give up, gate back to Gatemoodle, try something else."

Maggie nodded.

The other time they were here they had been waylaid by goblins. Dan strung his bow and made sure his quiver was positioned for easy arrow grabbing. Then he started off in the direction that had the easiest slope. His first thought was that they should stay on the hillside, because down by the stream the trees would block their view so they might walk right past the caves. But the vegetation had other ideas. It grew incredibly thickly and gripped their legs and feet so that every step was laborious. Plus almost instantly they were soaked to the waist by melting frost. At least downslope they had the help of gravity, and downslope they went.

The damp tamarack branches grew low to the ground, and Dan wasn't real keen on struggling through those. Luckily, the grasses and weeds thinned near the bottom, and Dan spotted a narrow path following the valley floor just outside the branches. Someone else didn't relish fighting through the trees. But who? Dan knelt to examine the path.

"Maybe just a game trail," he said. "But it looks a little too wide for that. I can't make out any individual footprints. If it's humans, they're real skilled at not leaving marks; I don't think I can walk it without crushing some of the weeds on the side. Goblins or dwarves are smaller, so them? In any case, we won't get anywhere unless we follow it." He pulled an arrow from his quiver and held it ready as they started down the path.

It had been early morning when they entered the Shadowland; when the sun was nearly overhead the path dipped under the tamaracks and crossed stepping stones to the north side of the stream. The trail left the rocks and crossed a damp spot before starting up the hillside, and Dan spotted a footprint. Whoever it was had been wearing a moccasin or some other soft-soled footgear. Dan put his foot beside the mark.

"A little bigger than me," he said. "So probably human. That's good, I guess."

"I guess," said Maggie, looking in all directions. She put her own foot beside the print.

"What?" asked Dan.

"I did not want to tell you because I hoped I was wrong. But the feeling is growing: Sister again. Not this print, but in the same direction."

Dan groaned. "She must have stuck to the Beast even as it went where it comes from. I bet they're both in the cave. Well, at least we're headed the right direction."

The afternoon wore on as they followed the trail up the hill, down the other side, and along another stream valley. Now and then Dan had the neck-prickly feeling that someone was watching and they paused to look and listen until the feeling went away. They started up the next, higher hill. The day seemed to grow colder even in the sunshine, and plants grew less lushly. Rather than dropping down the other side of this hill, the path turned right and continued just below the ridge line. It felt dangerously exposed to view and Dan paused, looking for another route. Something felt familiar. In his mind Dan stripped the landscape of its vegetation and substituted the dry grass and small shrubs of their previous trip.

"Maggie, I think we've almost reached the caves. The fire-drink those dwarves gave us when we reached the cave burned away the truenaming enough that I was able to notice things, and I remember the shape of these hills. The cave should be in that far one—maybe it's that dark spot."

Dan pointed to a distant hill, and just as he did a fire sparked to life by the dark spot. He couldn't be sure, but it looked like figures moved in front of it. He turned to Maggie and raised his eyebrows.

Maggie shielded her eyes. "Two men stand in front of the cave. Tall men dressed in hide tunics and leggings. Their faces

are painted or else tattooed. They hold long spears. Now a
woman steps out of the cave to join them, and a child. They call
into the cave as though others are there."

"No one was ever living here when I came before," said Dan.
I didn't think we'd have to get past—"

They heard footsteps behind them and whirled. A man
with a striking combination of blue eyes and dark skin loped
toward them along the trail. Dan fitted arrow to bowstring but
the man shook his head and smiled briefly before his face filled
with tension. Instead of raising his spear the man slowed, made
a chopping motion with his hand, and barked, "Ez!" Then he
pointed north, perpendicular to the trail, and said,
"Han daude!"

"What do you mean?" asked Dan, but the man merely
pointed again and ran past them, toward the cave.

"A Cro-Magnon man, and it seemed like he was expecting
us," said Dan. "We're the first people to be in contact with a
Cro-Magnon in thousands of years, and he has a message for us
that we can't understand because of course he speaks the Old
Tongue. But why isn't Inland helping us understand him?" Josh
used to call it Inland Google Translate; all Inland languages
became whatever language the Outland visitor spoke.

"There is so much here we do not understand," said
Maggie. "Such as why do I feel Sister not in the cave but in the
direction he pointed?"

THEY SPENT the night in a dry level spot on the south side of the
next ridge, just below the top. A slight depression in the hillside
sheltered them from the cold wind that whined down from the
north all night long. Just before dawn the wind dropped,

leaving a blanket of air so frigid that their breath had frosted the bearskin robe that they slept under.

They climbed to the top of the ridge and gazed in wonder.

A vast rolling steppe stretched to the north. Nearby grew a few scraggly birches, but beyond was only tall grass rippling in the breeze. At the far end of Dan's vision the horizon glinted white. In the middle distance was a herd of ...

"Elephants?" protested Maggie.

"Woolly mammoths," said Dan. He laughed. "The ice age. We followed First Changing Beast to the ice age. I should have known! Those museum sculptures of First Changing Beast, the lion person and the prehistoric Venus, are from ice age Europe, and so was the projectile point Josh found the other time we were here. I should have known all along First Changing Beast wouldn't only go to the place he comes from, but to the era. I wish we could spend some time exploring. But it would be a crazy shadowlands ice age anyway, and I don't want to meet shadowlands Neanderthals—"

Maggie shook him by the shoulder and pointed. The mammoths had rambled along while Dan talked, going about their mammoth business, and beyond where they had been standing, two figures battled.

The terrain was surprisingly easy to cross. Although the grass grew knee high and in spots up to Dan's chest, it was easy to push through and the ground was dry and fairly even. Distance was hard to judge, though, and even at a steady run it was close to an hour before Dan could hear the fight. No thunder, no wailing and singing from weird ghostly figures, just booms when air and ground were thrown, and groans when it hit. It was Lion Man versus Sister.

Dan and Maggie stopped.

"Should we truename each other?" asked Dan.

"Just truename me. I'll be safe from her, and then after she's gone you can release me."

"No," said Dan. "Absolutely not. We both know what it feels like to be the only one truenamed." Like being less than dust under grinding boots while you moaned in shame because you deserved worse treatment. "I will not do that to you even for one minute. You'll be OK if you wait for me here where her voice can't reach you."

The grass was tall enough that Dan was able to stay mostly hidden by approaching in a crouch. If they had been watching for him he would have been obvious, but they were absorbed in their conflict, eyes only for each other. Like angry lovers, Dan thought, or like someone gazing into a mirror who hates what he sees.

At least it looked obvious which one was Sister. He crawled close enough to her that she would hear his Minik Mingarria, and then realized he had no idea what to do. It *wasn't* obvious which one was Sister, because if they had separated, FCB would be in its gender-ambiguous form, not this obvious male. And hadn't he truenamed the Sister part already? And what new command would be of any use anyway?

Suddenly the Sister avatar raked her face with both hands. Dan lurched back in horror but noticed that the lion man avatar beyond her flickered. Even as Sister turned her bloody face to Dan and held out her bloody fingers, Dan kept the corner of his eye on the other to see what it did.

"Clear your mind!" said Sister. "When we go, reach us by having her follow me. It will have enough power there to separate us."

"What are you saying?" cried Dan.

Without replying, Sister turned back to her opponent. They blasted each other as the flickering Lion Man solidified into a duplicate Sister. But for a fraction of a second Dan thought he had seen a different form.

Dan ran back to Maggie and shouted, "She said I should clear my mind and then we could reach them by you following her, that FCB would be strong enough there to separate them. I don't know what that means but the weirdest thing is I think it really was Sister saying that." He shuddered when he added, "She scratched her face until she bled and I think that freed her for a second because the other one flickered into regular FCB—when you can't tell it's a man. But why would Sister help us free FCB?"

"Can you not see?" asked Maggie, clenching her teeth and frowning as she gestured at the fight. "She suffers and wants us to free her too."

Dan thought about Sister's self-wounding and nodded. Usually he thought Maggie went too far in her sympathy for Sister, but this time it made sense.

Maggie continued, "And you must clear your mind so they will go to where FCB truly originates. Remember how our version of the shadowlands got mixed up with Sister's before, stopping her from reaching the Beast? Now your version of the Shadowlands has gotten mixed up with the Beast's version and directed it here. You said yourself a moment ago that you knew all along he came from the ice age."

"You must be right," said Dan. "Wow, I wonder where he's really from. Maybe—"

Maggie touched his forehead. "You are supposed to clear your mind," she said.

"Oh, right." But thoughts kept zooming through his brain: what they'd been through, where they were now, where they might go next ...

"How?"

"Look at me," said Maggie.

"That doesn't help. Now I think about you."

Maggie pointed at her eyes and said, "Deep breaths."

Maggie's green eyes beckoned. Always there had been something about her that was beyond thought. As much as Dan loved her shape and her touch, as much as he loved the things they did together and the things they said, there was always something deeper that he never tried to describe even to himself because he knew it was beyond the grip of language. A deep green pool, soothing and sensuous, both warm and cool, and still less than that and more ...

"Look!" said Maggie.

Dan followed her pointing finger. The avatars of Sister and FCB had vanished.

Maggie took Dan's hand and said, "Now we will follow Sister."

To wherever First Changing Beast came from.

16

WHERE THEY CAME FROM

*T*he warm breeze carried scents that seemed familiar even though Dan had never smelled them before. On all sides stretched grasslands like they had just left, but drier and spotted with strange trees like giant broccoli. Small spring-propelled antelope bounded away, and a herd of zebra eyed Dan and Maggie before moving off more slowly. Big birds circled the blue glint of a distant water hole.

"Africa," said Dan.

Maggie laughed, although her face was drawn tight. "Even I can see that."

A deep cough sounded, not near but not far either. The zebras changed direction and began to trot.

"That was a lion," said Dan. "I always wanted to go to Africa, but in a Land Rover with a guide. There's all sorts of animals here that would be happy to eat us, and that's not even counting any Shadowlands specialties. We better find FCB and Sister quick. Where are they?"

The last bit of humor was gone from Maggie's face. She

raised her shoulders and slumped them. "I no longer feel her direction. It is as though she is here but not really here. Not the feeling of her being mixed with FCB; this is something different and I do not understand it."

The lion coughed again, and without speaking Dan and Maggie turned in the direction opposite to it and began to trot. The ground soon rose slightly and they passed a rocky escarpment. Trees were more numerous although there were still wide grassy avenues between them. The air was filled with the hum of insects and calls of innumerable birds, big and small, bright and plain. Monkeys peered from the treetops. Dan saw what he thought was a troop of baboons on another escarpment. A couple of big ones, probably males, jumped up and down and hooted and growled, and Dan and Maggie curved farther away, but then Dan stopped and stared. The "baboons" had just moved away on their hind legs.

"What is it?" asked Maggie.

"I wonder how far into the past we've gone," answered Dan. "Those must be australopithecines."

"Remember me? High school dropout before I was a fairy? Never watched nature shows?"

"I know, sorry. Humans evolved from some version of those things, but their fossils come from a couple million years before us. I guess nobody really knows when they died out."

"We cannot keep running aimlessly," said Maggie. "We must find shelter and think how to find her, or else go back to Gatemoodle. Can you even make a millions of years gate?"

Dan didn't want to think about that. "Looks like it's late afternoon. Let's find a place to spend the night and figure out what to do. Damn! We're wasting my last weeks before I might have to leave Inland."

"What is he doing?" asked Maggie, pointing.

One of the australopithecines, if that's what it was, had returned to the escarpment. It hooted and beckoned them.

"When Graciela and I fought Sister in the museum, someone like that helped us," said Dan. "His name was, well, Nameless. I think we should trust it."

Maggie was already striding toward the escarpment. Despite what he had just said, Dan nocked an arrow before following her, only to find that climbing the escarpment was tricky enough that he needed both hands. He shouted for Maggie to wait as he put the arrow back in his quiver and scrambled up, wishing she weren't so much faster than he.

Dan caught up and they peeked over the lip of the ledge at the same time.

"Go back down?" whispered Dan.

Just then the lion called from the bottom of the escarpment, a cough that turned into a full roar. The apeman jumped and hooted, communicating, "Get up here and let's flee!" as clearly as the most fluent English speaker. Trouble was, the rest of the troop, twelve or fifteen strong, were just behind him and they didn't give off a welcoming vibe. Two of them held rocks, several held sticks that they banged against the ground, and most of them glared. Two or three held babies who glanced at Dan and Maggie, grimaced, and buried their faces in their mothers' shoulders.

The lion roared again. Dan and Maggie scrambled onto the ledge. Their "friend" made shooing motions, the rest of the troop backed up, and they all ran upslope, Dan and Maggie to the left, their friend in the middle, the others to the right. One apeman threw its rock toward the lion, giving Dan a moment of hope that the threat display had only been meant for the big cat, but several others shook their sticks at Dan and Maggie as they ran.

Beyond the escarpment was an upland rising steeply into broken ledges and ravines. The apemen seemed to know where they were going, following twists and turns of the landscape without slowing. One ravine was so narrow that Dan and Maggie found themselves mixed in with the troop, and one of the creatures began swatting Dan with its stick. Dan put his hand on his sword hilt but he knew that if he slew this one, the others would overwhelm him. Their friend screeched at the one with the stick, but that one just hit Dan harder, and Dan stopped, flattened his back against the wall, and tried to fend off the stick with his hands. Maggie shoved her way next to him. The troop halted and began screeching. Dan thought this was the end, but his attacker abruptly fell back, wrinkling his nose. The others jumped up and down, contorting their faces and brushing hands against noses.

Then Dan smelled it. A whiff of mold and decay from farther up the ravine, as if some corpse moldered in a damp basement. He forgot the sticks and the apemen and choked out, "Oh my God, Maggie, are they dead?"

Maggie looked as horrified as Dan felt as she said, "Is that why I cannot sense her?"

The troop slowly marched back the way they had come, screeches fading. Only the one remained. He hooted softly, paced back and forth in front of Dan and Maggie, and pointed up the ravine. Then he reached up, patted both of them on the cheek, and followed his troop.

Wordlessly, Dan and Maggie proceeded up the ravine. The smell grew stronger until Dan could almost taste it. He spit, but it didn't help. And it wasn't only the smell; there was an atmosphere of wrongness that made Dan's skin crawl. Maggie stopped, put her hands on her knees, and took a few deep breaths. Then she nodded at Dan and they proceeded. There wasn't enough room to walk side-by-side without scraping the stone with their shoulders, but they did so anyway.

The left side of the ravine grew higher and higher while the right side fell away, until they emerged on a flat promontory before a west-facing cliff. The late afternoon sun illuminated a panel of pictographs on the cliff face, but something else demanded notice first.

The promontory extended for thirty or forty yards, and on the outer portion grew the expected grass with a few trees. But something was all wrong in the zone in front of the cliff, and from there emanated the stench. The grasses were bent and covered with pale yellow slime. Closest to the cliff it was almost as if they had melted, leaving a vile carpet. A little farther out plants bent double, and even as Dan and Maggie watched they seemed to sigh and surrender, sinking into the yellow mat. In the middle of the decay was a larger mass. First Changing Beast? Sister? Dan and Maggie crept forward and then exhaled in relief. Patches of bark were still visible, and a few discrete branches reached upward from the blob of slime molds and rot that had once been a tree.

Dan turned to the west. Warm African sun struck his face, and warm wind caressed him even if the aromas he had noticed when they first arrived were swamped by the death behind him. There was no way that mold and fungi could thrive in this heat and light, yet he turned back and there they were.

"Morbid fungi," muttered Dan.

"I have picked many a delicious mushroom for us to eat," Maggie reminded him. "Fairies know the ways of mushrooms and growths that love the damp. Yet never have I known something like this. Why did the australo things bring us here? What do they expect us to do? I do not sense Sister. I do not see First Changing Beast."

Dan ran along the edge of the decay, searching for First Changing Beast, searching for Sister, searching for anything that would make sense. He reached the northern edge of the promontory and then looped back along the perimeter, inspecting the downward slopes. Huge buzzards circled below, bright red and green birds darted from tree to tree, a monkey scampered along a branch, and large animals meandered the distant veldt. Normal Africa. Beautiful Africa. Dan sat and dangled his feet over the precipice. There were probably man-eating lions and leopards and hyenas down there, but up here he was safe.

Wait a minute. Why wasn't he trying to figure things out? Why wasn't Maggie yelling at him to get it together?"

Dan stumbled to his feet. When he got back to Maggie, she said, "It spreads even as we watch and do nothing."

"And I'm afraid something about the air is making me stupid. I didn't want to come back from the view below. I can't think of anything to do."

Maggie nodded. "It breathes out stupidity and defeat. It tells me to walk back down the ravine. Walk, or run." She looked west. "Can you not help us, Sun?"

Dan couldn't decide if it was by coincidence or what, but the sun had dropped almost to the horizon and now sent its rays horizontally against the cliff, and in that light the pictographs shone brightly. Humans, hunters holding spears, little more than stick figures. Slender antelope with long horns. Elephants and a skinny cat, leopard or cheetah. Spirals and handprints. More hunters and a speared zebra.

But two figures in the center of the panel, drawn double the size of the others, shone most intensely in the setting sun. It was obvious that they were more recent than the others because they were painted on top of them. One looked like a drawing of the lion person statue that Dan had seen in the natural history museum, a Paleolithic prototype for First Changing Beast as Dan had usually seen it. The other was a human, a stick figure like the others and yet completely different. A faint swelling represented breasts, a simple triangle a skirt: this one was a woman. All the other stick figures had been hairless and painted black; this one was painted in white, with a simple yellow swirl around the head for blond hair.

"Did the australos paint them?" asked Maggie. "Take us up here to show us their paintings, show us that they had seen them?"

"I don't think so. I mean, who knows what's possible with shadowlands weirdness, but only full humans like us can do art. But no one could paint them unless they saw them, so they must be here. I forgot to look in the trees!" Dan ran to the closest tree, but even as he reached it yellow slime crept up the trunk. With a whisper the tree dropped all its leaves and Dan could see its bare branches were empty. He watched with his mouth open and backpedaled as the wood softened and slumped to the earth.

"Dan!" Maggie ran and seized him by the shoulders. "Dan! No one painted them. That *is* them!"

"What do you mean?"

"It is why I feel like they are here and yet not here! They are here as rock art and no longer as living beings. The nearby earth dies because First Changing Beast no longer breathes."

The truth of this struck Dan as hard as the stench of death, and he said, "I once heard First Changing Beast say that the power it gave to the Earth was the power that the earth gave to it. Like they are the same thing in different forms." He backed away from the spreading rot and continued, "Anyway, we've failed. Sending FCB back where it came from was supposed to

give it power to separate from Sister, but this is all we've done."
He gestured at the cliff. "Sister even told us to do this, tried to
help like one of the good guys." He shrugged. "Failed like one of
the good guys."

They stared in silence and the light began to fade. Maggie
gasped and said, "I am not sure that we have failed. See! They
are separate. Sister is a blond woman, and the Beast is in the
shape you know best. That must mean that Sister was right:
here where it comes from, First Changing Beast had enough
power to separate from Sister's truenaming."

"Then why are they stuck in a cliff?" asked Dan.

Maggie turned to Dan, eyes wide. "It is you! It is your truenaming that holds them now."

"Maggie, you are so brilliant!" said Dan. He stepped to the
limit of the decay, which now stretched almost halfway to the
end of the promontory, and cried, "I release you, Minik
Mingarria!"

Nothing happened.

"I have to get closer," said Dan, eyeing the slimy yellow
ground.

"Oh, I am faster, I wish that I could do it," cried Maggie. "Be
swift, return swiftly!"

Dan ran for the pictographs, twenty yards away. He
expected the slime to be slick and burn like acid, but instead it
was gluey and cold. He couldn't move faster than a brisk walk
because he had to wrench his foot from the ground with each
step. It was cold like he was striding barefoot on ice, ice that
crept up his bones: now his ankles, now his tibias; halfway
there and it was into his thigh bones and Dan stumbled,
planting one hand in the slime before regaining his feet. Now
the ice was in his wrist, his elbow, his hips, seeking for his heart.
Dan was seven yards away, then six; he didn't know how close

he needed to be, but as he felt the first ice needles prick his heart he yelled as loudly as he could, "I release you, Minik Mingarria!" And as he fell forward, in his last moment of awareness, in the last light of the sun, the paintings of the blond woman and the lion person vanished.

DAN AWOKE with the full moon shining on his face. His mind slowly wrapped around what this portended. To rise above the eastern cliff the moon had to be almost directly overhead, which meant it was about midnight. Which meant he had been unconscious for several hours. It was hard to think clearly, but that didn't seem right. It had only been one night after the new moon when he had called to the fairies east of the sun and west of the moon, but he could only think of two days that had passed since then. Which meant he had been asleep almost two weeks. That couldn't be right either, but the moon above didn't stop being full. One full moon gone of the three that remained to him.

The second thing Dan became aware of was that it wasn't cold anymore. He patted the ground—no slime. He sat and looked, relishing a warm breeze. The plants hadn't grown back, but the ground seemed to be healing, soft brown soil. The stink was gone.

Where was Maggie? Dan jumped up and saw her lying where she had stood to watch him run toward the cliff. Now he ran to her and gently shook her. No response. Dan laid two fingers against her cheek; thank God she was warm. He didn't think he could stand to lose her. He kissed her gently and she opened her eyes.

"Prince Charming!" said Maggie, sitting up and smiling.

"Thank you for awakening me, my prince. But what are we doing here?"

"I've been trying to remember that. Whatever it was, I'm glad just to be here now with you."

"Me too," said Maggie. Her eyes glowed moss green in the warm moonlight. Dan leaned forward and they kissed again.

"I know what you were doing here," said another voice. A familiar voice. But whose?

"You came here to free First Changing Beast."

Was it First Changing Beast talking? The lion person's voice was deeper, but Dan had never heard the woman avatar speak. Perhaps it was her.

"And to free me."

Sister then. Their enemy. But hadn't she done something helpful recently? And her voice sounded gentle as she said, "Thank you, Daniel."

But then came that laugh Dan remembered, like poison in a mountain stream.

Now her voice sounded different too. "You are mine, Maggie Magpie!"

Maggie shrieked. Her eyes faded. She slumped to the ground.

Sister strode into view, ghastly scars on her face, and seized Maggie's hand. Finally Dan's mind worked and he shouted "Minik Mingarria!"

But they were already gone.

"Nooooo!" Dan's bellow echoed off the cliff. He kicked at the ground, then knelt and ripped up handfuls of grass. He ran to the nearest tree and tore at its bark until his fingertips bled, and then tore some more. He ran to the cliff and scratched at the pictographs, noticing that the speared zebra now bled with his blood. He bellowed again and finally slumped to the ground and leaned against the rock face.

"How could I be so stupid? How could I be so stupid?" He said it over and over again like a chant. "Why didn't we true-name each other before I released Sister? Why didn't I true-name Sister as soon as I knew it was her? Thinking she had become good, how stupid! How stupid! I know this place made it hard for Maggie and me to think, but that's no excuse.

"OK Dan, enough drama. Time to figure out what to do."

Dan folded his arms and stood in thought for a minute, and then spoke out loud again. "It's simple really. I kintravel to Maggie, and I locate Sister, and I truename her, and I slit her throat. That will take care of the stupid idea of me loving Sister once and for all." Dan pulled out his sword to have it ready, and began to concentrate on an image of Maggie full and clear enough for kintravel. That last kiss before Sister jolted them should do.

The warm green eyes. The soft lips. The strong, dark, shining woman they belonged to. Dan sculpted the image in his mind and began to fall into kintravel, but at the last moment he thought of Sister's laugh and jerked back to the promontory.

He had interrupted the kintravel on purpose. "I'm still not thinking straight," he said to himself. "Sister's no fool, and me kintravelling after them is exactly what she'd expect. Maybe she's set a trap to kill me the instant I appear. Maybe she's forced Maggie to reveal my truename, or maybe she's put Maggie in a cage and traveled far away and I'll use up all the time I have left in Inland trying to catch up with her. So it's not going to work to go blundering after Maggie.

"But then what do I do?"

A lion roared. The sound seemed to come from the ground below Dan, from the cliff before him, and from the sky above.

Dan had forgotten all about First Changing Beast.

He knew it was First Changing Beast, because what normal lion could roar a roar from all directions? And what normal lion could roar a roar that didn't make Dan fear that he was lunch? This roar filled Dan with respect and excitement, this roar made Dan believe that he could find the strength to do what needed to be done.

Now came another roar, this time from behind. FCB must be in lion person form. But when Dan turned he saw not the lion person but a great lion, at least twice the size of a normal lion, appear on the edge of the promontory; whether it had bounded up from below or simply appeared out of the air Dan couldn't tell.

And beside the lion was a woman so tall that she was able to wrap her arm through its mane and around its neck. Here in Africa, here where it was born, First Changing Beast appeared as male and female, human and animal, all at once.

The woman was garbed in only a short top and a loincloth made of animal hide, and in the moonlight her skin shone black. Her hair was in cornrows studded with white seashells, and her face was wreathed in laugh lines.

They ran to Dan, the woman as fleet as the lion, both of them with muscles rippling.

The lion lifted one enormous paw and placed it on Dan's head. Dan knew without a smidgen of doubt that the lion could crush him like paper, and yet he still felt no fear. Instead he felt infused with strength and joy, like he was special and at the same time exactly the same as everything else in the world. It was like being with Aslan, except that Dan was pretty sure

Aslan wouldn't hang around with a scantily clad African woman.

Then the woman let go of the lion's mane and hugged Dan. It was sexy and yet at the same time not, more like a jolt of vitality, an infusion of what made plants turn to the sun and made the sun smile back at them, a draught of motherhood and fatherhood too.

The woman released Dan and laughed a rich and throaty laugh. Then she began to speak in a language full of weird clicks that she made with her tongue. If there was ever a time that Inland Google Translate would have come in handy, this was it. But then the lion began to purr, and the woman's click talk and the lion's purr together wove meaning for Dan. Not words, nothing so precise, but emotions and intentions. There had been one eon or many of joy when seas rolled and retreated, mountains rose and fell, forests grew and died, animals and people loved and lost and loved again, cycle upon cycle upon cycle. But machines had come that clashed and cut, and machine minds that yanked the cycles into a straight line. Then had come an eon of drought and despair, cramped and creeping, sore and still. Then, not long ago, there came flashes of pain and weakness: a visitor, a thief. They must escape this drought to be safe from the thief. Even then they would not be what they once were.

The woman and the lion fell silent. Then the woman laughed, and the clicking and purring began again: Not yet, sang their song. Then they wove in Dan's mind a wedding, two weddings, a fairy paired with a mortal, and another pair as well.

Again they fell silent. The woman laughed, more quietly this time. Then they gazed into Dan's eyes, the large brown eyes of the woman and the great golden eyes of the cat.

It was Dan's turn to laugh. Now was the time to finish his

quest! Time to free First Changing Beast. Something in what they had said didn't sound so good, something about them still being weak after they made it back to Inland. Sounded like Sister still had enough of their power that they wouldn't be able to just zap her and make everything right. But that was good news about the wedding. Dan had no problems with a double ceremony as long as he got to marry his fairy. And if they were trying to tell him that the wedding would be the final restoration of their power, so much the better.

The specifics were totally unclear, but Dan had reached the final stage. He was going to defeat Sister and free Maggie. He was going to marry Maggie, be with her forever, and have the freedom of Inland. And to set this final stage in motion, he needed to free First Changing Beast.

"Let me think for a minute, guys." They still gazed at him with those big eyes. The woman was smiling. Dan wanted to make a gate to Outland for them right away, but he had to decide where. Making gates was exhausting, and he wouldn't be able to turn around and instantly make the gate to Inland. Even if it was just for a short time, showing up in the regular world with this giant African woman and giant lion sounded like a problem. He'd like to meet up with Josh and Alice, bring them through the gate to Inland to be Best Man and Maid of Honor, but even stalwart Josh might freak if he suddenly saw Dan with these companions, and Alice would freak for sure.

Dr. Green? After all, he would soon be free to return to Inland as Prince of the Fairies, so he'd better get used to weird things. But it would be awfully cruel to his patients who were already worried about their minds if they saw Dan with FCB, and he didn't know where to find Green after hours.

The Green Goblin? But he might be with his conventional boyfriend.

Finally Dan decided on the Goth Woods, middle of the night. The only people there at that time were usually drunk, stoned, or both, so they could attribute the sight of FCB to too many chemicals. Might even do them a favor by scaring them straight.

"OK, guys," said Dan. "I think you know this already, but the Shadowlands are the land between, and to set you free I need to take you to both the lands around it. That means we'll be in Outland for a bit first. I'm going to take us to a place where I hope you won't be seen by anybody who will be scared of you. But just in case, since you are obviously masters of taking different forms, if you could look like something smaller or more conventional, that would be great."

As Dan created the gate to Outland, the woman burst into peals of laughter and the lion roared. Dan was pretty sure that even the lion was smiling. The gate shimmered. The woman took Dan's left hand and gestured toward the lion. The lion bent its neck, and Dan reached up and grabbed his mane.

They strode through the gate.

ACKNOWLEDGMENTS

Thank you to Donna, Joey, Susan, Jane, and David